Blood of Hades

The Vampire Queen

Makenzi Rivera

Author's note: This book contains adult and dark themes including physical violence, death, consensual and nonconsensual sex.

 Chapter 1

A blood-curdling scream echoed through the fog. Callie grasped her ears at the piercing pain, only to realize the screams were her own. She was acutely aware of her heart racing. She tried to run but continuously stumbled.

The ends of her hair smacked her face as she whipped around to catch sight of her predator. She had only caught a glimpse of the slender, pale man but knew she would be dead if she didn't hurry.

Another fall, but she felt warm sand scrape her palms and shins this time. She had reached the end of the path. She looked around frantically but was surrounded by the ocean with nowhere to escape.

The fog disappeared as he stepped closer. Callie opened her mouth to scream again, but no sound was heard. She was frozen in horror as he leaped toward her.

In reality, Callie was sitting on the balcony of a high-rise apartment, watching the ocean and reliving her never-ending nightmare. She attempted reading to calm her mind but eventually placed the book upside down in her lap as she couldn't shake the ill feeling of her nightmare.

She had found copies of the *Vampire Chronicles* book series by Anne Rice at her in-law's house, and they piqued her interest. As a teen, she had become mildly obsessed with the popular vampire movies and books of the time. She decided to borrow the series based on nostalgia for her earlier years.

However, she had dreamt of a mysterious vampire man for the past few months. At night, she would jolt awake after dreaming of him following and finally approaching her. As soon as he reached her, she would awake in a cold sweat.

At first, she shook it off and figured it was expected to dream of these fictional characters when she would read before sleeping. As the months went by, the dreams became more frequent and vivid. Her most recent nightmare was the most realistic and frightening one she had. Just last night, she had dreamt of him drinking her blood! He held her in his arms and ripped into her throat. She awoke screaming and scared the hell out of her fiancé, Justin.

"Again Callie? I thought we agreed you were done reading those stupid books. All they do is give you nightmares and make me nearly piss myself when you wake up crying."

Callie, startled from her daydream, turned toward Justin, who stood in the middle of the sliding glass doorway. If only he could understand how real the dreams felt to her. That's why she had become obsessed with vampires, as he called it, to see if there we5re answers to why she had these dreams. Justin would jokingly say it was the evil spirits capturing her mind. Deep down, she knew her subconscious was yearning for something more in life.

Callie smiled and nodded her head. She closed the book and stood up to kiss him on the cheek.

"You're right, my love. Enough with this vampire nonsense."

"That's more like it. Now, put on that sexy black dress, and let's go celebrate ourselves."

*

Callie was an attractive but not overwhelmingly stunning woman in her mid-twenties. She had thick reddish-brown hair that reached just past her hips and almost matched in color with her brown eyes. She had a fantastic smile but rarely used it, succumbing to what others would call a 'resting bitch face.' Her attitude generally matched her unphased face, having dealt with life's traumas at an early age she rarely held a positive outlook on the world.

Justin was painfully average-looking but held a good physique from consistently working out. He had short blond hair that had been longer in his younger years, which all teenage girls seemed to fall for. On the other hand, he loved life and all the up-and-down emotions that came with it. He prided himself in always being the person to cheer others up.

They were having dinner at Ocean Prime to celebrate their eighth anniversary. They had met in high school and were friends for two years before Callie gave in and started dating him. Justin was her rock as she grieved the death of her parents. Callie was forced to move to Florida following their passing. With no other relatives besides her bum of an aunt, she was moved into her custody. Moving from a small town in South Carolina was sad and strange, but Justin immediately welcomed her. They started dating their sophomore year and have been inseparable ever since. Callie practically lived at Justin's house; his parents had taken her in like their own daughter.

They were engaged after Callie graduated college and rented a small home near downtown Tampa. Justin had surprised her with a California trip for their anniversary, hoping to lock down wedding details as they had already been engaged for two years without real talk of getting married. Callie loved Justin, but he didn't ignite passion in her anymore. Sure, Callie wanted to marry him, settle down, and raise a family with him. But simultaneously, she wanted to change her name, cut her hair, and start over with a handsome stranger. Maybe that is why vampires had enthralled her so recently, the danger and excitement of something new.

She laughed at something Justin said and gazed around the restaurant, watching the other people. She saw a lavish older couple dressed in all white, sharing a large Mahi filet. They stared lovingly into each other's eyes as the man cut a piece of the fish and fed his wife.

How cute, she thought. *At least I have that to look forward to with Justin.*

Callie stretched out her hand and watched her ring sparkle while only half listening to Justin's story. Out of the corner of her eye, she caught a flash of blond hair. She turned slightly and saw a handsome man sitting alone at a table. He wore a black suit and had a large steak on the plate before him. His chin and nose were finely chiseled, almost like the face of a statue. His ice-blue eyes penetrated her, and she felt the heat rise into her cheeks. He looked so familiar, and she couldn't turn away from his gaze.

He began to cut his steak while keeping his eyes locked on her. Callie gazed down just enough to see his plate covered in blood. Her eyes widened, and he raised the corner of his lips ever so slightly. Callie's heart began to pound as she melted at his handsome elegance, but then it seemed to stop when she noticed his unusually sharp teeth. Her breath ceased as the realization smacked her that this was the man from her nightmares.

Quickly, she turned back to Justin and squeezed his hand. She trembled and tried to control her breathing so she would not spiral into a panic attack. Justin frowned and encouraged her to eat her meal, which she no longer had an appetite for. Callie glanced behind her shoulder again, but this time, the man was gone.

Am I going crazy? I must be going crazy. He doesn't exist. Vampires aren't real! Maybe I need to start seeing a therapist again. These nightmares are getting out of control.

"Callie, what's wrong? You look like you've seen a ghost."

"I think I'm having a panic attack." She started to hyperventilate, and her food threatened to exit her stomach. He rubbed his thumb across her hand and tried to make eye contact, but her eyes darted around anxiously.

He quickly settled the bill so they could leave, assuming the loud and crowded environment was the cause of her anxiety.

*

Afterward, they strolled around the bustling town while Justin discussed their wedding plans. Callie only nodded in agreement as she couldn't erase the mystery man and his sharp teeth from her mind.

It was now later in the evening, close to midnight, and the wilder groups of people started to make their way out onto the streets. A group of clearly drunk men stumbled in front of them and bumped into Callie. Her small Dior shoulder bag fell onto the sidewalk, and she huffed as Justin shoved the drunk.

"What the hell, dude?"

Before Callie could grab her purse, the handsome blond man stood before her, dangling it from his finger.

"I believe you dropped this, ma'am," he said slowly and quietly. He smiled, keeping his lips tightly closed over his teeth.

Her eyes nearly popped out of her head, and her legs began to tremble. Now that he was directly in front of her, she felt faint. He was tall, much taller than Justin, who was just under six feet. He must have been wearing shoulder pads because they practically bulged out of his suit.

Or maybe he is just that muscular. Callie blushed at the thought.

His eyes were crystal blue, more pure and light in color than she had ever seen. Gazing into them, she felt as if she were being dragged in, about to crash into the clear abyss.

Suddenly, she came back to reality and to Justin, who gave the stranger an up-and-down look.

"Thank you," Callie said quickly and snatched the purse from him.

"Now, you should return to your little flat, don't you think, Justin?" The blond man winked, and Callie's jaw dropped open.

How does he know his name?

"Why would I do that? My fiancé and I are enjoying the night together," Justin responded catatonically.

The blond man chuckled and outstretched his long arm to pat Justin's shoulder. "You need to leave here. Go back home to Tampa. Tell your friends and family that you broke up with Calypso because she cheated. It was for the best."

Callie whimpered and felt she was going to pass out. Not only did this stranger know Justin's name, but her own! She detested her real name, making everyone call her Callie instead. Her mother's obsession with the ocean led her to be named Calypso, but she was chronically embarrassed and reminded of having a sea monster's name.

Justin turned on his heels and started to walk in the opposite direction without looking back at Callie.

The man put his arm around her waist and walked toward the beach. She felt frozen, but her legs moved with him. She had no control over her actions.

Who is this man? What happened to Justin, and why did he say I was cheating? Why is this man lying, and how did he know our names?

Walking through the sand with the blond man felt surreal. It was almost exactly like her dreams. Suddenly, a chill passed through her, and she began to shiver.

Could this be...no. Vampires aren't real. You are just crazy and had too much to drink, she told herself.

This was a dream; it had to be! It felt like hours had passed since Justin had walked away from her, but it couldn't have been that long, could it?

You are asleep, Callie. I recognize him because I dream of him every night. Tonight is just...a nightmare.

It felt so real, though, the coarse sand scraping her toes and the sea foam gently kissing the soles of her shoes.

She didn't know how far they walked but realized they were alone. There were no lights or buildings, just the sand, the ocean, and the mysterious man. He let go of her back and turned away, gazing into the sea.

He remained silent for what felt like hours while Callie anxiously scratched her hands. She eventually vomited and heaved until he faced her.

"I am afraid I am not the Vampire Lestat you dream of, Callie." His deep voice pierced the air, shattering the silence that surrounded them. "My name is Raphael. I know you are confused, but this will all be clear to you soon. You will know why I have come here and why I have watched you the past few months."

"W- watch me?" she stuttered.

"Yes, Callie, I watch when you dream. Your face is so peaceful and perfect until you dream of those terrible monsters." He chuckled, and the chill she had felt earlier ran through her spine again.

"This can't be real," she wailed as she dropped to the sand and began to clutch at her hair. She was going crazy, that was it. It was impossible that her stalker now stood in front of her, peering down at her shrunken body.

"Oh, mon chérie, it is more than real," Raphael whispered. This was the first time Callie noticed his slight French accent.

He grabbed her by the chin and lifted her to stand on her feet, but he was so gentle that she felt no pressure. His hands encircled her back and pulled her into him. Her breasts pressed into his chest, and she gripped his forearms. His muscles were as firm as stones underneath his suit. Her feet lifted off the ground, and Raphael held her in the air, just inches away from his face. She stopped breathing and was adrift in his beautiful blue eyes.

Her heart pounded with fear, but her stomach fluttered with attraction to him. The conflicting feelings made her nauseous, and his hand sliding up her waist brought her back to the present.

With the quickness of lightning, he ripped her dainty

dress to reveal her small but plump breasts. He kissed the tops of them, which elicited a gasp from her. Raphael kept eye contact as he opened his mouth and gently bit into them. She felt a slight pain at first but melted into ecstasy. She threw her head back with a moan but quickly regained self-control to face her stalker and saw his lips dripping with her blood. His bright white fangs gleamed in the moonlight, which sent another shiver down her spine.

"Now sleep, mon chérie," Raphael said as he kissed her lips. She tasted the sweetness of her blood on his tongue, and she pulled herself in for more before melting into a deep trance.

Chapter 2

Raphael was a sophisticated man, over 600 years old, but only twenty-eight when he was turned. He enjoyed the styles of the modern century, the advanced technology, and the buzz of the city. It starkly contrasted his childhood, hand harvesting grains and vegetables and slaughtering cows, with his brothers and father.

He pushed the old memories out of his mind. There was no need to dwell on the past. What was important was the present, and he had finally found *her*. He searched for ages after hearing of the prophecy in a small Greek town outside of Athens. He remembered every detail as if it were yesterday.

Raphael had felt lost after being turned. He had no companions, no meaning, or purpose in his life. The beautiful woman who captured his attention and turned him said he would be the king. *The king of what?* He had thought. It wasn't until years later, while he wandered through the Greek countryside, that he learned its meaning.

After conversing with a couple of drunks early in the morning, one told him of an old witch who lived on top of a hill in the countryside. "You'll know when you reach her," he stuttered. "There is a view of the mountains, and no person or animal dares to go near the old shed."

Raphael set out the following night, desperate for any help or advice this supposed witch could give him. He spotted the shed after walking twenty miles, which he cleared in mere minutes.

A broken-down shed sat atop a hill with the famed Mount Olympus in the background. The wind howled around him and brought a chill, though the night was relatively quiet and calm. The smell of a nearby boiling pot of herbs was enough to make him shrivel his nose.

As he climbed the steep hill, his palms began to sweat. A witch couldn't hurt him, right? He laughed. He was a creature of the night, a monster. He could snap her neck in a second.

As soon as he approached the door, it flung open to reveal a wrinkled old woman. She wore a tattered shawl around her shoulders and beckoned him inside.

"I have been waiting for you."

He sat uncomfortably in a wooden rocking chair while she lit a few candles around the small room.

"Madame, pardon me, for I do not know your name, but what do you mean you have been waiting for me? Do you know who I am?"

"Of course I do. You are Raphael, the one healed by God."

"God?" Raphael laughed so hard it shook the thin and rotting shack. "I hardly believe that. Don't you know what I am? I am a monster. I drink the blood of the innocent, and I kill to feel emotion!"

"God does not mean that you are pure. Gods are good and evil, but you shall learn that in time. Raphael, I am the eldest witch in the land. I know when the Gods fight or when a prophecy is born. I have much to share with you, but I am so tired. Please." She stretched her wrinkled wrist over the table, offering it to him. He stared blankly at her, perplexed by her actions.

"Madame, I am unsure what you wish of me."

She shoved her wrist in his face, her tiny arm trembling.

"Drink from me, beloved, and you will understand. Please, only a little. I am so weak."

The sight made Raphael sick to his stomach. He had murdered beautiful young women in their sleep and thrown the carcasses of men into the ocean without a thought. But to drink from this poor, elderly woman hurt his morality.

He hesitantly lifted her wrist to his lips and gave a gentle bite. Her blood was unlike anything he had tasted before; it was smooth and not salty, unlike human blood. Suddenly, everything went black, and an enormous amount of pain exploded in his head. He fell backward off of the chair, crashing into the floorboards.

Ancient history filled his mind. He saw the names and

faces of the Greek Gods: Zeus, Poseidon, Hades, and Hera. He saw the birth of the first vampires; a young boy and girl were strapped to logs with a fire blazing underneath them. Raphael heard their screams and smelled their burning flesh. A man in a hooded cloak slit his wrist with a knife and let his blood drip into the screaming children's mouths. They both tore out of the ropes and jumped toward the hooded man. They bowed at his feet, then jumped into his arms and drank from his neck.

The following vision was of three elderly women performing a different task. One woman spun a golden thread on a wheel, another drew out the thread with her long fingers, and the final woman cut the thread. In this vision, he could hear screaming and the shaking of the Earth as if there was an earthquake.

Raphael's eyes opened suddenly, and he saw the hunched witch standing over him.

"Long ago, the prophecy told of a blond man who would be born again of God. This man would become king and rule over all of his kind. He would find a queen, and together, they would reign. You are him of which the prophecy speaks. Your name means healed of God, which you are. The dark blood of Hades flows through you, son."

Hades, the ruler of the underworld? This was too much for Raphael to process. He had heard the myths growing up but attributed them to his poor family's delirious fantasies.

"Hades created your race with the help of ancient witches like myself. He wanted a creature of the night to do his dirty work and bring him souls. But his creation did not come without a price. The prophecy speaks of you, Raphael. Once you find your queen, you two will become unstoppable. You must be mindful, as she will betray and kill your master one day."

"Does this prophecy happen to mention who this queen is? What land does she hail from? Does it provide a name, or am I supposed to wander the Earth for eternity asking for the Queen of Vampires?"

The witch cackled and sat back down in her small chair.

"You will know once you lay eyes on her."

"You are full of delusions, old woman. I have no master and no claim to this so-called prophecy and witchcraft you put in my head!" Raphael hissed at her and stood up, dusting himself off. He stormed out of the house and into the night, leaving the old witch to cackle.

Raphael forcibly met his master soon after that night. He became intoxicated under his power, spending every waking moment pleasing him or executing an order he was given. He never forgot about his queen, though.

He searched for decades, gazing deeply into every woman's eyes that he passed. He didn't know what he was looking for. A feeling, perhaps, that this woman would be his queen.

He traveled to America in the early nineteen hundreds, shortly before the human world collapsed. He feasted on the poor and homeless, forgetting about the conversation with the witch. He did not think of witches or queens for years. He was too involved with Hades and his missions to spend time searching for his queen. That is until he met her. His first love, the first vampire he created. Heartbreak and tragedy followed and he fled to California to engross himself in the ways of humans. In 2016, he left the mountains of California to visit the beaches of Florida.

Quite ironic, he thought, to be the living dead in the land of sunshine. He preferred the East Coast with the waves and coarse sand, but he still visited the West Coast now and then. After all, he had to spread out his victims. The police would become suspicious if there were too many murders in one area.

He was strolling through a park shortly after dusk in Tampa, looking for his next victim. He saw a young woman sitting on a bench underneath a streetlight, reading a book.

How peculiar, he thought. *You should not be here alone; I will feast on your innocent blood.*

The girl tossed her gleaming reddish-brown hair over her shoulder and looked at him. Raphael made himself invisible, so she looked through him. His heart dropped. Her face was exquisite, resembling the ancient Gods he had seen in the vision from the witch.

Could this be? After centuries of looking for her, could this be his queen? He couldn't make another mistake, not like last time.

He focused on her and noticed the book she was reading, *Interview with a Vampire*. He grinned, thinking how perfect his queen was reading a book about vampires. She would learn the truth about them soon enough.

*

Callie slept in Raphael's ornate king bed. The massive oak frame held a red silk canopy that draped over the sides and onto the floor. She had been sound asleep for almost twenty-four hours. As soon as the sun set, Raphael watched over her. He marveled at the slightest changes in expression as she slept. Her face shone bright even in the poorly lit room. Her lips were as pink and luscious as ever. She was so beautiful, his queen, and he wanted to devour her.

He dreamed of draining her body of blood and then having her drink from him, a complete blood transfusion. Just the thought of the sensual act made his body stiff and brought the heat of a fire. Raphael began to pace, anxiously waiting for his queen to awaken. He had so much to tell and show her and was impatient to start their life together.

While she slept, he attempted to see into her mind, but it was closed off, unlike before. Oh, how he had loved entering her dreams at night, peering into her subconscious and entering her mind. He would feed early in the night to withhold enough energy to sustain himself until dawn. He knew when Callie would fall asleep, even when he was hours away from her. At first, he had to be next to her to enter her dreams. Callie's mind quickly stopped fighting him and even longed for him to enter her mind. As the weeks passed, he had to leave her, as his passion had grown too strong.

Suddenly, Callie's eyes fluttered open. She sat up to examine her surroundings; she was in a bed that should have belonged in a royal palace. The thick comforter that covered her was exquisitely soft, making her want to melt into the bed. The room otherwise was very minimal, with no windows and only a red Persian rug covering the floor. It was pitch black in the room and quiet enough to make her ears ring.

The previous night's memories flooded her mind, and she noticed that her black dress was gone. She wore a soft cotton nightgown that hugged her sides. She lifted the dress to check the top of her breasts and was not surprised to find a small bruise with two holes. She felt a presence in the room and looked over to see Raphael lurking in the doorway.

"Where have you taken me?" she demanded.

"This is my private penthouse. I have many houses, places to hide and to live, but this is one of my favorites."

"Are we still in Santa Monica, or am I in hell now?" Raphael laughed and slowly approached the bed.

Callie's heart started to pound, and he heard it. He reached his hand out and motioned for her to follow him.

"Just kill me already." She shrunk away from him, and his lips turned to a frown.

"Nonsense, now get up and follow me," he spoke sternly.

Callie hesitantly grabbed his outstretched hand and let him help her out of bed. Although he was tall and muscular, he was so gentle with her.

Raphael strolled through a narrow hallway, and Callie looked at the pictures on the wall. There were many paintings of the countryside, and she recognized a Monet. He led her into a large living room with windows that spanned from floor to ceiling. She rushed forward to look out and saw they were elevated above the ocean.

Raphael came from behind and placed his hand on the small of her back.

"I love to watch the storms roll in. To feel the thunder

shake the floors, to feel the danger."

Callie laughed, then remembered she had been kidnapped by a vampire.

"I understand how you feel, mon chérie. I too was lost, scared, and confused. Only I had no one to turn to, nobody to confide in or keep me company in the nights. But we have each other, and I promise you will grow to trust and love me. You were made for me, Calypso."

It was hard for Callie not to melt as she listened to his thick voice speak such romantic words. Her heart ached for him, ached to be touching him, but her mind felt foggy.

"You speak so romantically for a vampire," she spoke slowly. She paused, feeling the anger and heat rise through her body. Her hands began to shake, and she turned to the window to focus on the crashing waves below.

"Why did you kidnap me? What did you do to my fiancé? And why are you trying to seduce me?" Her questions rolled out and took her by surprise.

"Mon chérie, please sit." He led her to a highbacked velvet chair and sat across from her in an identical chair. He crossed one leg over the other and leaned back, his pose exuding elegance and comfort.

"My name is Raphael Capon. I come from a family of farmers. We were not poor but not wealthy by any means. My mother bore three children in total, all boys. We lived in the countryside of Northern France. When I was twenty-eight, I traveled throughout Europa, and aside from war overtaking the country, I missed my family dearly and decided to return home. On my journey, I stopped in a small town. I don't remember the name now. I entered a tavern and saw one of the most beautiful women of my life, spare you. Her blonde hair and bright blue eyes captured me. I immediately introduced myself as a high-class merchant, which I was not. She let me entertain her for a few hours then asked me to accompany her home. Once we were in private, she shoved me against a tree and bit my neck with a strength I believed was impossible for women."

Callie shuddered at the image and fidgeted in the chair. Raphael maintained eye contact with her as she squirmed.

"She turned me into a vampire in the year fourteen twelve. She told me I was the one, that one day I would be the king. Years later, I learned the meaning of her words from an old witch outside of Athens. I was chosen to be the King of Vampires."

Callie had been studying the room to escape, but his final words grabbed her attention and brought her eyes back to him.

"You see, we are very independent creatures but still need order and someone to keep us in place. There has been much chaos throughout our kind, but soon, there will be peace. I have been waiting for my queen to rule with me. You are the one, Calypso." He smiled slightly, trying to calm her nerves, but only brought fear into her eyes.

"I have brought you here to teach you, to tell you our history, and to prepare you for a lifetime of honor and power. Truthfully, I have been watching you for months. I stumbled upon you one humid evening in Tampa and knew you were mine, my queen." Raphael raised her hands to his mouth, gently kissing them. His fangs lightly scraped across her knuckles.

"I have not turned you yet, so you will have time to come to terms with the death of your human life. I promise you will enjoy your new life much more."

A warm tear escaped from Callie's eyes and rushed down her cheeks, splattering on her bare legs.

"Your fiancé will go home and do exactly as I told him. As a vampire, we have the power of mind control and altering. It is better this way; he would not understand what you are or how to tell others. He needs to think your relationship ended badly to move on with his life. Calypso, you need to understand that while you will stay beautiful and perfect forever, he will become nothing more than a memory in years to come. He lives one lifetime, and you will rule the Earth for millennia."

Callie stayed quiet for ages. She did not move or shed any

more tears; she just sat in silent contemplation, trying to take everything in. Her obsession had become a reality: she was becoming a vampire. She was going to become the Queen of Vampires, which she did not understand. At least if she was stuck like this for eternity, she was with someone so handsome. Raphael chuckled and stood up, pulling her up as well.

"Would you like to explore the nightlife here? The city is so beautiful at night."

Callie's mind still raced after Raphael's story. She didn't know what to feel, but she knew she felt nauseous.

Raphael sensed her nervousness and rubbed her back with his cold hand. "At least for food, Calypso. You must be starving. I know you didn't touch your meal last night."

Callie gasped as Raphael's hand reached her lower back. She had nearly forgotten that she first saw him only a night ago. It felt like she had known him for longer, in another lifetime.

"I-I have no clothes, and I'm really not that h-hungry," Callie stammered.

"Check the closet in your room. I believe you will find your size there."

Callie backed away slowly and walked through the hallway and into the bedroom. She was surprised to find an entire wardrobe inside the closet: long velvet gowns, short mini dresses, sweaters, purses, high heels, and boots, all Callie's size.

How could he know my size? He knows my name and size and has watched me sleep at night. What on Earth is next with this demon?

Callie dressed herself quickly, not wanting to make the vampire wait. She chose an elegant red sweater, skinny black jeans, and black combat boots. She found a bathroom in the hallway and splashed some water on her face, confirming that this was real life. She momentarily looked at her reflection in the mirror, tossed her hair over her shoulder, and turned around. Raphael stood in front of her, wearing a similar red sweater and black jeans.

"A vampire's intuition," he said as he winked at her. He held the door open for her, and they entered a dimly lit hallway. They approached an elevator, and Raphael inserted a key to open the doors.

"I have the top-floor penthouse," Raphael explained. "There is no access to this floor except for my trusted workers who have a key. Granted, I will not keep you locked up here during daylight hours. You may come and go as you wish if you return home to me by sunset. You mustn't be out alone at night; vampires exist, as you know." They exited the elevator and entered the parking garage. Callie's eyes widened as she viewed a line of expensive black cars parked along the back wall.

Raphael pushed his keys, and a black matte GWagon roared to life, the headlights almost blinding both of them.

"Ah," Raphael sighed, "I will never tire of that."

Callie watched the lights move past her as they drove through the city. It felt surreal, like she was watching a movie. The previous night on the beach kept replaying, so she was too focused to speak. She was so mad, so scared, so confused, and her draw and pull toward Raphael made her feel disgusted at herself. How could she lust for a monster? One who had already flipped her life upside down and was now leading her toward death.

They arrived at a Japanese restaurant, the best in town, according to Raphael. She ignored walking in, sitting down, and Raphael ordering for her. It was as if Callie was stuck in a trance, watching the last twenty-four hours of her life flash by. She tried to figure out where she had gone wrong.

"Tell me what is on your mind, mon chérie," Raphael said as he reached across the table to hold her hand. She stared at his long, slender fingers. They were smooth and pale, with no blemishes or wrinkles. His nails were finely manicured, better than her own. She looked up, getting lost in his beautiful blue eyes again.

"When will you do it?" she asked quietly.

"I will explain the process to you the best that I can, mon

chérie. I am not going to turn you until you are ready. You must accept this transformation; you must want to become a vampire before anything happens."

"Why is that? So you feel fine on your moral compass?" Callie crossed her arms and looked away, her cheeks burning from staring into his eyes.

"No." He chuckled. "You must accept this as a human to make the transition easier. I have seen it happen too many times over my years, where someone is turned against their will." He paused as if he wanted to say more but held back.

"You don't want me to off myself once you turn me into a blood-sucking monster, right?" Callie leaned forward onto the table, winking at Raphael, using her charm to disarm him.

"Yes, you are correct, Callie, but...it's not that simple. Don't worry about that now; you have enough to take in. Let's not shatter your reality anymore this evening."

Just as she was about to respond, their food arrived. Callie didn't realize how starved and weak she was until she started eating. She closed her eyes and ate almost embarrassingly quickly while Raphael barely touched his plate.

Callie finished eating and wiped her mouth with a white silk napkin before asking, "What, you don't eat food as a vampire?"

"Yes, I can, but I don't need to. I prefer the taste of my other meals."

Callie snorted. She couldn't believe how casually he talked about killing people and drinking their blood.

"I don't want you to think of me as a murderer, Callie. Do I kill people? Of course, but many of them deserve to die. I have made many mistakes in my long lifetime, but I am not ashamed to admit that. You do not have to kill either unless you want to."

"Why on Earth would I want to do that?" Callie nearly shouted back at him. She was furious; this handsome stranger was going to kill her and make her kill others! She knew that no matter how attractive he made it sound, she would become a monster.

Raphael sighed. He was inside Callie's mind, of which she was unaware. He didn't know how to make things easier for her. She was right. After all, she would become a killer. You cannot be a child of darkness without stepping into the realm of cold-blooded killing.

"I am going to give you time to accept your fate. Once I feel you are ready, I will transform you. I will wait as long as I need to, weeks, months, years if I have to." Callie blankly stared back into the abyss of his blue eyes.

Please let it be quick. Please don't let me live years under the spell of this monster.

"It is quite a simple process," Raphael continued. "I will drink from your blood, and you will drink from mine. I will make it as quick and painless as possible, but your human body will die. Since you shall have my blood in your system, you will survive and be reborn as I am." Callie stayed quiet and asked their waitress for a drink as she passed by. The waitress returned with vodka on the rocks, as Callie had requested, and she downed it immediately, almost puking as she did.

"Oh God, why must you drink such vile liquid? Perhaps a scotch next time?"

Callie started to laugh and couldn't stop. Her stomach ached as the movements constantly waved through her body. She was so loud that her laughs echoed off the empty restaurant walls.

"You drink blood, but you want to lecture me on my alcohol choice?" Callie scoffed. "Trust me, it tastes like shit, but I'm just trying to get drunk. After all, you just described how you were going to kill me."

After Callie's outburst, Raphael quickly settled the bill, leaving too large of a tip. He helped her into his car as she stumbled. They sped off into the night, and Callie began to feel sick to her stomach. Some amount of time had passed, and she wasn't sure how long they had been driving as she spaced out, imagining dying. The car stopped abruptly, and Callie looked out the windshield to see they were parked in front of a cliff. Raphael opened her door and helped her out as soon as the car was parked.

"I know you are scared, mon chérie, but there is much to look forward to with this transition. Your life is just beginning, and you shall have many more opportunities than you ever would in a human lifetime. You will see the world in a new light; it will be amazing, I promise you."

Callie's head was swimming. She wanted to believe his words, and she was becoming a little more open to it, but she couldn't accept the fact that she would have to die and, in turn, kill others.

"Stop saying these things!" Callie shoved Raphael with all her strength, but he hardly moved. "I don't want to die! I want to live my meaningless human life! I don't care who you are or how much money you have. Leave me alone!" Her voice echoed into the night. She was acutely aware of how quiet the night was, spare ocean waves crashing below the cliff. It was just her and the Vampire King alone in the night.

"I'm losing my patience with you, Callie." Raphael stepped toward her, and she slowly backed away. "You have lived a tragic life, yet you want to continue it. You want to work your whole life, ruining your physical body. You want to age, get wrinkles, and struggle financially with a man who will never please your longing soul."

Tears welled up in Callie's eyes, and she felt them rush onto her cheeks, warm and salty.

"You think I am a monster?" Raphael asked, baring his fangs at her. "I will show you a monster." He jumped forward, throwing her onto the ground.

Callie yelped and scrambled backward, kicking up dust as she tried to escape him. She kicked dust and rocks into his face, which unphased him as he continued to walk toward her.

Every sense was heightened for Callie. The pain in her palms as rocks dug into her skin. Her racing heartbeat and shallow breaths. The cool, salty breeze that whipped around her.

It was almost exactly like her nightmare, only this time it was real.

She was unaware that she reached the cliff's edge and was about to fall off the side. She locked eyes with Raphael as he lunged towards her again. She screamed and expected immense pain, but he only grabbed her shirt.

Callie whimpered as he lifted her off the ground and brought her to eye level. Her mind went blank as she saw his terrifying face; evil seemed to consume his eyes and his fangs seemed to reach for her skin.

He hated toying with her and causing distress, but it was the only way he knew how to change her mind. He lifted her over the edge of the cliff. She screamed and struggled to try and kick him.

"I hold you so close to death, and yet you still struggle. Do you want to die tonight, Callie?" His tone seemed to mock her, and Callie was terrified of how quickly he had turned into a monster.

"I would rather die a human than die and become what you are," she spit in his face. He released her, and she fell into the darkness.

All the air exited her lungs as she plummeted below. The rush of air was so great that she could not scream or react. In the mere seconds, her body tumbled through the atmosphere at lightning speed. She thought of the cold and impending death that awaited her, wondering if her parents had felt the same way. At least she was away from him, the monstrous man whose face would be the last thing etched into her mind.

Finally, Raphael swooped down, wrapping his hands around her waist and bringing her body close to him. He hovered just above the jagged rocks sticking out of the waves. Callie's eyes were tightly shut, but when she felt the ocean spray hit her face, she opened them. She was not dead; in fact, she was floating, wrapped tightly in Raphael's arms. She automatically gripped his biceps out of fear, and he flew up into the night sky. He raced upward, and Callie pulled closer to his chest as the cold air tore around them. The wind was deafening, and it felt like he was flying as fast as an airplane.

Raphael eventually landed on a tall skyscraper in the city. Callie's legs were weak underneath her, and she refused to let go, trembling in his arms. She looked over the edge of the building and saw the millions of lights twinkling below them. It was beautiful and terrifying at the same time.

"I am sorry for giving you such a fright, mon chérie," Raphael whispered. His voice was calm and seductive and made her legs even weaker. "Yes, I can be a monster. I can rip the flesh from a human and enjoy it. But I would *never* hurt you, Callie. You are my queen. I know you are."

Callie had mustered enough courage to release him from her death grip. She slowly lowered herself, sitting against the building as far away from the edge as possible.

"Well, I guess I'll have to overcome my fear of heights." Raphael chuckled, and Callie kept her head down, staring at the lights as they blurred in her vision. "I didn't know vampires could fly," she said quietly. Raphael sat down next to her and placed his hand on top of hers. His skin was cold and sent goosebumps racing up her arm.

"There are many things you don't know and will come to learn. Flying is not available to everyone, so to speak. We gain power with our age, of course. But you and I are special, Callie. We...get extra strength and powers. You will be able to do things other vampires would need centuries to accomplish."

They stayed silent for a while, Callie still reeling from falling off a cliff. She felt as if she had truly died, she couldn't feel her heartbeat or pulse. She couldn't tell if she was breathing either, her body was in complete shock.

She contemplated jumping off the building and dying for good, but decided she did not want to experience the terror of falling for a second time.

"You know this is the only reason I choose to live in the city," Raphael finally spoke. "Watching all of the lights is quite magical."

"I'm surprised. I figured a man of your age wouldn't appreciate the technology and pollution of this century," Callie joked. Raphael smiled slightly, pleased that she was beginning to warm up to him.

"I have been through it all, mon cheri. Of course, I love these extraordinary pleasures of human life. My favorite is to sit up here so far away from everyone, yet I can step into their minds. I can hear the cluster of voices or the endless traffic if I wish. Or I can completely close myself off and be alone." He blushed, feeling vulnerable after opening up to her.

Callie still felt nauseous from being thrown off a cliff and flown through the air. Raphael sensed it and reached out his hand to her.

"I believe you have had enough excitement for one night. Come, let's return to my penthouse. The sun will be here soon enough." Callie stood up slowly, her legs threatening to buckle underneath her. Raphael pulled her close into him, and they took off.

Callie didn't open her eyes until they were back in the penthouse, which she didn't understand. Perhaps they had flown in through a window or secret entrance she didn't notice earlier.

"The car..." she said slowly, looking around and taking in her surroundings again.

"Don't worry." Raphael chuckled. "I'll have someone fetch it, and it will be waiting for you downstairs in the morning if you wish to drive it. Speaking of the morning, I will not be here, of course. But you may go as you please. Take whatever car and money you wish. Spend the day shopping; perhaps you are not satisfied with the wardrobe I have acquired for you. All I ask is that you return when the sun sets so we may enjoy the night together."

Callie nodded and let him lead her back into the bedroom she had woken up in. She was so exhausted all she could do was kick off her boots. She had no energy to take off her clothes and nearly collapsed into the bed. Raphael pulled the covers over her as her head sank into the silk pillow.

"Wait," she mumbled and pushed herself up. "Where do you go when the sun rises?"

Raphael stayed quiet and slowly leaned in as if to kiss her, his long blond hair brushing against her cheeks. Callie slipped into a deep sleep as he stepped away, marveling at the beauty of his queen before disappearing.

Chapter 3

When Callie awoke, she was surprised it was already noon. She stripped her clothes from the previous night and took a shower. As the hot water pelted her body, she kept turning her head, half expecting Raphael to be behind her. The memories of the previous night replayed in her mind: the evil look that twisted across Raphael's face, her body tumbling through the cold wind as she was thrown off the cliff, and how safe she felt flying in his arms. She hated herself for the mixed turmoil she felt in her body and vomited before exiting the shower.

She quickly scanned the closet he prepared ahead of her arrival. She wandered into the living room and spotted a shiny pair of keys waiting for her on the kitchen island. Next to it was a black titanium credit card named Raphael Capon. She smiled and left the penthouse, looking behind one last time.

Once she entered the parking garage, she noticed the line of sleek black cars against the wall. The G Wagon they had taken the previous night was there, along with a lifted Ford Truck, a Tesla, a Lamborghini, and a few others she couldn't name. She didn't need to be told that these were all Raphael's cars. She wondered how he acquired this money, and then the image of bloody bodies entered her mind. She shook her head to clear the image and pressed the keys, seeing that her ride for the day would be a Range Rover.

Callie drove to the nearest cafe and ordered a double shot of espresso, knowing she would need the energy to stay awake all night. She briefly debated running away but figured it was useless as he managed to find her in Florida before she knew he existed.

After she ate, she decided to go shopping. After all, the vampire had offered her his money. She started her spree at Michael Kors, not knowing how much money he had left for her. She quickly moved on to Prada, Louis Vuitton, and Saint Laurent. She spent thousands of dollars carelessly, becoming more reckless as the day went on.

She never had so much money to throw away and felt no shame in using someone else's. She was going to die soon anyway, so what did it matter if she spent two thousand on a pair of sunglasses?

*

By eight o'clock, the car was filled with bags, and she was unsure if she had drained his bank account. She was stuck in traffic only a few blocks away from the penthouse. She knew the sun would set in a few minutes, and she wouldn't be back in time.

Fuck...I can't believe I'm going to be late. Will he seriously throw me off a cliff tonight for not obeying him?

Callie flew into the parking garage, nearly denting the car on the concrete wall. She stuffed bags inside of each other, rushing to gather everything she had bought. She ran into the elevator and was thankful it was empty. The ride to the top floor was excruciating, and by the time it opened, her whole body trembled. She stepped slowly toward the single door at the end of the hall. The door swung open, and Callie rushed inside and dropped all of the bags.

"I'm so sorry," she exclaimed, tears threatening to spill out of her eyes. "The time got away from me and...and—"

Raphael appeared to soothe her and brush the frizzy hair out of her eyes. "Did you think I would be upset at you?"

"You told me to return at sunset, and I wasn't."

"I'm not going to kill you over a few minutes, mon cheri. Not after I've waited an eternity for you. Now, go get ready. We have reservations at the finest steak house in town."

Callie sighed in relief and her body felt weakened over the heightened adrenaline. Raphael's cold fingers brought her grace as opposed to fear the night prior. She went into the bedroom still unbelieving that she was alive.

She picked out a short black dress with lace along her neckline. She put on black socks that reached just over her knees and the same boots she had worn the previous night. Pulling her hair over to one shoulder, she imagined Raphael's lips grazing the side of her neck. Once she calmed herself, she walked into the hallway.

Raphael looked as handsome as the previous night, but this time, he wore a red button-up shirt with the sleeves rolled up. She nearly gawked at his biceps, which seemed to explode out of the sleeves. He left a few top buttons undone, and she turned away, trying not to stare. As they exited into the hallway, Callie turned back toward him.

"Wait, why are we taking a car if you can fly?"

"I like to drive when I am living as a human. I love feeling the attention and stares from the bourgeoise when I pull up.

"You don't need cars to be stared at," Callie blushed. "And why do you have so many cars, and why are they all black? Is that your evil color?"

Raphael laughed. "Why yes, I prefer black, red, maybe some deep purples. Every knight needs multiple steeds, Callie. These are my twenty-first-century steeds."

He paused; the only noise between them was Callie's racing heart. "My first horse was black, and I choose black vehicles in honor of him."

Callie was taken aback by his answer, not knowing he had such fond memories inside of him. The elevator opened with a ding, breaking the awkward silence between them.

Raphael walked toward the sleek black sports car that Callie could not identify. He stepped in front of her and opened the door, which swung upward.

"Spider Mclarin."

Callie sat down, and her eyebrows furrowed together. She began to piece all of their previous conversations together. He always said something that she questioned or thought about.

"Yes, I can read your mind, Calypso." Her head jerked as he appeared instantly inside the driver's seat. "You will be able to read minds once you turn as well."

Callie felt hurt and sank into the cold leather seat. She turned slightly so her dress rose, revealing more of her thighs. She wanted to see how far she could push him before he would bite. "Well, knowing that I will never have private thoughts around you is wonderful."

"You allow me into your mind. At first, I had to be next to you and force myself in. As time went on, you opened yourself up to me. I could enter your mind being thousands of miles away."

"Wait..." Callie responded. "You were next to me? You came into our bedroom?"

"I'm surprised you are just now making this connection. You never wondered why that handsome blond man was in your dreams every night?"

"I-I..." she stammered.

"Oh, the ecstasy I felt, sitting alone in my penthouse. Closing my eyes and hearing your soul call out to me. Begging for me to enter your mind."

Callie turned away from him, hot tears stinging her eyes. She felt naked and violated. Moments later, they pulled up to the restaurant. There was a long line of people in elegant suits and dresses waiting outside. Raphael placed the car in park and opened the door for Callie. She got out, refusing his hand, and avoided looking at him. Raphael led the way and walked confidently in front of the line of people. As he opened the door for Callie, a man who was waiting touched Raphael's arm.

"The line is back there, man!" Raphael turned his head slowly, scowling at the stranger.

"Don't touch me, peasant. We are royalty, unlike yourself."

The man gawked as the two walked into the restaurant. They were seated immediately, and Raphael ordered glasses of wine for both of them.

Callie pouted as she examined their surroundings. Everyone was dressed luxuriously, and the waiters had an air of elegance about them. The sizzling smell of steak and potatoes made her mouth water.

"You can't be mad at me, Callie," Raphael spoke finally, swirling the red wine around. "I had to enter your mind before I chose you."

"Choose me, like a slab of meat." Callie downed the wine and slammed the glass onto the table, still refusing to make eye contact with him. A few couples from nearby tables turned and stared at their commotion.

"I had to make sure your mind and soul were truly what I felt when I first saw you."

"And what is that? Oh, please tell me what my mind and soul spoke to you, Lord Vampire."

Raphael chuckled. "I appreciate your humor, Callie, but you must contain it. Not for me but for others."

"Who?" She scowled. "The vampires you claim I will rule over?"

"We can discuss this later. First, let's eat."

The waiter endlessly brought food to their table. Callie ate salad, bread, and superfluous meat and vegetables. They finished the meal with a flaming desert, and Raphael excused himself. Callie felt tipsy from the multiple glasses of wine but was still dismayed over her invasion of privacy.

What could my soul say to him? All I remember is dreaming of him every night, but I thought it was the vampire Lestat from the books I read. I can't believe he watched Justin and I sleep! I wonder if he ever drank from us.

Callie fidgeted in the seat, wondering what was taking Raphael so long. She suddenly remembered she had her cell phone in her small clutch bag. She took it out, deciding to go on social media. She hadn't been on her phone since Raphael had taken her, though only a few nights ago. The first picture that popped up was of Justin. It was his selfie at the gym. 'Focusing on myself and my gains,' he had captioned it. She closed the phone and looked around the restaurant again, not seeing her tall blond companion.

"Excuse me," she said to the waiter as he passed their table. "May we have the check?" She hoped to speed up their exit from the restaurant.

"The bill has already been paid." Callie was confused. Where was Raphael? She stood up and exited the restaurant, looking around out front. She saw only people walking by and a small line still waiting to enter the restaurant. She could not find the car they had taken earlier. By now, she was angry at him for leaving her alone. She turned and quickly walked down the sidewalk past the bustle and commotion. She saw an alley up ahead and decided to turn down it, desperate to find him.

Raphael stood in the shadows, leaning up against the wall of another building. She almost ran to him, then stopped abruptly within a few feet of him. As her eyes adjusted to the darkness, she saw that Raphael had his mouth against a stranger's neck. She gasped, and he heard, turning around to reveal bright red blood rolling down the side of his lips. She recognized the victim as the man from earlier who had grabbed Raphael.

"Is this what you do to humans you don't like?" She asked, furious she caught him in the act. "Aren't you supposed to do this somewhere more private?"

Raphael laughed and shoved the stranger against the wall. He looked unconscious, or maybe he was frozen in a stupor. "Yes, Calypso, I feed from the humans that disrespect me. Most do not, as I am terrifying to look at."

Of course, you are terrifying, you are a damn monster.

A shiver ran down her spine as she focused on the bright red blood dripping off of his lips. Lips that she wanted to kiss, though they had just committed an atrocious act.

"You aren't terrifying," she responded. She hadn't meant to open her mouth, as she was still mad, but the words slipped out.

"You really think that?" The smile grew on Raphael's face. "Even while I stand here with a man half dead and his blood on my face?" He wrapped his hands around her waist and pulled her into him.

"No matter how much you infuriate or terrify me, I can't seem to resist you," Callie whispered. She became lost in his deep blue eyes again. They seemed to put her into a trance, and she wondered if this was how his victims felt. She couldn't resist him and pulled his face down to meet hers. She kissed his lips and was surprised they were not ice cold like the rest of his body. She melted into the embrace, and he pulled away quicker than she wanted him to.

"Let's get out of here," he whispered, resting his forehead against hers. The stranger, whom they had forgotten about, fell to the ground.

"Will he be okay?"

"He'll wake up soon. I did not drink enough to kill him, thanks to your interruption." The two of them walked down the alleyway, holding hands. "Callie, would you like to go on an adventure tonight? If you would let me, I'd like to show you part of my world, our soon-to-be world."

"Where are you going to take me?"

"We'll have to fly, I'm afraid. No cars allowed at the vampire bar."

Callie laughed. "Vampire bar? Let me guess, all-night specials on Bloody Marys?" Raphael pulled her close again, and they took to the sky. Callie buried her face into his chest and gripped tightly, even though she didn't need to.

The wind was deafening and cold, but she felt more secure than she had been the previous night. They landed quickly. Dust swirled around them, making Callie cough. She stepped away from Raphael and scanned the surroundings. They were in the middle of the desert, it seemed. Rocks and sand surrounded them, with no plant life or any signs of humans for that matter. She heard the thumping of bass music and saw the shadows of a building up ahead. Her heart began to beat faster.

A vampire bar, they will smell me! They will know I am human and rip me to shreds. This was a mistake.

"Calypso." Raphael grabbed her arms and spun her around to face him. "I would never bring you into harm's way. Yes, everyone knows you are human. I have already announced our presence."

"Announced?" She stepped back in confusion and the dry sand and rocks crunched beneath her feet.

"When I was made king, I was blessed with many powers. I can send messages into the mind of every living vampire. I let everyone here know that the king was arriving with his soon-to-be queen. Nobody will harm you; they dare not disobey the king."

Callie felt more reassured and followed behind Raphael, making sure not to stray too far from him. As they walked up the creaking wooden stairs, she felt a heat rise around her. She held her head high but kept her gaze averted, knowing every move was watched with extreme scrutiny. She couldn't bear to look at those around her. Raphael led her to what she presumed was the dance floor. The music changed to an old tune, that sounded early nineteen hundreds.

Raphael wrapped one hand around her waist, and with the other, he held her hand in the air, leading her through a waltz. Callie rested her head against his chest and tried to stay calm. It was hard when every dead soul stared right at her. Some of them looked like they wanted to bow down and kiss her feet, and others looked like they were one second away from ripping her head off of her body.

"Pay them no mind," Raphael said once the song had ended. "Let's get you a drink; maybe it will help to calm your nerves." They walked over to the bar, where a young woman polished glasses.

"What an honor to see you tonight." She smiled as Raphael leaned against the bar. She was covered in tattoos, and her bright orange hair made her look more alive than the other vampires in the club. "What can I get for you, darling?"

"Uh, do you have martinis here?" Callie asked. She could see the empty glasses scattered along the bar, all stained red. She could only assume blood was on tap.

"Sure, we could make that work, honey." She set down the towel and glass she had been vigorously wiping. She grabbed two bottles and began to pour the liquids into the same glass. She grabbed a lime and knife from behind the bar and chopped thin slices of the lime.

As Callie reached her arm forward to grab the drink, the bartender picked up the knife and attempted to slam it into Callie's hand. The knife barely grazed her skin as Raphael grabbed the handle. He flipped the knife around and threw it back at the bartender, severing her head completely. Callie screamed in terror as the head rolled onto the floor and her body collapsed.

"Anyone else care to make a foolish mistake?" Raphael boomed, turning around and outstretching his arms. "I come here, and you make a mockery of me. Next time, all of you will burst into flames." He grabbed Callie's hand, and they rushed out of the bar.

Callie was shaking by the time they were outside under the stars again. "I don't understand," she wept.

"Not everyone respects us. I am so sorry, Calypso. I did not think anyone would be so ignorant as to act out."

"What did she want from me?" Raphael took a moment to wipe the tears from her eyes. He had too much to tell her and knew it would break her heart to reveal the truth. He couldn't hide it forever, but tonight was not the right time.

"Not everyone approves of us. They resent the king and will be against you once you become queen. Not all vampires, of course, but a select few. They don't listen to the rules and would rather be on their own to create chaos in the world."

Callie sniffled and looked back at the lone building. The dust began to swirl around them again, but she felt no wind. A deep gray fog rose from the ground and began to take the form of two bodies. Callie stood behind Raphael and tried to control her convulsions. After an attempted murder and now this horror, she was ready for the nightmare to end.

"You shouldn't have brought her here," a deep voice echoed from the fog. There was no face that Callie could make out, just the shadowy figures.

"I don't need permission from you," Raphael growled. Callie had never heard him so angry. The fog laughed a resounding boom that sent shivers down Callie's spine. "She's not the one you are looking for. She deserves to be a housewife, not following in your shadow of death and destruction."

This made Callie furious. Her nostrils filled with rage, and she momentarily forgot her fear. She clenched her fists together and stepped out from behind Raphael. "You don't know me," she spoke with a tense jaw. "You don't know who I am or what I can do."

"No, we don't know you," the fog responded. "But Hades already knows what lies in your soul." Callie stepped back in confusion, and Raphael rushed at the fog. He yelled something in Latin, expecting the fog to disappear. Instead, the gray cloud rushed toward Callie's heart center and entered her body.

Pain gripped throughout her body, and she dropped to the rocky ground, clutching at her heart. She felt as if she couldn't breathe, or if she did, her whole chest cavity would implode. A deep laugh echoed in her ears, leaving her deaf to Raphael's scream of terror. Then, out of nowhere, it was silent, and the pain was gone, as quick to leave as it had come.

They were left alone in the darkness once again. Callie stayed quiet, staring at the endless stars, trying to catch her breath. Raphael tried to get her to stand up, but she grounded herself as much as possible.

"It's time to go," Raphael grabbed her roughly, but Callie dug her heels into the ground.

"What the fuck was that Raphael?"

He stayed quiet and continued to drag her across the rocky ground.

"I nearly died; tell me what happened!" she screamed. "You've been lying to me! What was that? Some sort of spirit? Talking about Hades, as in the Greek God?"

Raphael spun around and looked Callie in the eyes. He was furious, and she saw the red veins popping in his eyes. "You really want to know?" His voice boomed into the night. "Those were Hades' demons from Hell. I tried to chase them away, but they went inside you."

"Went inside me?" Callie freed herself from Raphael's grip and stumbled away from him. He tried to step forward and grab her, but she jerked away again, flailing like a wild beast. Her hair was messy, and her nostrils flared. She was covered in sand and had the look of a killer. Raphael decided to let her stay free and calm down.

"Why would they go inside of me?"

Raphael stayed quiet long enough to make Callie's heart stop, finally breaking the tense air. "The demons went inside of your soul so that Hades could judge it, just as he does with all of the souls that go to Hell."

Callie's mind swirled as a whole new dimension of life was confirmed. "What happens now?" Her knees were quaking, and she was ready to drop into Raphael's arms and fly out of this horrific night.

"This doesn't change anything. You will still become the Vampire Queen; he just knows you now. I tried to avoid this for as long as possible, but that bastard can't wait."

"Wait," Callie snapped back up, ready to fight. "You knew about this?"

Raphael had enough of the games. He scooped her up in his arms, leaving only inches between their faces. "I am the servant of Hades. Creature of the Night, Vampire King of Hell, the devil's slave, and you, Calypso, are going to become the queen."

They rocketed into the sky, and the breath was stolen from Callie's mouth. He had his arms so tightly around her that she could not pound or kick him. She eventually resorted to biting his chest and ripped away part of his flesh, to her surprise. This made him stop mid-flight, and Callie felt dizzy and nauseated.

"Don't play this fucking game with me," Raphael grabbed her hair and yanked her head back, the blood splattered onto his face. "See? You like this," he continued. "You were born to be a vampire."

"No! I'm not giving my soul to the devil!" Callie screamed and continued to try to fight against him. "Let me go! Kill me right here!"

"Don't you get it?" Raphael's screams echoed in the middle of the night. "Your soul is doomed. If I let you go now, you will fall right into Hades' hands. Now that he has tasted your soul, he is waiting for you. Turning into a vampire will save your soul. You'll serve him instead of having him torture you." He pulled her closer to him, and she finally stopped struggling. She sobbed into his chest and repeatedly said no.

Callie was unaware of it, but they teleported back to the Santa Monica penthouse. Raphael decided it would be too much to fly back in her shocked and disheveled state. Teleporting took much of his strength, but he would use all of it to get her home safely.

He gently laid her down in the bathtub, turned on the shower, ensuring the water was warm but not too hot, and undressed her.

"Is this okay?" He asked her. Callie didn't respond as she was in a comatose state. Her face was frozen in terror, her hands balled into fists, and her muscles were utterly tensed.

Raphael tossed aside her clothes and gently washed away the dirt and blood from her hair. Brown muddy water ran down her face, leaving lines down her cheeks. He brushed his thumb across her skin to clean the imperfections. She finally moved and touched his cold, white cheek.

"Please tell me it's not true," she barely choked out the words. "Tell me my soul can be saved. I can go to heaven!"

He hung his head, and his shoulders drooped, feeling defeated. "There is no heaven, Callie. All souls go to Hell." Raphael cringed as her wail pierced his ears. He hated to see her in pain; it wasn't supposed to happen this way. She was supposed to fall in love with him first, and he would ease her into the dark path. She would have wanted to become a child of Hades, but instead, she had been thrown into the fire and was burned and afraid.

"I have to go," he said quietly and stood up, turning away from her naked body. She was terrified to be alone; she could end up in Hell at any second.

"Wait, don't leave me! Where are you going?" She stood up and reached out to him, but he was already gone.

Her body began to tremble, and she let out another long and painful wail. The water turned scalding hot and pelted her skin.

hapter 4

Callie woke up in bed hours later without remembering how she had gotten there. She had no memory after Raphael left her in the shower. She was clean and wore a white cotton nightgown that went past her knees. It looked ancient, from the medieval ages, and probably was, she decided.

She heard a loud thump from the living room, and the hairs on her arms stood up. Could it be the demons from the previous night, ready to drag her to Hell? She sprung out of bed and quietly opened the door to slink into the hallway.

"Raphael?" she called out but knew he was not there.

"So sorry, miss." A middle-aged woman popped around the corner, making Callie jump from surprise. "I'm the cleaner, Maria," she stuck her hand out to shake, but Callie didn't take it.

A house cleaner? I'm sure he feeds on her, the scumbag.

Raphael had become a liar in her eyes overnight. From hiding the truth about her transformation, to having to sacrifice her soul to Hades, what else could he have lied about?

She circled Maria quickly, looking for any bite marks on her body or apparent cover-ups. She found nothing and marched into the kitchen with her arms crossed.

"Sorry you scared me," Callie spoke but did not look at Maria. She didn't trust her yet. "How long have you worked for him? He never mentioned you."

"My grandmother worked for his father many years ago. She had my mother shortly after, and she took over for the Capons when she was of age. Now I am here," Maria spoke cheerfully while dusting around the living room.

"Oh wow," Callie ate a bowl of fruit she found in the fridge. She was on the verge of losing it, hearing her vampire captor had a family line of indentured servants.

"So, how did your family start working for him?" She sat on the chair closest to Maria and stared intently at her.

"Well, his father helped my grandma from a bad situation

in Ecuador. All he asked was for her to work for him for a few years. His father treated her and my mother so well, so she asked to be kept on after his father passed and Raphael moved back into the area."

"Very interesting," Callie crunched obnoxiously on an apple. "So Raphael must have treated your mother great then for you to work for him as well."

"Oh yes," Maria responded. "He has always been very generous, and it is an easy job. The Capons have greatly helped our family, so I cannot thank him enough." She paused for a moment before turning back toward Callie. "I'm not surprised Raphael forgot to mention me coming today. He is such a busy businessman, as you know. I am so happy to finally meet you. He has spoken so highly of you. How amazing for you, finishing law school."

Callie stiffened. She had attended college for two years in an attempt to be accepted into law school after earning her bachelor's degree. However, the bachelor's proved to be challenging enough, and she dropped out, never pursuing the degree. Her failed attempt occurred almost four years ago. Had he been stalking her that long?

"Oh, thank you." She laughed nervously and twirled her hair strands. "Raphael must have talked about me for a while then."

"Yes, about a year now. So noble of you to complete your degree while helping your ailing family."

Callie's eyebrows furrowed together and her lips twisted. "Is that what he said about me?"

"I never meant to pry, ma'am. I remember the day he told me you had finally finished school and would be moving here with him. He was so happy; I hardly ever see him smile."

Callie smiled and nodded, then stood up quickly. She put her empty bowl in the sink and returned to the living room. She began to look at the tall bookshelves that sat next to the windows. The shelves were built into the wall, which she hadn't noticed before. She scanned the titles, looking for something to pop out at her. Most of the books were old with browning and tattered spines. She recognized a few titles—*Frankenstein, Dracula,* and *Republic* by Plato. Others had no title on the cover or were in a foreign language. She squatted down to the bottom shelf, and a thick textbook caught her eye. *Greek Mythology.*

She took the book and nearly ran back into the bedroom. She jumped onto the bed and opened the cover, desperate for answers.

Callie read for hours, learning about the incredible family tree of the ancient Gods. She remembered a few of the stories from school, but only this time, they were real. There was not much information on Hades, for which she scoured the whole book. It mentioned the defeat of the Titans by Hades and his brothers Zeus and Poseidon. She could only imagine these figures were real as well. She learned that the three brothers had split the land equally, and he ruled over the souls and underworld. She could find no text speaking of his evil besides the story of Persephone.

She sighed and flipped around so her legs lay on the wooden bed frame. She hadn't found any incriminating information but was still unconvinced that this immortal God held her best interests. She was hurt by Raphael keeping the truth from her, especially when she was almost coming around to the idea of becoming his Vampire Queen. Perhaps she could get back at him.

Eventually, she noticed the golden sun streaming into the hallway and knew the sunset was approaching. She had tuned out Maria, who left and returned with groceries. Callie went to the bathroom to clean up and noticed her cell phone on the sink. Aside from checking Justin's social media the previous night, she had barely used it.

She grabbed it and instantly regretted it. She had dozens of texts from people she wouldn't consider friends, but they were very concerned about her cheating on Justin and abandoning

Florida. None of the texts were from Justin, which disappointed her slightly. She left the phone where she found it and returned to her room to change.

Moments later, she walked down the hallway, her black heels clicking against the polished wooden floors. Callie bent down to return the textbook to its place on the bookshelf. The tight red dress she wore slid up her thighs.

"Getting ready for dinner with Mister Raphael?" Maria called out from the kitchen.

"No." Callie smiled and grabbed a set of keys from the basket on the island counter.

"Oh, he left a note saying he would return for dinner. Expecting you to be here, of course, miss."

"That's alright, he'll know where to find me," Callie smirked, then walked out the door to Maria's amazement. Callie nearly ran to the elevator and pressed repeatedly on the down button. She didn't have much time before Raphael would be on the hunt for her. With the help of social media, she was able to find a party at a college campus nearby.

Unfortunately, she couldn't figure out how she would get there as the keys she grabbed didn't unlock any of the cars. Frustrated, she threw the keys in the bottom of her purse and stomped out of the garage. She called a taxi and arrived at campus ten minutes before the sun went down. She threw a wad of cash at the driver and stumbled out of the car.

She heard a commotion behind the school buildings and headed in that direction. The stench of cigarettes and beer let her know she was successful in her mission. Callie spotted a younger fraternity brother at the door of the building, keeping tabs on who entered the party. She walked up to him with a smile, doing her best to charm him.

"Hey there, beautiful. What sorority are you in?" Her plan had worked; he had fallen for her looks.

"Tri-Delta," she responded and tossed her hair over her shoulder.

"Step right on in." He stepped away from the door and motioned her to enter.

"I'm actually a new recruit. I was wondering if someone could show me around?"

"I'm not really supposed to leave the door unattended, but I'm sure my brothers wouldn't mind if I show you around." He instinctively wrapped his arm around Callie's waist, and they walked inside together. The brother talked about how he had joined the fraternity, but she didn't listen.

She quickly scanned the room for Raphael but didn't see his tall frame.

"Can I get a drink?" Callie interrupted him. He held her hand and led her to a corner with a large punch bowl.

"Come on, Cody, you know the rules!" A blond brother handed Callie a cup of punch and rolled his eyes at her counterpart.

"Chill, bro, I was just showing her around."

"It's totally fine." Callie turned to Cody. "I'll hang outside with you. Maybe we could smoke?" Cody's face lit up in a smile, and he took her by the hand again.

"You know you are too pretty to smoke."

Callie smiled and shrugged her shoulders. "The way I see it, we are all going to die anyway."

"You've got a little dark side to you," Cody joked. They stepped back outside as the twilight settled in. They moved around to the side of the building, and Cody pulled out a pack of cigarettes. He handed her one and lit it, getting too close to her face. He finally asked her name and who her big sister was.

"Oh uh...Emma," Callie responded quickly. She figured there had to be a sorority sister with that name. Cody began another boring and pointless story, and Callie did her best to listen and laugh at appropriate times. She kicked back one leg against the wall and slouched against it, letting the harsh tobacco smoke fill her lungs. She wasn't a frequent smoker but had smoked as a teen when she fell in with the wrong crowd. Justin had been the one to pull her out of the bad habit years ago.

Callie became overwhelmingly aware of the buzzing of the dim light above them. The sound seemed to fill her ears, then stopped abruptly. Her heart skipped a beat, and she knew Raphael had arrived. She dropped the cigarette and crushed it with her heel, then took Cody by the hand and drew him into her. He knew what she wanted, and she knew what she was doing to him. Their lips met, and it was terrible, but she gave into him, letting his thin and bad-tasting tongue into her mouth. Cody tried to continue, but Callie had to move her head away after a few seconds.

Cody stepped back, and Callie saw Raphael watching them from the corner of her eye.

His blond hair was tied back into a neat bun, something she had never seen before. He wore his usual black pants and a black button-up shirt. A few of the top buttons were undone, revealing his pale and muscular chest. She quickly averted her eyes after making eye contact with Raphael.

"You think toying with a fraternity brother will make me jealous?" Raphael questioned, his face free of any emotions.

She tried to control her smug grin; she had struck the nerve she intended.

"That's not my intention; why don't you look into my mind and figure it out?" she responded harshly. Cody looked confused but didn't say anything and continued to puff on his cigarette.

"If this is the life you want, please be my guest."

Raphael put his hands up and stepped back, turning away from them.

"That's not what I want." Callie tried not to sound too desperate. "I want you to kill him for me."

She had gotten his attention now. He turned back toward her, and she saw the anger creep into his face.

Cody's eyes popped, and Callie grabbed his arm tightly. Raphael stood in front of her instantly, and she had to look up to see him.

"So you tease him, making him think he's the one you want. All with the purpose of me ripping his heart out?" Raphael growled. "Is this the sick game you get off to?"

Cody's mouth opened, threatening to object, but Raphael silenced him with a flick of his hand.

"This isn't a game." Callie let go of Cody and placed her hands on Raphael's face. "I want to see how far you will go for me. I want to know that you will kill for me."

Raphael laughed and stepped back, removing her hands from his cheekbones. "You want me to kill *Him* for you," he said quietly. Tears sprung into her eyes, and she was suddenly overrun with guilt.

"I will do everything in my power to protect you, Calypso. But I can't kill Hades. That just isn't possible." He paused, seeing the sadness in her face, and then continued. "So, would you like me to kill him right here, feet away from this lovely party?"

"No." She sniffled and wiped the corners of her eyes. "He didn't do anything wrong; he doesn't deserve to die."

Raphael nodded and touched his hand to Cody's head. "Go back to your party, tell all your friends about the skank you kissed." Cody instantly turned and walked away as if the events had never happened.

"Now for you." Raphael kissed Callie's forehead and hugged her, trying to provide some comfort to the pain she was feeling. "Let's go back home," he whispered. "I have a lovely meal waiting for you." Callie shook her head but didn't respond, afraid to say anything else. "We are going to teleport, so it might feel different. We did last night, too, but I assumed you were too distraught to notice." Raphael wrapped his arms around her, and by the time Callie opened her eyes again, they were standing in the penthouse's living room.

"Why did you fly me around all those times if you can instantly travel places?" Callie asked as she sat down at the dining table. Raphael moved to the stovetop and began cooking a large white fish filet.

"I'd spoil you; you'd want to travel in such luxury all of the time." He laughed. "As you know, we can fly after years of practice and strength, but I have teleportation powers as well, and so will you."

The warm aroma of the food was enough to make Callie drool. Quickly enough, Raphael plated their meal and brought it over to the dining table. He poured two glasses of red wine and sat across from Callie.

"Let me present to you our meal for the evening. Swordfish salmoriglio paired with wild grain orzo and delicious red zinfandel."

"This looks and smells amazing. I didn't know you could cook."

"What, because blood is my main meal I can't cook? I've been around too long not to pick up on it," Raphael smiled and drank the wine as Callie ate. "I stopped by Nova Scotia to get a fresh catch. They always have the most clean and flavorful fish out of any region."

"And I just ditched your dinner," Callie averted her gaze but continued to shovel the food into her mouth.

"I'm not upset. Maria was much more upset. I'm sure she was ready to take your place tonight." Raphael swirled the almost empty glass in his hand and winked at Callie. Light rain pelted the glass windows, making the dim interior more cozy.

"Oh my God, how did I forget about your indentured servant? She told me you brought her grandmother from Ecuador, and the whole family has worked for you since. Or your dad first." Callie laughed.

"It's true, you know. I was in the jungle of South America when I heard her cries for help. I killed her abusive husband; she wasn't present, of course, and I brought her back with me. She couldn't work for me right away as she was late in her pregnancy. I bought her a house and provided well for them. They rarely saw me, and I didn't need help with my properties until recently in the modern century."

"I find it hard to believe that nobody questions you. How you get your money or why they only see you at night." Callie glanced around at the minimal luxurious furniture and decorations in the room.

"I'm an international businessman," Raphael's response was suave. "Her family has been paid so well there is no need to question me or where my money comes from."

"Where does it come from anyway?" Callie had nearly finished the meal but was more engulfed in the conversation. She felt ashamed for asking so many questions, but more would pop into her head each time she asked one.

"You read my *Greek Mythology* today, didn't you?"

Callie's eyes widened, and Raphael chuckled. "So you learned that Hades is the God of the underworld or the underearth. Which means all rocks, minerals, and gems are under his power." Raphael took the last sip of wine and continued. "Hades is a God of wealth and luxury. He rules over money, silver, and gold, to be exact. As his servant, I will never run out of money, nor will you. Before I met Hades, I would steal wealth from my victims. But there is no need for that anymore."

"Is it true what the book says about him?"

"What exactly are you referring to, Calypso?" He made eye contact, and her heart began to beat faster.

"Well, it made it seem like he's not evil. The book even mentioned that he is a God of fairness. In the myths about him, oh, are all of those real? And the other Gods?"

"I'm sure there is some truth to the myths. Yes, the Gods are real. I haven't met anyone besides Hades and a few glimpses of Hermes. He's delivered a few souls to Hades."

"Wow," Callie was stunned but not surprised. "Oh, uh, it seems he isn't evil aside from kidnapping Persephone."

Raphael stiffened at the name, but Callie failed to notice. "I don't think Hades is evil unless you want him to be. He can take on the part of an evil devil very well, but he doesn't have to be that way."

Callie nodded, her heart still beating fast, and she took deep breaths to try to calm herself. Raphael stood up and walked over to the large television to turn on the soundbar. A slow, old-time song started to play. Raphael pulled Callie out of the chair and into his chest.

"This isn't how I wanted it to happen," he whispered into her ear. One hand held the small of her back, and the other held her hand to his chest, slowly leading her around the room. "I wanted to make you fall in love with me first." As he kissed her earlobe softly, he couldn't help but feel tempted to bite into her neck.

"I'm already falling in love with you," Callie whispered. Every hair on her body stood straight up. It was against her human nature to love a monster, but she couldn't resist his allure.

"You shouldn't be. It hasn't been enough time. I didn't mean to rush into this; it's my fault."

"Stop," Callie placed a hand on his cheek. "I wanted this and you, you said so yourself. My soul was reaching out for you."

Raphael broke apart from Callie and pinched the bridge of his nose. "Yes, Callie, but I upheaved your life, shattered your view of the world, gave you a terrible fright..." His words were interrupted as Callie stood on her tiptoes to kiss him. He pulled back immediately, placing his hands on her shoulders to push her back to the ground.

"I don't care anymore." Callie looked up to him with pleading eyes. "I want you to take me away from my human life. I'm so terrified, Raphael, but I want to spend eternity with you."

The words made his skin vibrate with electricity, but his heart sank. This was what he had wanted after all, but now he rethought his offer.

"You want to spend eternity with me, living luxuriously like we are now. You don't want to spend eternity shrouded in darkness, living kill to kill."

"I don't care about the darkness or sacrificing my soul to Hades. I've had enough trauma in my life, you know this. I can handle everything; I'll do anything to live like you! Your life is perfect." Her eyes glistened and pleaded with him. The rain had ceased and the only noises were their beating hearts and pumping blood.

"I'm far from perfect, and I apologize for giving you that picture."

"How can you say that? You have everything you want! Endless riches, your looks are impeccable, you have endless time to do whatever you please, you rule over the entire race of vampires, for God's sake, Raphael!"

Raphael's face fell as he watched her eyes twinkle with the imaginative picture she had painted for herself. She was so far from the truth, but he knew if he told her, she would be heartbroken.

"Come on," Callie grabbed his hand and stood tall to kiss him again. "You've been watching me for a year. You can't tell me you don't want this."

"You need to stop, Callie; we can't do this yet."

"I'm not doing anything," she laughed, stroking her hand down his chest.

"I don't want to hurt you, but you are hard to resist, especially being this close." He wrapped his arms around her and laid his head against hers. Her smell and blood rushing through her veins was intoxicating. He knew that he only made it worse, speeding up her heart rate and making her release pheromones.

Callie stepped back and turned to walk into the hallway. She shimmied one shoulder out of the spaghetti strap, then the other. She turned, seeing Raphael quiver with his hands clasped before him.

"You washed me naked in the shower just fine, but you can't take a little teasing?"

"Different intensity. You know you are beautiful, and I desire you. You don't need to prove anything tonight."

"But I want to. Take me!"

"Callie, I can't." Raphael was frustrated now and ready to

put her in a trance. "I have killed so many women..." He trailed off. The memories flashed back to him. Images of bloody women torn apart abused his mind. "Ripped right in half. Or decapitated."

Callie was silent, pondering what he had revealed to her. "Then turn me into a vampire; we'll be able to have each other."

Raphael's mouth dropped open and he shook his head in defeat. He rushed to her and placed his hands on top of her head, transferring his memory to her.

It was a few months after Raphael had spoken with the witch. He had left his local region and traveled northeast. He settled in a small town outside of Russia, still governed by a king with a castle. Raphael had killed him and become the new ruler over the land, only he had become a God. The people worshiped him and brought him offerings of beautiful young women every night. The particular memory he placed in Callie's mind was the night he was captured by Hades' demons and dragged to Hell for the first time.

As Raphael's hands transferred the memory to Callie's mind, she saw the vision with her own eyes. She was viewing from Raphael's point of view but felt as if she were in the memory.

Callie blinked her eyes repeatedly and moved her head, seeing the brick castle walls around her. It was dark, and she struggled to see. Suddenly, the room was filled with a giant light resembling fire. As the shadows flickered off of the walls, Callie was finally able to see the massacre. The room was moderately large but plainly decorated, with only a Persian rug and a large wooden bed. The bed frame held four tall posts, and Callie saw a blonde woman with her arms tied to two of the posts.

Callie seemed to move closer to the woman and saw her chest ripped open. The cavity was a mess of blood and guts, with her heart missing. Callie saw a shriveled organ next to her legs, presumably her missing heart. Callie felt herself moving, scanning more of the bare room. She noticed multiple women piled on top of each other on the floor. A large brown puddle spread across the cold wooden floors. Just as she thought she couldn't view any more horror, she looked upward to find another woman hanging from the ceiling.

Her thighs were ripped open, and blood dripped down from her center. A drop of blood splashed onto Callie's forehead, and she heard a hideous screech. Two shadowy figures appeared in the corner, and she recognized them as Hades' demons. They rushed into her, and she felt immense pain throughout her entire body.

With the last image, Callie collapsed, and her vision returned to the present. She shook and breathed heavily while Raphael stood away and wrung out his hands.

"I didn't mean to frighten you, but you should be aware of what I am capable of."

"I saw the demons." Both Callie and Raphael were surprised that was all she spoke of.

"The night I met Hades," Raphael sighed. "I had been acting as King of that land. Hades heard and was not happy about my rise to fame. That's when our relationship began."

"How did Hades hear about what happened on land?"

"As King, I demanded sacrifices every night. Youthful women from all over the country would come and beg to be offered to me. I was sending so many souls to Hell, he couldn't help but notice me."

Callie was stunned, but she still stood up and faced Raphael. "I don't care about what happened hundreds of years ago."

"This has been a mistake, Callie. I wanted to take it slow with you, and I did. From when I first saw you, I left you alone, only checking on you once every few weeks. I didn't start entering your mind until a few months ago. What does it matter now? I tainted your soul."

"No, Raphael," Callie's voice was cut off as he flicked his hand.

"You need to leave and go back home. I've made a mistake

bringing you into this life."

"What am I supposed to do now? You ruined my life! I can't just go back to Justin and forget about you. You can erase my memory, but what about yours? You'd drive yourself to madness watching me live without you."

"I know this is difficult to accept, but I am trying to save you from harm." Raphael gritted his teeth together.

She was right; she couldn't leave him now. He had let her in too much; she penetrated every thought of his, and he would never be able to exist without her. But he couldn't accept her fate with Hades. There had to be another way. "How? I already told you I don't care!"

"Calypso!" Raphael shouted, his frustration boiling over. He couldn't think like this; he had to leave.

His voice pierced her ears, and she doubled over in pain. Just as she was about to protest again, he was gone.

She was left afraid and alone for another night.

Chapter 5

After collapsing to the floor and weeping, Callie decided to end her self-wallowing and sleep. She tossed around in the empty bed, replaying the night in her head.

All she could see was Raphael's look of disappointment at her boldness and stupidity. Of course, he wanted nothing to do with her. She had acted like a child.

Just as she was about to give up on sleep, she noticed a faint change in light in the hallway. She knew dawn was breaking and the sun would rise soon. She jumped out of bed and exited the penthouse, instinctually finding the random door in the barren hallway that opened to the rooftop stairway. Her beating heart matched the sound of her slippers slapping against the metal stairs. As she pushed the door open, the sun's golden rays nearly blinded her.

Callie reached the rooftop in perfect time to watch the giant blazing fire rise into the sky. She was terrified that this was the last sunrise she would ever see. She lowered herself to the cold and rough concrete as she took in the beauty and colors of the sky. She stared into the sun until her eyelids forced themselves shut, and her eyes wept. Callie realized how exhausted she was once the sun had fully risen over the skyline and distant mountains. She had much less energy coming down the stairs and fell asleep immediately after climbing into bed.

*

She jolted awake around two in the afternoon but felt rested. Her dreams consisted of Raphael pleasuring her as she begged him to drink her blood. It had felt so real, as if her body had really been touched by his cold hands. She wondered if he had created the fantasies in her mind or if they were born of her own desires.

Callie quickly got ready as she didn't want to miss any remaining daylight. She exited the building with only her phone and a water bottle and began jogging toward the beach. She ran a mile along a paved trail beside the sand and water. Callie never enjoyed running but forced herself to do it in high school. She had joined the track team purely out of spite and hatred for herself and the world around her.

She found exercise equipment along the path and walked over to it. As she did pull-ups, she forced herself to stay in the present moment and feel every muscle exert itself. The sweat began to bead around her forehead and roll down her face. She grunted and struggled under the beaming hot sun, knowing she would never again feel the pain she currently endured. It was such an unusual feeling to yearn for something not yet gone.

Callie drank her water and decided to lie down along the beach, thankful for the time to rest in the sand. The sun's rays seemed to surround her, making her look angelic. She decided to go on her phone one last time to say goodbye to her human life. The sun was not yet set but was beginning to fall in the sky, bringing beautiful colors. She took a picture of the sky and posted it on Instagram, captioning it 'starting a new adventure.'

Within minutes, her phone buzzed with notifications, likes, and comments. Callie knew that posting her location in Santa Monica would confirm that she had broken up with Justin and started a new life with her California lover. What Raphael said made sense; she knew Justin would never accept her becoming a vampire.

Callie checked her text messages before turning the phone off, and one unread message surprised her. It was from Justin's mom, Anne.

Hey, hon, we just wanted to reach out to let you know that we still love you, and we always will. You will always be a part of our family. Please reach out if you ever need anything. Justin will come around someday, too. Love, Momma Anne.

The tears flowed out of Callie's eyes even though she tried not to cry. Justin's family had taken her in since her aunt abandoned her at best. His parents always took both of them to and from school, cooked meals, and even bought Callie new clothes. Justin was her best friend before they dated, and she hadn't realized how long their history was. She reread the text, choking up at the words Momma Anne.

She threw the phone on the sand, done with that part of her life. She knew she had to release herself from her human attachments. After turning, she wouldn't be able to return to the past.

Callie wiped her remaining tears and moved herself into a sitting position. She was never a big believer in God, even after her parent's death. Her mom had pressured her into religion, but she never truly felt the faith. Now was as good of a time as any to send a prayer into the world. She sat silently, trying to think of the words to justify her actions.

Please, God, if you are out there, hear my plea. Help me, God, I don't want to be a monster. Help me find the good in this. Help me find the light. If I had a chance of seeing my mother and father again I wouldn't do this. But knowing about Hades changes everything. I can't go on like this, being human, knowing that no matter what I do, I am condemned to a hellish fate. At least as a vampire, I can avoid this and spend eternity bringing good things to the world, right?

The giggling of a group of girls nearby distracted Callie from her focus. She readjusted herself and noticed the bright orange hue the sky had taken on. The sun was close to setting and had become a deep blood red. Callie looked around at the other beachgoers to see if they observed the same red sun. Nobody was struck with such awe besides herself.

She laid down on her back and watched the clouds coruscate as the color changed from yellow to orange and pink. The colors seemed more vibrant to her, and Callie was lost in the beauty, taking in every beautiful detail and second in the glorious light. Birds flew by, and she cried over the simple beauty they added to the landscape. The sun had set, but Callie did not realize it as she watched the sky continue to shift and add purple and blue hues. Only when the clouds changed color from pink to a deep blue did Callie recognize it was nighttime.

"Fuck!" she exclaimed and jumped up from the sand. She grabbed her phone, left the water bottle, and ran back toward the buildings. She couldn't get back fast enough as the darkness crept in.

By the time she made it into the elevator, she was breathless and shaking. She could barely turn the key and tried to calm herself on the slow journey upward. Once the doors opened, her vision was blurred, and she could only see Raphael's door at the end of the hallway. She walked quickly toward it and was relieved when the door swung open as she approached.

Callie ran inside, but the foyer was empty, so she shut the door behind her and walked toward the living room. Raphael sat in one of the high-backed chairs, drinking a glass of wine.

He was exhausted but outwardly showed no signs. He had traveled around the world, staying in the night to resolve a solution for Calypso. If he had friends, he would have confided in them, but since he could no longer speak with them and didn't trust Hades, he was left to his own thoughts. He would turn her into a vampire, as she wished, but he knew the transition would be difficult for her. He vowed to make it as easy as possible and hide her fate with Hades for her own good.

"I see you have not left yet." Raphael struggled to keep a smile off his lips.

Her body felt weakened from her recent rush of adrenaline. Her mind swirled with chaos but she sighed and calmed herself.

"I'm not leaving. I'm sorry about last night. I wasn't thinking straight. I do want to become a vampire but for the right reasons."

"What would that be?" He drew the words out slowly, his eyes narrowing and focusing on hers.

Callie stood up straighter and tried not to focus on the fact that he eyed her. She felt his ice-cold gaze on her skin, making her tremble.

"I'm ready to let go of my human life. I have lived through so much pain, and I am ready to let it go. Raphael, I am terrified, but I know you can guide me through this.

You obviously know what you are doing."

"You understand by doing this that you are subjecting yourself to a life of darkness and committing yourself as a servant to Hades?"

"I understand," she responded quietly. Raphael grinned and put his empty glass down. He then went into the kitchen and removed a screaming tea kettle from the stovetop.

"It's good you haven't eaten today; it makes the process easier." He poured a cup of tea and handed it to Callie. "These are natural herbs; they will help with the transition."

The cup scalded her hands, but she held it tightly and sipped slowly.

Callie gagged. "It tastes like death."

"That means it is working," Raphael responded. "I trust you made the most of your last day as a human."

"Thank you, I did," Callie responded with a smile. "I saw the sunrise and sunset, and I think they were the most gorgeous colors I've ever seen. I pushed my body and worked out even though I hadn't done that recently. I guess I wanted to feel my weakness and effort."

Raphael nodded and finished his glass of wine. The redness shone differently than in his usual glass, and Callie could only assume it was blood.

"You should change. The night is young, but we have much to accomplish."

"What should I wear?"

"An outfit to die in," Raphael's lips curled into a malicious grin that Callie couldn't help but fall for. She finished the tea with a large gulp and went into her bedroom.

How odd that I consider this my room now and my home when I was a stranger a week ago.

Callie settled on a low-cut black dress, black knee socks,

and her favorite black boots. She tied back her hair in a long braid. After all, she didn't want it to get in the way. After anxiously smoothing down her dress, she walked back into the living room where Raphael awaited.

"Gorgeous doesn't even begin to describe you, Calypso," he whispered. Her cheeks instantly flushed, and she looked away from him. "I have something for you to complete your look."

Raphael's hand opened to reveal an impressive red stone attached to a golden choker. The color was unlike anything Callie had ever seen. It seemed to glow like the embers of a fire mixed with the beauty of the dazzling sun.

"Oh wow." She was speechless at the beauty. Callie slowly turned and felt Raphael's ice-cold fingers slowly brush across her neck. He clasped the necklace, and Callie held the stone in her palm. "Where did you get this?"

"It is a rare and unique stone, and you will never find anything like it on Earth. I climbed through the depths of Hell to find it for my queen."

Raphael stiffened, and Callie knew it was time. She took a deep breath and tried to calm her racing heart.

"Come, a new life awaits us." He held his hand out, and Callie grabbed it, finally feeling secure enough to touch him without fear.

Her body jolted, and they appeared on an empty beach. It looked the same as the first night they had met.

"I have a veil of protection around us. This is why you cannot see any buildings or people. We are still in the city, but it's as if we are in another world. Nobody around can see or hear us."

"Why didn't you teleport us somewhere that's actually private?" Callie tried to calm her nerves but burst out with nervous laughter. The waves crashed loudly next to them and almost drown out her voice.

"It takes more power to teleport farther away. I will be transferring much of my energy to you tonight. I like to stay close to home in case anything happens."

"What would happen?"

"Oh, you never know. You might enjoy my blood so much that you decide to fully drain and leave me as a dried corpse." Raphael grinned, and his fangs seemed to grow longer. The sight made Callie stop breathing. "Any last words? Prayers to God?"

"I was never one to believe in God." Callie cleared her throat. "But I did pray earlier. I'm sure you already knew that, though." The hairs on her body stood up, and she felt a sinking pit in her stomach. The bitter taste in her mouth made her nauseous.

I'm so afraid, but I want this so bad. I want to be free. I want to have power and control over my life. I want to be with him.

Raphael felt the chaos and turmoil in her mind and physical body. He kissed her neck gently, bringing her back to the present moment. She gave into him, extending her neck and pressing her body into his.

"Are you ready?" Raphael whispered into Callie's ear and wrapped his arms around her waist. This time, he kissed her lips and pulled away. Her body tensed as he pulled away, fear bouncing in her eyes.

Raphael roughly bit into his wrist, leaving a giant gash. Callie nervously grabbed his hand and brought his oozing wound to her mouth. She wasn't sure what to do, so she began to lick his blood.

"No," Raphael pushed her head closer against his bleeding wrist. She latched onto his flesh, and his blood flowed into her mouth. "Suck first, lick at the end." Callie obeyed and sucked against his wound, pulling his blood into her mouth and swallowing it. She looked up at him, and his face glistened in the moonlight. To her surprise, the blood was thick and had a distinct taste, but not salty. Callie pulled away when his wrist suddenly healed, and she no longer felt his bleeding tissue.

She wanted to speak, to say something about the unthinkable act she had just committed but her mind was blank.

Raphael took her in his arms again and leaned back as he kissed her and bit her neck. As his fangs gently pierced Callie's skin, they both moaned. She jumped slightly but instantly melted into his arms. Raphael slowly bit deeper into her neck, feeling her jugular vein dance against him.

Her back arched, and her nails dug into his back. It felt like she had waited so long for this moment of indescribable ecstasy.

His fangs finally pierced her jugular, and he opened his throat to receive the rush of blood. It tasted so sweet and tender; he had barely controlled himself the first night but no longer needed to.

Callie had felt a quick, sharp pain as he bit into her, but it instantly turned into ecstasy. She felt weightless and like she was floating but still in the safety of Raphael's arms. Every terrible memory of her life flashed before her eyes. It was as if she were watching a traumatic movie, but none of it mattered anymore. The only thing that mattered was how incredibly amazing she felt.

Raphael lowered Callie's body onto the cold sand. The wind picked up around them and seemed to spiral around their bodies. He was almost finished with her. He sank his fangs one last time into the top of her breast, sucking out the remaining blood from her chest cavity.

Callie's body was shutting down, each organ slowly ceasing to exist with the lack of blood in her body. Her lungs struggled to work as her body lay still, falling into the shadowy realm of death. Her body took a final gasp of air before her heart ceased beating.

Callie's physical body was dead. Raphael felt her soul leave her body as he gently lowered against the sand. He brushed his fingertips against her cheeks, marveling at her human beauty one last time.

Callie felt herself float out of her body. She could feel herself rise in the sky and saw her body and Raphael below. A bright white light shone through the dark clouds above her. She was filled with sudden joy as she quickly rose to the light. No matter how fast she seemed to rise, the light was still too far away.

When it seemed like she could reach out and touch the light, she fell back to Earth. She tried to scream but had no voice to call out.

Chapter 6

Callie slammed back into her physical body and was struck with immense agony. She writhed around, feeling every nerve in her body synapse. She felt her blood boiling inside of her veins. Every bone felt like it was being cracked and mended together. She sobbed uncontrollably and screamed in torment.

"You told me there wouldn't be any pain!" She was barely able to get out the words. Raphael stood a reasonable distance away, making sure to keep out of her reach.

"Your physical body is dying and being reborn."

Callie continued to scream and cry as the agonizing pain took over her body. Then, it stopped just as quickly as it had come onto her. She continued to sob as she rolled over onto her side.

"No, no," she wailed. Her high-pitched screams matched the tone of winds whipping around them. "I was almost in the light." Raphael crouched down beside her, still keeping his distance.

"I know what you saw, but it wasn't real."

"But I saw it!" Callie wailed, wounded mentally from her harsh death. She managed to collect herself enough to stand up and move just in time as large waves crashed over the beach. "What is going on?" she asked Raphael.

She didn't feel normal; every sense was heightened. It was as if every object had a faint glow around it. The stars were enormous and looked like they could come crashing down at any second. She was able to recognize constellations and planets when she had never studied them before. Her hands looked longer and slimmer, and her skin had already turned whiter.

"I know you feel strange now. It will take a while to get used to your heightened senses. Come, let's feed; you need your strength."

Callie trudged along behind him. Her body felt so heavy but at the same time weightless. It took all of her concentration and strength to put one foot in front of the other. She didn't know what to expect after her transition, but this was not it.

As they walked along the empty streets, Callie became annoyed. "You can take us out of this bubble now. I'm hungry, I think. I feel nauseous and so terribly thirsty."

"There is no veil of protection around us anymore. The streets are just that empty. Probably the hurricane."

Callie stopped in her tracks. A streetlight buzzed annoyingly and she wished it would explode. "Hurricane? What are you talking about? We are in California, not Florida."

"Apparently, one started brewing off of the coast of the Pacific Islands earlier today. It's supposed to hit us tonight."

"You aren't making any sense," Callie stopped walking as her vision blurred and spun. "Everyone was out here earlier."

"I can't make sense of it either. How did a tropical storm develop hours ago and suddenly travel over a thousand miles to hit a state where hurricanes historically do not happen?"

"Was the weather this crazy when you turned?"

"I don't remember, but even if it was, I doubt I would have a memory of it. I was too captured in the beauty of the woman who turned me. As well as the alcohol."

Callie remained silent as they walked along the streets. She smelled the human before she saw him; the raw stench of body odor and blood intoxicated her. She spotted a homeless man in an alleyway urinating.

"Do humans really have no shame? Absolutely putrid," she murmured. Raphael chuckled and waited for her to make a move. "Can't I just drink your blood? It tasted so delicious."

"Not yet. You are depleted; you need more than I can offer now. Don't worry; all human blood tastes the same. The rich and most innocent taste the same as the scum of this Earth."

Callie walked forward quietly, knowing the man couldn't hear her approaching. She grabbed him from behind, gripping his neck tightly, and he began to choke. She felt her fangs reach for his neck, and she pierced into his skin with no hesitation this time.

She sucked intensely and moaned as his salty fluids entered her body. As Callie drank, Raphael approached from behind and moved her hair out of the bloody mess. Watching her feed was such an incredible sight after dreaming of this moment for an eternity.

"Do you feel his body becoming weaker and the blood flowing slower?" Raphael whispered into her ear. "If you keep going, he will die. You need to fully drain his body, but you should know what it feels like."

Callie continued to suck at his neck for seconds, minutes, she did not know, but until there was nothing left but a cold and slightly shriveled corpse. Afterward, her body vibrated with electricity, and she looked down to see the blood splattered against her chest. The corpse lay against the wet alleyway with a gaping hole in its neck.

"We usually have to dispose of the bodies, but not in this situation. I've come to learn the police do not question a homeless man dying. Any other human would have an autopsy and investigation, but they don't seem to care for the worthless."

Callie took a few steps back, still reeling from her kill. She felt strong and powerful now. The fresh blood flowed through her veins, providing life and energy. She wiped the blood off of her face with the back of her hand.

"Oh, I feel incredible!" Callie exclaimed and jumped onto Raphael. He caught and swung her around, delighting in her joyfulness.

"Mon chérie," Raphael muttered the words into her mouth as they embraced. "Where shall we continue our journey on our first night together?"

Callie squealed as he spun and placed her back on the ground, the heel of her boot squelched against the blood on the pavement.

"Let's go dancing!" Callie's smile was contagious, and Raphael nodded in agreement against his better judgment. He held out his left hand, and Callie gripped it tightly. This time, she was prepared for the jolt to her body as they teleported out of the alley.

They appeared outside of a busy nightclub. The bass from inside seemed to send waves throughout Callie's body. She hung onto Raphael's hand long enough for him to grow nervous.

"This is overwhelming; we don't have to go in." Raphael's words cut through the booming music so Callie could focus her attention on him.

"No, I want to go in. I need to experience the music and lights," she trailed off, staring at the line of people waiting to go inside.

"Alright, let me know if it becomes too much, and we will leave. Trust me, it took a while until I was comfortable around this much commotion." Callie rolled her eyes and gave him a flirtatious smile before turning on her heel and bolting inside the club. Raphael laughed and shook his head; he was so happy to see her so enthusiastic. He had been so worried she may not transition well but was already taking her vampirism in stride.

Raphael raced into the building and stood to the side, trying to locate Callie. He spotted her in the middle of the dance floor, already shaking her body to the beat with two drinks in hand. They made eye contact, and she nodded for him to come over. Instantly, he was at her side, wrapping his hands around her swinging hips.

"What did you get for us?"

"Oh, I'm supposed to save one for you?" Callie laughed and took a sip from both straws before handing one of the drinks to Raphael. "I honestly don't know what it is; I just grabbed it from someone." Callie chugged the drink and then threw the cup onto the ground. "God, I am dying of thirst! Can we even get drunk off of alcohol?"

"Yes, we can feel a little buzz. It will never be comparable to drinking as a human; we never get to the point of stupid intoxication. But the thirst will never go away."

"Never?" Callie screamed a little too loud, and a few people nearby covered their ears in pain.

This is our curse. The thirst goes away after feeding, but it always comes back. No matter how much blood you drink, you will always have cravings and thirst. Remember this so you don't lose control.

Callie stepped back, unaware that her vampire companion could speak into her mind. As she stared back at him in total disbelief, he continued to speak.

I am speaking from my mind to yours. We have this special connection since we have shared each other's blood. If you share blood with anyone else, you would also have this connection. Go ahead, try it.

Is this how you got into my mind when I was human?

"Oh no," Raphael spoke out loud again. "That is a different process, which we will work on. It's been a while, and you need to feed again to keep your strength."

Callie gazed at all of the eligible humans surrounding them. Enthralled with her recent discovery, she decided to try something of her own. She scanned the crowd and put all her focus and energy into having a human come to her. A college-aged girl began to cut through the crowd and walk toward Callie. She was attractive, with sleek black hair and an olive complexion that brought out the light green in her eyes.

The girl walked up to Callie almost as if she were in a trance. Callie grinned and stepped closer to the girl, pushing her body up against hers. Raphael was impressed with Callie and let her know by looking into her eyes and nodding. He moved closer and pressed his body against the backside of the girl, squeezing her in between them.

Callie kept dancing and swaying with her new partner, though the tension was so high she could barely contain herself. She rubbed her hands along the girl's body, squeezing a protruding nipple. As the girl moaned and threw her head back in ecstasy, Callie bit into her neck. Raphael followed her lead and nipped into the other side of her neck.

Good girl, nice and slow like that.

"I hope you were calling me the good girl," Callie smirked and wiped the blood off her lips with the back of her hand. The girl was stunned, and Callie had to help hold her up. She went in to drink again, but Raphael protruded his hand to stop her.

"No more. We want her to be able to walk out of here." Raphael gave the girl a slight push, and she disappeared into the crowd. Callie was satisfied, feeling the blood expand throughout her body. The joy she had felt earlier bubbled up again, and she felt like a new person. The music seemed to get louder, and the lights became brighter. She could focus on each and every person's conversation if she chose to, or she could tune it all out and only focus on Raphael's gorgeous face. She trailed her fingers up his chest and brushed them against his sharp jawline. She kissed him roughly, feeling her emotions and attraction rise in her body.

"I've been waiting to kiss you for so long," Raphael spoke the words into her mouth as their tongues intertwined.

"I'm sure you have been waiting for more than that." Callie panted heavily as the bass grew louder and vibrated her body. Raphael grinned and pulled her closer to him, trying to neutralize all of the surrounding stimulation.

Callie laid her head against his chest and tried to steady her breathing. She did her best to tune out the loud music and focus on the sounds of the people surrounding her. She could hear shoes squeaking against the floor, ice cubes clinking together in glasses, and the murmur of people's conversations. She concentrated further, breathing even more slowly to separate words from the jumble of noise.

They continued slowly swaying as the crowd danced around them in a flurry. Raphael watched Callie's face in awe as she lit up and giggled while processing the new feelings in her body. He remembered how he had felt similarly, as if he were being reborn into the world. His memories were so ancient that they felt like a past life, something that made him who he is today, but he refused to ponder on or acknowledge.

Callie turned to a couple ten feet away from them. They argued, and Callie peered through the crowd to see a man push the woman standing across from him.

"You bitches, you are all the same. I told you not to text him, you stupid bitch!" The white man's face was red from anger, and Callie could see the veins popping on his forehead.

Raphael could feel Callie start to pull away from him, so he tightened his grip around her. "Let them be, mon chérie." He whispered into her ear, letting his lips drag across her neck, trying to convince her to stay with him.

"Let me just talk to him; help this girl out." She batted her eyelashes and smiled at him, knowing her charm would win him over. Raphael's lips tightened across his face, and he nodded slightly, allowing her to leave.

I won't kill the guy. Callie winked as she slipped through the crowd and disappeared. She appeared next to the angry man, who was now texting on his phone as the girl sobbed and spoke incoherently.

"Hey, are you okay?" Callie took the girl's hands and looked into her eyes.

"Brian, he—he," she hiccupped over her words.

"Bitch is too drunk to even speak."

"It seems like Brian has had too much to drink tonight," Callie said between gritted teeth. She crushed the glass in his hand, and the shards sprayed against his clothes. He jerked himself away.

"What the fuck!"

Callie grinned widely, making sure to lick her tongue over her sharp fangs. Unfortunately, Brian was too busy wiping the glass off of himself to notice. If he had just noticed, perhaps the following events wouldn't have unfolded.

Raphael came up behind Callie to assess the situation.

"Are we all good here?"

"I'm done playing games with you bitches." Brian harshly

pushed Callie and Raphael out of the way and approached the exit sign. Callie huffed, and Raphael grabbed her shoulder to try to calm her down.

"Come on, let's get out of here and go back home."

"I'm not done with him yet!" she hissed back at him.

Raphael's eyebrows furrowed together, warning her not to push him any further. "I'm just going to scare him out of being a terrible human being."

"I don't think anything could stop that," Raphael replied.

"No, you don't think *I* could stop that." Callie shoved him and turned on her heels, disappearing into the crowd. Raphael sighed and decided to let her win this one. He would wait for her to return and hopefully not have to clean up her mess.

Callie swung the exit door open too hard, and it banged against the wall, leaving an indentation. Brian walked out of the bathroom, shaking water off of his hands.

When he saw Callie, he grinned.

"I see you couldn't get enough of me, sexy little thing." He cornered her against a wall, and to his surprise, Callie grabbed his throat and slammed him against the wall. "Oh, I see; you like to play rough, don't you?"

"I want to know what gives you the right to go around calling women bitches?" Callie spoke between gritted teeth. She squeezed his neck harder, and he started to choke and gag. Brian shoved her with all of his strength but couldn't unlatch her. He resorted to spitting in her face, which made her step back.

"You *women* are inferior to us; it's that simple. Didn't your dad tell you that? Oh wait, you probably never had a daddy," Brian mocked her with a snide smile.

The last words infuriated Callie, and she finally broke. She grabbed Brian's head with both of her hands and yanked to the left, snapping his neck. His body dropped to the ground just as Raphael opened the exit door.

"Callie!" he shouted and dropped next to Brian's body. It was too late; he was already dead.

Callie stood back, her shoulders hunched and breathing heavily from the anger and adrenaline pumping through her body. Raphael stood up and quickly scanned for cameras in the small hallway. There were none, so he grabbed Callie's hand and pushed open the emergency exit door, silencing the alarms as they ran out of the building.

"What the hell happened?" he demanded. He walked fast, and Callie had to practically run to keep up with his long stride. He still tightly gripped her arm, and she tried to pull away from him.

"He said women are inferior to men!"

Raphael said nothing and continued to walk on without looking at her.

"Then he said that I didn't have a father," she continued. Nothing changed, and Callie grew more frustrated. "Can you stop and say something? Where are we going anyway?"

Raphael stopped and released her hand. "We are running away from the scene of a murder! God, Callie, you told me you wouldn't kill him! I should have trusted my instinct and never brought you here."

"I didn't mean to! He just made me so angry."

"So you snap his neck? If you are going to kill someone, at least make it worth it!"

Their argument was cut short by a piercing scream. They both recognized it to be the girl Brian had fought with. Callie's face dropped; she knew his dead body had been discovered.

"What do we do now?" she whispered.

"We don't do anything. We leave here and go back home."

"But didn't you say we have to dispose of the victims?"

"Yes, Callie," Raphael sighed. "But what were we supposed to do in this situation? Drag two hundred pounds of dead weight out of the club to throw him somewhere? Or should we fly away with him, leaving a missing person report? It's best to let the police handle this one. I don't know what they will come up with as causing his neck to rotate fully."

Callie was stunned by Raphael's bluntness and anger at her. He grabbed her hand, and they were jolted to the beach where they had stood hours before. The wind was treacherous and deafening against Callie's ears. She planted herself firmly into the ground to withstand the high speeds.

What are we doing back here?

"You want to act out and show your powers? So show me, Calypso." Raphael rose into the air until he hovered above her. He looked like a possessed angel with his rangy body that seemed to omit a golden aura. He motioned for her to join him, but she had no clue how to start flying. She jumped up and was immediately slammed to the ground by the wind. Multiple pieces of trash flew by her, and sand stung her eyes.

"What am I supposed to do?" she cried out.

"Oh, come on, don't let a little hurricane beat you." Raphael continued to hover above her, almost teasing her.

Callie stood back up and lifted her arms to the sky. Nothing happened. She squeezed her fists until her whole body shook, but again, nothing happened. The wind continued to whip around her, but all she could hear was Raphael's booming laugh.

"Do you take pleasure in seeing me fail?" Tears streamed down Callie's face.

"You are thinking too hard about it. You can do anything you put your mind to."

Callie wiped her tears, embarrassed that she had cried in the first place. She took a deep breath and closed her eyes.

She imagined herself floating in the air like Raphael. When she opened her eyes, she was off the ground and at his level. Raphael smirked at her and then suddenly turned to fly into a waterspout that had developed offshore.

She was unsure of how to control herself but kept her mind focused on her flying. She threw her body forward and shakily jolted behind him. The wind whistled around them and thrashed her body from side to side.

As they approached the waterspout, the wind became

more unbearable. Raphael led the way and tore through the clouds, leaving a path for Callie to follow.

Just when Callie thought she couldn't handle the winds anymore, Raphael broke through the center of the spout. Callie flew in behind him, and immediately, the winds stopped. Raphael grabbed her hands to help steady her as he sensed her weakness.

"I told you it wasn't that hard."

"Are you insane? You just flew into the middle of a storm! I don't even understand how I am flying."

"It's just like I told you, Calypso. One of our greatest powers is, in fact, our minds."

Callie nodded, and then the dizziness overtook her. Her eyes rolled back in her head as she dropped toward the ocean. Raphael swooped down and grabbed her limp body, immediately teleporting them back into the penthouse.

He bit open his wrist and shoved it into Callie's mouth. Her body was unresponsive, and her tongue rolled out of the side of her mouth.

Raphael's nostrils flared as he shook her body and pressed his wrist into her mouth again. His heart stopped until he felt her teeth latch on and suck his blood.

"I pushed you too far, mon chérie." He kissed the top of her head and stroked her hair. "I'm so sorry." He repeated over and over.

"I don't know what happened." Callie pushed herself into a sitting position and was surprised to see such a worried look on Raphael's usually stoic face. "But I feel fine now."

"Go clean yourself up. I'll meet you in the bedroom."

Callie slowly trudged into the bathroom and shut the door behind her. It took her minutes before she could look at herself in the mirror. Once she finally raised her gaze, her mouth dropped open in shock. Her face had completely transformed, and she didn't recognize the woman staring back at her.

Any sign of acne or whiteheads had disappeared. Her complexion was very pale, which she had expected. What bothered her the most was that she looked perfect now. Her forehead was smaller, and her brows were more defined. Her nose was skinnier and turned slightly upward. Her eyes were the same brown color but seemed to have flecks of gold and even red in them now. Callie had constantly struggled with bags and dark under eyes, which were nonexistent now. Her cheekbones were high and lifted with a slight rosy tone. Her jawline was more defined, just like Raphael's.

She couldn't help but rub her hands, which seemed longer and skinnier, along her face. She was mixed with emotions of disgust and amazement. Her face was perfectly symmetrical, and she couldn't stop staring at herself. Eventually, she drew herself out of her wonder and scrubbed a wet washcloth against her face and chest. She didn't have any blood stains on her but still felt the need to clean herself from her impurities.

She suddenly felt exhausted and knew the sun would rise soon. She removed all her clothes and looked at herself in the mirror one last time. She was a much skinnier version of herself, although she was already slim to begin with as a human. Callie opened the door and walked back into the bedroom. She was surprised to find the Persian rug thrown back to reveal a small opening. She shimmied down the hole and dropped down onto a cold concrete floor. It only took seconds for her to be able to see in the total darkness.

Raphael stood in the corner with his hands behind his back. His long golden hair fell down his back, and she noticed he was naked as well. Callie looked around the large room and saw it was completely empty except for a large black coffin in the middle.

"So this is where you come every night." Callie broke the silence, and Raphael turned around. Callie tried her hardest to keep her eyes on his face and not trail downward.

"I told you I have the top penthouse and also the floor below. I remodeled it so there is no entry except from our flat above. I had all of the windows removed and imported Italian stone."

"Perfect for a vampire's lair." Callie paused to clear her throat. "I'm sorry for disappointing you tonight."

Raphael walked over to her and embraced her. He kissed the top of her head, and she melted into his cold, robust body. "You didn't disappoint me, mon chérie. I know you reacted to your emotions, which are so hard to control at this point in your journey. I promise it will get easier. Come, let's lay down."

Raphael helped Callie into the coffin, which was lined with soft animal fur. He lay next to her, and Callie was surprised by how much space they had.

"I didn't have time to make your own," Raphael whispered as he moved a strand of hair from her face.

"It's alright. I don't mind sharing with you."

Raphael smiled, and his white fangs shone in the darkness. He pressed his body against her, and Callie buried her face into his neck. She began to kiss him and rub her fangs against his jugular.

"Don't get too excited," he whispered into her ear. "We don't have much time left."

"What happens now?" Callie asked, her heartbeat deafening them both. Raphael kissed her slowly, and they both descended into a deep sleep.

Chapter 7

Callie awoke the following night in a daze. She didn't feel rested and was surprised she had no dreams. She felt like she hadn't slept at all, rather just lay in the darkness with no thoughts or movements. The daytime had seemed to draw on for an eternity; it felt as if years had passed since the previous night.

She was alone in the coffin and exited promptly to jump through the narrow hole up to the penthouse. She dressed herself quickly, feeling ashamed of her perfect naked body. As she walked out of the bedroom, she glanced into the bathroom mirror and screamed in horror.

Her face, which was so beautiful and awe-striking merely hours ago, was now gaunt and hideous. Large dark circles hung under her eyes, and her skin was pulled so tightly across her face that her cheekbones seemed to peak through.

"What happened to me?" she exclaimed as she entered the living room and found a too-calm Raphael. His hair was pulled up into a tight bun on top of his head, and he drank a glass of blood.

"This is what happens to us without blood. We desiccate." He paused, drinking from the glass that stained his lips red. "Since you are new, you must feed much more frequently to keep the blood in your system. I, on the other hand, could go weeks without drying up like you have." Raphael handed Callie the glass, and she downed it instantly.

"I've seen you drink blood every night, though. I need more."

"Of course, it tastes delicious and feels amazing, as you know." Raphael grabbed a decanter from the fridge and refilled the glass for her.

"Why do you have bottled blood anyway? It tastes better fresh."

"I have my means of accessing humans and getting their donations for times like these. I thought it would be best to stay indoors after our adventure last night."

Callie nearly spat out her drink and slammed the glass on the kitchen island.

"Wow, seriously? You're going to keep me locked inside here now?"

Raphael couldn't help but let a smile creep across his face. He wrapped his hands around her waist and pulled her in for a deep kiss. "Don't fret, mon chérie. You are not my prisoner. I have so much to tell you, and I'm sure you have many questions. Come, let's sit."

They sat across from each other in the high-backed velvet chairs. Callie finished the second glass and felt her skin return to her new Goddess-like complexion.

"Tell me about Hell and Hades. When will I get to meet this famed underworld and God?"

"Easy now, no need to rush in." Callie could see the visible change in Raphael's expression. "We won't go to Hell until we have the ceremony for you to become the queen."

"When will that be exactly?" She retorted.

"Once you are ready," Raphael chuckled and shook his head. "You still have much to learn before you are ready to rule over an entire race." Now it was Callie's turn to have disappointment on her face. "You've just become a vampire last night, mon chérie."

"I know," she sighed and tossed her hair out of her face. "But what is the whole point? Why is Hades even involved? You haven't told me the meaning of this vampiric royalty either."

"Hades is our master, Calypso. He created the vampire race thousands of years ago. It started with two of them and they were his loyal partners. The other Gods forbade Hades from creating us, but he ignored them. The Fates, which I'm sure you are familiar with, told of a prophecy of a king and a queen stemming from the first vampires."

"So the first vampires aren't the king and queen? Do they still exist?"

Raphael grimaced and nodded. He crossed one leg over the other and stretched his arms along the chair. "Yes, they still exist, and that is part of our purpose. As I said, they were originally his loyal partners. They did all of his bidding, no questions asked. I'm unsure what happened; I wasn't born yet, but they betrayed him. So, in short, our purpose is to destroy the first vampires."

Callie's eyebrows furrowed. "Why can't Hades kill them?"

"He could, but I'm sure he doesn't want to kill his creation. Besides, that is what the prophecy declared. That the king and queen will kill the first two. I wasn't aware of this when I was turned. The woman who turned me simply told me I would be a king. With no knowledge of Hades, I was stuck wandering around the countryside for years killing and stealing, acting as a king, before Hades dragged me to Hell and crowned me as the King of Vampires."

Callie sat in quiet contemplation, trying to imagine the first vampires and why they betrayed Hades. "So what about Hell? Is it as bad as it seems?"

Raphael sighed and stood up to pour them another drink before answering. The hum of the refrigerator bothered Callie, and she tapped her feet impatiently.

"Yes and no. It depends on who you are and how you end up in Hell. I could go on for hours describing the details, the hierarchy, the torture, but you will never fully understand until you see for yourself.

"Hell is such a broad term to use, but we will call Hell the entirety of the underworld for explanation purposes. There is lots of barren land with nothing but lost souls wandering around. Then there is actual hellfire, which is constantly incinerating the most evil souls. There are sections where souls are trapped in their own guilt, so they relive the worst moments of their lives or of what they can imagine.

"Then there is Hades' castle. It is quite spectacular, given the amount of detail he created. There isn't as much torture and depression inside of it, except for his torture chambers. But it is just a marvelous castle where we will spend our time in Hell. There isn't any need to go into the land outside unless, of course, Hades sends you on a mission."

"That's not at all what I was expecting. But is there really no redemption for the innocent?" Callie's eyes began to water at the thought of all souls, particularly her parents, being sent to such a terrible demise. The living room seemed to grow smaller and constrict her.

"There is redemption for pure souls. The Elysian Fields, or a false heaven, if you will. Hades is the judge of all souls. He decides if they are sent out into the barren lands, if they get tortured by his demons and monsters, and some evil souls even join his ranks. But for the pure souls, he sends them into paradise. It's not real, of course. Nothing so beautiful could exist in Hell. It is a mirror of sorts; the souls enter after judgment and can never return. We can look into the mirror and see the beauty but cannot enter it."

"Have you seen it? Can you communicate with any of the souls inside the Elysian Fields?"

"Yes, I have stared into the Fields for countless hours. I'm sure there is more landscape than I perceived, but I stared at beautiful golden grains of grass and a lake. I believe you could communicate with a soul, but I have never seen any there personally."

"Were you trying to find someone?"

"Yes," he responded curtly. "My mother."

Callie stayed quiet as she no longer had any questions. Raphael's explanations did nothing to calm her down and made her more anxious about the future. He sensed her uneasiness and reached out to hold her hand. He stroked her cold palm with his thumb and smiled at her. "Come here, it's going to be alright. I've had a change of heart. Maybe we should leave this damned place after all and get some fresh air. How would you like that?"

Callie nodded. "We should get going, I would hate to turn into a hideous monster again. Where will you take me tonight?"

"How about San Francisco? There are plenty of filthy night creatures out." His fangs protruded as he smiled, and Callie felt a strong physical pull to his body.

"Are you kidding me? That's a six-hour drive! We'll never make it before the sun rises."

"Have you forgotten about our Godly powers already?" Raphael kissed the top of her hand and winked. Callie rolled her head back and immediately burst into laughter.

"Do you really think that I can fly that far? I barely got a hang of it last night, and I think you forgot I passed out."

"I believe in you," Raphael said, grasping her hand. They walked out of the penthouse and climbed the stairs to the rooftop.

We are going to run and jump off of the building and fly into the night. Just follow me. If you are scared, I can hold your hand.

Callie felt the hairs raise along her arms as Raphael spoke into her mind. She swallowed hard and took off running before Raphael started. She had to show him that she wasn't afraid after all. She closed her eyes tightly as she dove off of the rooftop. She dropped about twenty feet and her heart caught in her throat. Finally, she caught herself and flew above the building to meet Raphael. He waited momentarily to make sure she was stable and then sped off into the clouds.

Callie felt stronger flying that night, and the winds were much less tumultuous than the previous night. She could control her movements better, although she still held her arms out as if she were a bird soaring in the sky. Raphael stayed yards ahead of her, and no matter how hard Callie tried, she could never fully catch up to him. She squinted her eyes and put all of her strength into flying until her body shook with weakness.

Their high-speed chase brought tears to her eyes, and she felt a sense of relief wash over her when he finally began to descend into the city. The glow of a million cars and buildings meant nothing to her as they dropped down into San Francisco.

Raphael chose a dimly lit park to drop into. He landed

lightly on his feet, making no sound, while his counterpart clumsily dropped and skidded against the pavement. She stayed on her knees for a few seconds while she caught her breath.

"That only took us half an hour. Not too bad for your second night flying."

Callie nodded and stood up shakily. She was ravenous and wanted to feast immediately. Pains rocked through her entire body, particularly her stomach, and made her want to claw her insides apart.

Raphael held her hand and walked over to a cold metal bench.

"I don't need to rest; I just need to feed," she hissed at him as a few solo people walked by on the path. Her desire to feed increased as she caught a whiff of their hot, pumping blood.

"I thought that we could test out another one of our powers. What do you think about that?" Raphael put his arm around her, pulling her in close, and she heard the blood pumping through his veins. "I want you to calm and empty your mind as if you were meditating. Once you focus on your breathing, you can start to shift your focus onto another person and into their mind. Try with me."

Callie slowed her breathing and cleared her mind as she was instructed. Once she felt calm and focused, she looked deep into Raphael's ice-blue eyes and tried to pull thoughts out of his mind. Instantly, she received a vision of Raphael staring at her back the night she and Justin went to Ocean Prime.

Raphael could tell by the frown on her face that she had received his vision. He laughed and leaned in to kiss her, his fangs dragging across her bottom lips.

"Excellent, my queen. Now, use this as we walk around looking for a victim. I want you to pull thoughts from their minds and only feast upon the most vile you can find."

Callie and Raphael held hands and slowly strolled down the dark park path. Scarcely any people were out walking, and Callie was disappointed in their thoughts. She couldn't convince herself or Raphael that the insomniac mother, night shift nurse, or recently divorced father were worth feasting on. They approached a busier area of the park next to the main street, which had more benches and chess tables. The quiet hum of the night intrigued Callie. Distant sirens in the city, the clack of chess pieces against the table, the snoring of a man yards away.

A few homeless people were scattered amongst the sitting arrangements, and their odor made Callie hold her nose shut. As they stood in the shadows observing two homeless men play chess, Callie was suddenly intrigued by a new man who began to walk along the path.

She could easily sense the fear and anger that reeked from his body. He walked too quickly and kept checking behind him as if he were being stalked. Callie entered his mind and quivered as she received the thoughts of his recently failed date. The man had planned to drug the girl he met online, but she sensed his bad vibes and escaped the situation by lying and telling him she was going to the bathroom. Now he was left angry, horny, and ready to pounce on the next unsuspecting woman he could find.

"He seems vile enough to me, wouldn't you say?" Callie whispered to Raphael. He grinned back at her, and Callie stepped out of the shadows and onto the path.

"Excuse me, sir?" She made her voice high-pitched and frantic, and her victim caught the bait. Callie could hear him lick his lips and wheezing as he quickened his pace. He was so enthralled in her beauty that he didn't notice the deadly fangs in her gorgeous smile.

Callie grabbed the man and pulled him closer as she ripped his jugular vein open. She moaned loudly as the blood gushed into her mouth, which caught the attention of a few of the homeless crowd. An elderly woman who sat on a nearby bench began to scream. Her loud howl pierced Callie's ears and she dropped the corpse of the man she fed on.

Callie grabbed her ears and winced in pain. Raphael stood behind her, seemingly unaffected, watching the scene.

Make her stop! Callie screamed into his mind.

Pay her no mind, finish your meal.

She scowled as the lady continued to shriek. She dropped down to feed on the man again, then decided against it. Why shouldn't she enjoy her meal in peace?

Callie rushed over to the inconsolable woman before Raphael could stop her. She grabbed and slammed the woman into the ground. Her skull cracked open, releasing a large pool of dark, clotted blood and a terrible smell. Callie stood over the body, heaving as the two chess players turned to see the commotion.

"Calypso, no!" Raphael dropped down to the elderly woman but knew he was too late. He sighed as the faint sound of sirens grew closer toward them. "We need to go now!"

"Wait, at least let me feed on her." Callie was utterly unaware of the damage she had caused and the danger she put the two of them in.

"NO!" Raphael's voice deafened Callie and the unsuspecting humans around the park. "Leave her be; the police won't suspect a vampire if there is only one neck wound. We need to leave now."

The sirens seemed to close in on them, and their approaching lights blinded Callie, though they were still a few blocks away. Raphael gripped Callie's hand, and they teleported back to the penthouse's roof.

He sat down against the roof's wall and pulled his hair out of the bun.

"You look very attractive like that," Callie's sultry voice did nothing to affect him.

"You seriously have nothing else to think about?" Raphael's anger was like a slap to her face. "You put us in serious danger back there."

"What, you really think the police are dangerous?" she giggled.

"We both know we could kill them in seconds, but that is

not the point. I told you to kill one person, not two. Besides that, you wanted to make our kind known by wounding your uncalled-for murder. The more the human race discovers us, the harder it is for us to exist the way we do. Let alone Hades strongly disapproves of such occurrences."

Callie sighed before speaking. "I'm sorry, I don't know what happened. Her scream infuriated me, and I acted instinctively. You don't think the police will suspect a vampire?"

"Humans are incredibly dull to the supernatural. Even if there is evidence of such, their brains would rather come to any other conclusion than the forces of something higher than them." Raphael had calmed down but was still disappointed by Callie's actions.

She felt his feelings toward her and moved to grab his hands, trying to make amends. Her heart leaped as their skin touched and she searched his beautiful blue eyes. Overcome with guilt, adrenaline, and longing towards Raphael, she moved one of his hands to her hips and leaned in to kiss him.

As soon as their lips met, erotic fireworks exploded inside of her. She leaped onto his lap while kissing him passionately. Raphael met her back with equal lust and action.

Grabbing her tightly around the waist, he carried and slammed her up against the doorway to the stairs. She moaned into his mouth as the cold metal pressed against her spine. She was lost in their twisting tongues as they stumbled down the stairwell. The pain from being thrown around the stairs only enhanced the intensity she felt for him.

Finally, their entangled bodies made it inside the penthouse and down into their lair. By the time they rolled down the narrow hole, they were both naked and ready to rip into each other's bodies. Both of their hearts beat together as one feverous organ.

Raphael pulled on Callie's hair as he thrust into her. Screams of pleasure vibrated off of the cold stone walls. A fantastic sensation crept through her entire body, something she had never been close to experiencing before.

They moaned in the pleasure of exploring each other's bodies for hours. With one last thrust, Raphael collapsed onto Callie's heaving body, and he finished by biting into her swollen breast.

Callie was frozen, still feeling the euphoria of their consummation. Her past orgasms as a human were laughable compared to what she had just experienced.

"That's it, no mess?" she joked once she finally caught her breath.

"Makes it easier," Raphael sat up and grinned at her. "No mess and no worry about children."

Callie didn't realize she would never be pregnant once she became a vampire. She had never given pregnancy or children much thought in her human life, anyway. Justin had talked of a family, but she always pushed it into the back of her mind.

"I'm sorry for earlier." Raphael kissed her forehead, then stood up, bringing her back to the present moment.

Callie felt extreme fatigue take over and knew the morning was on the horizon.

"Thank you for an amazing night," she responded softly. They climbed into the coffin and wrapped their arms and legs around each other, becoming one. As Callie drifted into her slumber, she couldn't help but feel the cold, empty stare of the old woman's eyes as life drained out of her.

Chapter 8

As the short summer nights came to an end and fall closed in, Callie began to dread the long nights. Each night was the same; she would awake feeling depleted and angry at herself and the world.

After gulping down cups of blood, she would sit and listen to Raphael's agonizingly dull stories about her duties and expectations. The only useful information she retained was to obey Hades, never question or talk back to him, and never make another vampire without his permission.

Callie would try to change the subject to something lighter, like discussing the human race or even asking Raphael about his human life, but he always disregarded her and brushed her comments away like she was an annoying child. She felt discouraged that she couldn't reminisce on her past life, which was still so recent.

Afterward, they would venture into Santa Monica or nearby towns to feed and practice their powers. Over time, Callie became exceptional at flying, jumping, and running at incredible speeds. She could easily extract strangers' feelings and thoughts just by looking at them. Raphael taught her to change their memories so they wouldn't remember the trauma of being fed on.

Callie tried not to kill, but every night ended in a blood bath. She managed to spare a few humans she fed on but lashed out at strangers walking by who dared to judge her. Sometimes, it was a victim who struggled too much while she fed. Other times she was pissed at Raphael and killed on purpose to infuriate him. In her first month as a vampire, she killed sixty-six humans.

Raphael viewed her as a monster as she fed too roughly. Instead of piercing the vein, as he taught her, she continuously ripped the entire vein out of the neck, causing a quick death. Besides that, she was a sanguivorous creature. He thought of himself as a romantic, causing his victims to swoon as he gently pierced their skin and slowly drained their life force. On the other hand, Callie would roughly grab her victims, causing pain and terror in their remaining seconds. He was forced to clean up her mess multiple times a week, which caused tension in their relationship.

As much as they both tried to deny it, Callie loved to kill. This act, which she had prayed to have morality over, completely overtook her life. She couldn't help it; it was in her blood. The power intoxicated her as she held a fragile human life in her hands; the feeling of destroying it was almost more satisfying than drinking their scrumptious blood.

After the feeding and killing frenzy, they would return to the penthouse and have passionate sex. Raphael tried to punish her for her misdoings, hanging her from the ceiling in chains while he whipped her, but it only played into both of their erotic fantasies. Callie acted as his submissive servant only while they were naked. Raphael would rarely orgasm; his most thrilling actions included feasting on Callie's blood and delighting in her screams of pleasure. By the end of their romp, Callie had fang marks covering her neck, earlobes, breasts, and thighs. She could never feed from him, though, which he made very clear.

More recently, however, Callie would fall into a tremendous guilt spiral for her murders. She would drop to the ground, screaming and sobbing as she relived the memories of her past kills. Raphael would try to bring her out of it but did little to help the situation. Callie would fall asleep, wishing that she would never wake up.

After dealing with her outbursts for a week straight, Raphael decided to switch up their routine. He laid out an elegant ruby-encrusted dress for Callie to wear on their bed above the lair. Callie slowly stumbled out of the coffin, alone like every night, and trudged upstairs. She rolled her eyes when she saw him waiting for her in an elegant gray velvet tuxedo with intricate red designs.

"What is the meaning of this?" She scowled at him.

"I thought we should switch up our night. I made

reservations for us at the best steakhouse in Los Angeles."

"I've heard that before," she mumbled as she pulled on the dress. After adjusting the fabric on herself, she headed to the fridge to grab the decanter of blood, but Raphael appeared in front of her and grabbed her wrist.

"You are fine without a drink. You have not desiccated the past few nights. Have you noticed?" Callie shrugged and turned away from him.

"Does it matter if I've noticed or not? I still feel like shit when I wake up."

Raphael failed to contain his laughter and kissed the top of her head. "I'm afraid that is a matter of your perspective and attitude."

Raphael teleported them outside of the restaurant, as Callie insisted. They cut the corner and walked into the restaurant, with every pair of eyes following them. Not only were they more pale and beautiful than everyone, but they also held an air of elegance and power.

After being seated, Raphael ordered the most expensive bottle of Cabernet Sauvignon. Callie began to pour herself a glass when a waitress rushed over to them.

"Oh, please, madam, let me take that." The woman grabbed the bottle out of her hand and finished pouring the glass. She filled up Raphael's glass and began to discuss the elaborate specials for the evening. Callie ignored her, and Raphael didn't respond as he stared at his partner.

"I'll, uh, give you two a few minutes," she mumbled awkwardly and walked away. The tension was nearly unbearable for Raphael, but Callie felt at ease.

Callie finally broke the silence. "Why did you even bring me to this drab, meaningless dinner?"

Raphael raised his eyebrows and the corner of his lips in a slight smile.

"I thought you would enjoy the decor and luminescence of the wealthy Californians."

Callie rolled her eyes and scoffed at his reply. The restaurant could be considered luxurious to an uneducated human, but Callie knew better. The elaborate gold that seemed to stretch along the walls like a vine was fake, and the deep red lighting did nothing but give shadows to wrinkles. She knew the rich and famous flocked to this type of restaurant, the kind that overcharges for cheap ambiance and medium-quality food, but she was extremely unimpressed.

"Nothing impresses me anymore. The second I tasted your blood, the veil was lifted from my eyes. I'm far more annoyed with the pesky human race that I could actually care about them or any of their far cries of architectural meaning."

"Well, this is news to me," Raphael said, sitting back in his chair and stretching out his legs. "Usually, you practically beg me to discuss human emotion and nature with you."

"Things change. I hate humans. Now I see why you never want to discuss them. They are meaningless fools."

"Callie, Callie." Raphael shook his head. "You are missing the point of human existence."

"Which is what?" She laughed. "Every single human has trauma and is restless. Not one person is actually happy in life, and before you interrupt me, yes, I know that. My eyes merely glance at someone, and their life's trauma and internal mess are dumped on me. I don't care, nor do I want to know, about the deaths, the addictions, or the financial struggles they all have in common. It's quite disgusting, and I don't pity them anymore."

The waitress returned eagerly and filled both of their empty wine glasses.

"I'll have your most expensive Tomahawk, bloody rare." Callie gave her order and flashed a devilish smile.

"I'll have the same, thank you," Raphael nodded his head, and the waitress turned on her heels.

"Your revelation means you are settling into your powers, Calypso. There is truth to all that you say, but humans still have a purpose and meaning on this Earth.

"Don't ask me what, for I haven't figured that out. But the Gods put them here, or at least allowed them to exist and form society as it is today. I don't see much meaning besides my own gain and Hades, of course."

Callie rolled her eyes at his name, and Raphael decided not to scold her. If he had to punish her for every mistake she made, she would never be out of the ball and shackles.

"My human existence was vastly different from what you see today," he continued. "My family were poor farmers, trying to raise cattle and crops during a time of drought and political uprising. My father was an asshole alcoholic, to say the least, and my mother was a rather sickly angel. I always blamed my father, who was so cruel to her. I was the eldest son, trying my best to protect my mother and keep away from my father. My middle brother was essentially a copy of him, or at least he tried to be. My youngest brother was the favorite, innocent and pure.

"I worked hard in the fields but received little recognition. Eventually, I grew tired of it and left our town to explore more of the world. I didn't get very far, and that's when I was turned."

Callie was surprised that he had revealed so much of his past life to her when he had never mentioned it before.

"Reflecting on the past is a weakness in my mind." Raphael read her thoughts and explained, "Especially my human life, which has nothing to do with or benefit me in the present moment. I ended ties with that person when I swore my loyalty to Hades."

The waitress interrupted again, this time with their meals. She tried not to cringe as she placed the large red steaks in front of them. Callie was upset by Raphael's last words and moved to grab her wine glass. She knocked it over, and the dark liquid quickly absorbed into the white tablecloth.

"I'll have another bottle," she spoke between gritted teeth.

"Are you sure about that? Seems as if you are tipsy enough." The waitress laughed as she blotted at the mess.

Callie turned her head almost robotically toward the

waitress and snatched her wrist.

"I gave you a command, and you are to follow it without question!"

"Easy now, don't break her wrist," Raphael scolded. Callie released her tight grip, and the waitress nodded. Her eyes fogged over, and she left to retrieve another bottle.

They finished their meal in silence, except for the rough clank of knives or the gulping of wine. Callie purposely ignored Raphael's attempts at eye contact and touching under the table.

"I need to get some fresh air," she finally said and stood up from the table. "Wait for me; I'll finish that wine."

Raphael decided it was best to give Callie space, so he stayed at the table for a few minutes. He silenced the surrounding merriment of the restaurant so he could close his eyes and meditate in peace. Something tugged at his chest, and he knew he had to check on Callie. He exited the restaurant quickly and returned to the back of the building where they had arrived. He was feet away but could easily see the picture.

Callie had the waitress's back up against the brick wall and was close to her face.

"Do you think it's funny, disrespecting someone of my status?" she yelled.

"No, ma'am, I'm so sorry. I was just trying to make a joke," the woman sobbed.

Callie grabbed the wrist she had bruised earlier and jerked her arm up, breaking her humerus. The woman screamed and dropped to the ground, clutching her broken arm.

Raphael appeared behind Callie and spun her around. Before he could open his mouth to reprimand her, she kicked and impaled the woman's face with her heel. Raphael gasped in horror as Callie struggled to pull her stiletto out of the woman's eye socket. Her face was crushed and barely recognizable.

"Oh my God," Callie turned around slowly, then dropped down next to the disfigured body. "She was a single mother." Callie had received her thoughts in the last breath the woman took. She was full of fear and worried about her daughter, who was home with a babysitter.

"Oh my God," Callie started to sob. Raphael squatted next to her and wrapped his arms around her sunken shoulders. "What have I done? What do we do now?"

"We do nothing. We go home. If we get rid of the body, the police will leave it as a missing persons case. Her daughter should know her mother is dead and not coming back. Why give her hope?"

"Please, let me do something. I know where her daughter is." Callie continued to sob.

"You've done enough to alter the course of her life. The rest is in fate's hands now," Raphael murmured, trying not to be too harsh. He heard the doorknob on the restaurant's back door start to turn and instantly teleported them back to the penthouse.

Callie lay sobbing and screaming on the living room floor. His plan to switch the evening events did nothing but make it worse. After her fit, she remained comatose on the floor. Raphael gently undressed and carried her down into the lair. He lowered her into the coffin and brushed a few stray hairs from her face. By now, she was sedated and would be until the following night.

A loud ringing rocked Raphael's ears, and he dropped his head. He had almost forgotten about Hell's council meeting, which couldn't have come at a worse time. He pulled his cell phone from his pocket and quickly made arrangements for the following night. The meeting could last days, and he couldn't leave his damsel in distress alone for that long. With no time to change out of his tuxedo, he gave Callie a departing kiss and teleported to the underworld.

*

Callie awoke the following night earlier than usual. She was startled awake and was surprised to find herself dressed in another pilgrimage nightgown on their upstairs bed. She had no idea of how she had gotten there, as her last memory was of sobbing on the ground. A faint noise from the kitchen pricked her attention, but she was not in a rush to investigate.

She rose slowly from the bed and trudged through the hallway, expecting to see Raphael in the kitchen as she always did. But instead, Maria was busy stirring in a large pot.

"Miss Callie, I hope I didn't wake you!" she exclaimed without turning around.

"Not at all. I sleep like the dead. What are you doing here?"

"Mister Raphael called me this morning to inform me of an unexpected meeting he had to attend and that you were coming under the weather with a nasty bug. He felt bad asking me to come over to care for you, but I insisted!" She continued to mix and throw herbs into the steaming pot.

"Unexpected meeting?" Callie mumbled under her breath. Maria turned around and gasped when she saw Callie's pale complexion.

"Oh my Lord! Please lay down; you do not look well at all!"

Callie laughed and sank into the velvet chair. She had never noticed how soft and inviting the chair was until this moment.

"What are you cooking for me, Maria?"

"This is an old recipe from my grandmother. This soup is full of nutrients and minerals. It has lots of herbs and organ meats."

Maria's cell phone began to chime, and she answered it immediately.

"Yes, sir, I am here with Callie now. I got in about an hour ago. No, she hasn't tried to kill me yet." Maria laughed.

Callie scrunched her eyebrows together and walked into the kitchen. "Let me talk to him," she demanded.

Maria handed the phone over and went back to managing the soup.

"My love, why didn't you tell me about this important unexpected meeting you had to abandon me for?" Callie said in a fake cheery voice and walked into the hallway, out of Maria's hearing. The darkness surrounded her and made the paintings on the wall seem to jump out.

"Callie, I don't have long to talk. I was just making sure that you hadn't murdered the housekeeper out of spite." Raphael's voice sounded faint and distant.

"Where are you? And thanks for the faith in me."

"I honestly don't know what to expect from you anymore. I had a council meeting come up. I don't know when I will return."

Callie's face scrunched in confusion. "What do you mean you don't know when you will be back?"

"Time doesn't exist the same in Hell, Callie," Raphael began to sound frustrated. "I have to go."

The call ended abruptly, leaving Callie worried. What kind of council meeting could exist in Hell? She had so much to learn and felt rather uneducated about the underworld.

She returned the phone to Maria, who served the soup in a single bowl.

"Not hungry?" Callie asked.

"Oh no, this is all for you. Trust me, I have had plenty of servings in my lifetime."

Callie graciously ate the warm bowl of liquid and organs. It had a bloody flavor but nothing compared to blood straight from the flesh. Once she finished, she brought the bowl to Maria, who was occupied washing the dishes. Callie smelled her blood pumping beneath her skin and resisted the urge to drink from her.

"Maria, if you had the chance of everlasting life, would you take it?"

"Such an interesting question! No, I would not take it. Our God gives us a certain time on this Earth, and I will enjoy it as such." Her cheerful demeanor and smile annoyed Callie.

"You actually believe in God, then?"

"Why of course! There are too many miracles in my life and my family to not believe. I am grateful every day."

Callie ended their conversation by walking away. She became incredibly bored and had to pace around to control her murderous urges. If Maria had answered her question differently, she would have killed her on the spot. But she decided to follow the rules for once. Maria left soon after, leaving Callie wondering how long she would be alone.

She flipped through old books and stared at paintings on the wall for what felt like hours. Eventually, she decided she would return to her coffin and sleep. As she stepped down into the lair, she heard a loud thump on the floor above her. She jumped back upstairs and found Raphael panting heavily on the living room floor.

His shirt was tattered and bloody. His hair was a mess, and his scalp had missing patches. Callie froze in place as she examined his wounds. She dropped down to her knees, frightened at what could have caused him so much damage. He lifted his head, and Callie whimpered when she saw his left eye missing, completely ripped out of his socket, leaving a swollen and bloody mess. Gashes lined his face and neck.

She pulled him into her chest, not knowing how to comfort him. He immediately ripped the top of her nightgown and sank his fangs into her breast. She let him feed while she gently stroked his back. When he pulled away, she helped him up, and they slowly walked downstairs. Now it was her turn to undress him, and a single tear slid from her eye as she removed his crimson-stained shirt.

"Hades did this to you?" Callie cried.

"No, mon chérie," Raphael winced and kissed her forehead. His wounds were already starting to heal, but it was nonetheless traumatizing for both of them. Raphael stayed quiet and climbed into the coffin; Callie wrapped herself around him.

"Hell has a council of monsters, demons, and persons appointed by Hades. Their job is to enforce the rules and offer solutions to Hades. I serve as a member of the council. I begged to come home tonight to be with you, but some of the members were not happy about it."

"Was the meeting on my account?" Callie whispered.

"Not entirely," Raphael groaned as he shifted around in the coffin. "But you were a matter of discussion." Callie wept silently, and Raphael tried to sleep, but the nightmare of the fight kept replaying in his head.

Demons surrounded and held him down as countless others attacked him. They spit in his face and threatened to kill him if he ever brought the Queen of Vampires to Hell. He screamed back at them as the creatures tore into his flesh, treasuring their moments of defiling the coveted Vampire King.

Once they had all taken turns berating him, they quickly disappeared as Hades entered the room. He frowned, all-powerful and ever-knowing why it happened. He could have stopped it but allowed his subordinates to take their anger and fears out on Raphael to send a message to him. Keep your queen in line, or there will be grave consequences.

Raphael shivered as he blocked his mind from her.

He had to keep this secret from her; she couldn't ever know the truth.

 Chapter 9

The following night, Callie awoke as Raphael ascended from the coffin. She patted next to her and pulled down her ripped gown.

"Please, come stay and rest with me," she spoke seductively.

"I can't, Callie. They postponed the meeting on my behalf, and I can't make Hades wait much longer." He turned away from her and jumped upstairs, hurrying to put on a new shirt.

"I don't understand." Callie appeared behind him as he buttoned his sleeves. "They practically beat you to death, yet you still show loyalty to them?"

"I don't have loyalty to the council, only to Hades. I know he punished them after I left."

"How do you know that?" Callie demanded.

"He caught a glimpse of me as I teleported back here. I saw the fire in his eyes. We are all supposed to be civil toward one another, but...some of his servants have too much compassion for him. It blinds their judgment. Please keep yourself out of trouble."

Raphael disappeared, leaving Callie to ponder on his words. She decided against keeping herself out of trouble that night. It didn't benefit her to follow the rules the previous night, especially with the chaos that seemingly existed in Hell.

She quickly thumbed through her wardrobe and pulled out a sparkly red lingerie outfit she had bought during her human shopping spree. Callie never wore it, as she never needed clothes around Raphael. She changed into the matching set and covered herself in a thin robe. She quickly ran to the rooftop and soared off into the night, wishing she could teleport.

*

Callie landed in Los Angeles, which was close enough for her to fly to without feeling depleted. She knew she would be filled with rich blood soon enough. She had spotted a depressing-looking nightclub from above and decided this would be her spectacle for the evening. She walked in confidently and told the bouncer and manager that she was the new girl for the night.

"New girl?" The overweight manager laughed. "We barely have enough customers to keep these girls paid."

"Don't worry about that. It will be a full house tonight." Callie smiled, covering her fangs. She was already calling out to desperate and terrible men in her mind. The manager shrugged and walked her to the dressing room door.

Callie walked inside and saw only a handful of girls preparing themselves. A petite, short-haired brunette turned and smiled at her.

"Oh my God, you are so pretty!" she squealed.

Callie laughed and let her robe drop to the floor, revealing her perfectly smooth and slim legs. "Oh my God, I wish I had your height! You barely even need heels!"

Callie had forgotten that she would need stilettos to play the part of a stripper, but thankfully, she found a pair sitting on a table. They were black with red soles, perfectly matching her outfit.

A dark-skinned woman with curly hair turned around from the mirror and glared at Callie. "Excuse me, who do you think you are?"

"I'm Calypso, the killer of men. And you are?"

"I'm pissed that you are here! None of us have made any money tonight, and Mike has the audacity to bring some new bitch in here!"

The short girl playfully slapped her in the arm.

"Venus, be nice!" she hissed, then approached Callie. "Ignore her, she's just upset. I'm Crystal." She stuck her hand out for Callie to shake, but she laughed at the gesture. "Do you want me to do your makeup? Not that you need any, but to make you pop?"

"Sure, Crystal, maybe a red tint?" Callie sat in a chair and crossed her legs, feeling like elegant royalty.

"I don't know," she responded as she dug through her makeup bag. "The stage lights are terrible, and it would make you look washed out. How about purple?"

Callie grinned, one of Raphael's favorite colors. She could barely contain her excitement of what was to come. As she fantasized, Crystal lined her eyelids with a dark purple color, which made her brown eyes glimmer.

"Your lips are so plump and red," Crystal was enthralled with her beauty.

"Get out of her ass." Venus walked by and tapped Crystal on the head, breaking her spell. "It's showtime, ladies!"

Callie was the last one out of the dressing room and took a minute to study the surroundings of the dimly lit club. Crystal was bubbling with excitement as at least two dozen men were in the club as compared to the usual handful. She instantly approached a group of well-dressed Hispanic men and conversed with them. Callie saw that one of the two poles was empty, so she took her chance and climbed the stage.

She slowly stepped around the pole and stared at the men who began to notice her. A rap song began to play with the lyrics 'speechless in the presence of a demon.' Callie grinned as she seductively stroked the pole; the words couldn't be any more true.

The men who weren't occupied with dancers began to flock to the stage, drooling and emptying their pockets on the ground. Callie wasn't doing anything impressive either, just staring into their souls and a couple of spins and splits on the pole. When the song ended, she walked off the stage, and Venus, who was on the stage next to her, yelled to get her attention.

"Hey! Pick up your bag!"

"I don't need it," Callie responded without looking at her. "You can grab it." Venus was shocked, so it took her a minute to move to the other stage and grab the bills.

Callie spotted Crystal arguing with one of the men she had been talking to earlier. She walked up behind her and lightly touched her shoulder.

"What's wrong, babe?"

"He says he won't pay me for the lap dance I just gave him!"

"Sorry, puta," the man laughed and raised his hands out to the side. "A lap dance is supposed to make me horny, and you didn't even get me hard."

Crystal gasped, and Callie rolled her eyes.

"Don't worry, I'll take care of him," she whispered to Crystal.

"Come to VIP with me. I'll show you a good time and get you nice and hard." Callie dropped down and rubbed his inner thigh.

"No, Mama, I don't have money for a private room," he responded, but Callie knew he was lying.

"I'll do it for free, but why don't you pay my friend first?"

The man instantly reached into his pocket and begrudgingly shoved a twenty-dollar bill at Crystal. Then Callie grabbed his hand and led him to the VIP room, close to the front door, and closed off with a thick red curtain. She nodded at the burly security guard as he closed the curtain behind them.

The room was smaller than Callie expected, but it would still serve her purpose. The center of the room held a small stage with a pole and a long cushioned booth spread across half of the room.

Callie stepped onto the stage and lazily walked around the pole while her first victim got comfortable in the booth, spreading his legs and rubbing the top of his pants.

"What you did to my friend wasn't very nice," Callie said, sliding down the pole, sitting on the stage in front of him.

"She wasn't as beautiful as you. Look, you're making me hard already."

Callie faked a smile and moved her top down to reveal more of her breast and part of her nipple. "It doesn't matter; she provided you with a service that you are required to pay for."

The man laughed, and Callie hated him for it. She hated

his greasy, slicked-back hair, his faint stubble line along his chin, and his sickeningly overwhelming cologne scent.

"Come sniff this off me; let's have a good night." He pulled a small bag of white powder out of his pocket and unzipped his pants.

As he pulled his hard flesh out and sprinkled powder on top, Callie dropped to her knees to give him one last pleasure. She licked off the gasoline-tasting powder, feeling nothing, then proceeded to rip off his penis with her teeth.

Before the man could scream in pain, Callie crushed his windpipe in her hand. He made a horrible gurgling sound that was music to her ears. She spit out his organ and watched as his face began to turn red and then purple. She tightened her grip until the blood vessels in his neck and face began to pop. Once she was sure he was dead, she shoved his penis into his gaping open mouth.

His blood had squirted onto her nearly bare chest, so she wiped herself clean with the edge of his shirt. She dragged his body around to the back of the stage so it wasn't visible from the entrance of the room.

"There you go, nice and hard like you wanted," she spat on the corpse. After taking a moment to fix her hair, she walked back out to the main floor.

"Keep the men coming in here, and don't let anyone interrupt. I'm going to have a busy night," Callie told the security guard. He nodded in agreement and waved over a man who was staring longingly at the red curtain.

Callie grabbed his hand and threw him into the booth, straddling herself on top of his lap. She felt him rise against her, which was quickly stifled as she ripped into his jugular and drained his body. She was glutinous in feeding, desperate to refill her body with power and vitality.

The corpse rested on top of the first, and she wondered how many bodies she could stack behind the stage without becoming obvious. The sight of blood or smell of decay was irrelevant as she would entrap the men with her beauty. She planned on killing every rotten man who had unsuspectingly stepped into the club that night.

She continued to call men into the room and decided to kill them based on how terrible their souls were. For the more innocent men who committed only a few evil deeds, she spared a quick death by ripping into their necks. The more heinous—the assaulters and cheaters—she would rub up against and convince them to pull out their flesh. They all agreed instantly, not expecting to have their organ physically torn or bitten off.

One man tried to overtake Callie upon entering the room with her. She pretended to be weak and fragile, letting him climb on top and hold her down.

"Please, no." She practically giggled as he rushed to unzip his pants and hump her.

"You know you like it." His hot breath reeked of alcohol and smacked her nostrils.

She quickly pushed his face away, snapping his neck to the side. She finished the job by decapitating him and kicking his ugly head to the back of the room.

By now, it was early in the morning, and hardly any men were left alive in the club. The room reeked of blood and decay. Callie was occupied giving an innocent virgin a blowjob when she felt an ominous presence behind her. She threw her head back and laughed maniacally.

Raphael found no humor in the situation and grabbed a fistful of Callie's hair, yanking her off the man and pulling her up to stand. Raphael flicked his hand before the young man could react and made his heart stop, something Callie didn't know was possible.

She had never seen him in such a rage. His eyebrows furrowed together, and veins popped out of his face. His usual blue eyes had turned a blood-red color, which frightened her. He tightened his grip on her scalp, and she squirmed in pain.

"What is the meaning of this?" He pronounced every word

deep and slow, eliciting a wince from Callie with every syllable he spoke.

"I had to pull you away from Hell. I knew that killing all these men would elicit a response from you."

"Not only will it elicit a response from me, but from Hades himself and the entire council of Hell. They kicked me off the council after Hell was flooded with two dozen souls screaming of murder from a stripper vampire. How do you think that makes me look?" Raphael pulled her inches from his face, and she saw the murderous look she was so familiar with in his eyes.

"I went to Hell to vouch for you since you aren't progressing fast enough. Hades and Hell are ready for their Vampire Queen. I begged for more time for you to continue to adjust to your new life. You are supposed to be a queen who brings an end to chaos, but you are busy spinning tricks and prostituting yourself to humans." He spit in her face and released his death grip on her hair. Callie fell to the ground and was so stung by his words that she couldn't wipe his saliva off her face.

Raphael paced around the room, massaging the temples of his head. Callie was so ashamed of herself that she couldn't look at him.

"Get up. We need to clean up this mess," he growled. She obeyed and slouched behind his tall frame.

"Can I say goodbye to the girls and make sure they're alright?" Callie whispered.

Raphael was annoyed at her response but decided to allow it. He tightly gripped her arm, making her immediately bruise up, and dragged her to the dressing room. By now, the club was empty; not a soul was left, including the security guards and manager.

Raphael pushed Callie into the dressing room, and she stumbled, losing balance in her heels.

"No men in here!" Venus screeched.

"Oh my God," Crystal cried at Callie's disheveled and bruised appearance. "Is he your pimp?" she mouthed.

"Something like that." Callie forced a laugh as she took off the heels and tied her robe back on.

"There's been a gas leak in the building. You all need to leave immediately," Raphael boomed. The dancers looked confused, but they all hurried to gather their belongings and wads of cash. Crystal was the last one to leave, and she paused before exiting, kissing Callie on the lips, to both of their surprise.

"Thank you for tonight." She blushed, then ran out to catch up with the rest of the girls. With the club now empty, Raphael and Callie left through the emergency exit and stood in the alleyway.

The sky was starless in the city, and the sounds of traffic and barking dogs seemed deafening.

"At least the girls are happy with me," Callie joked, breaking the silence between them. Raphael frowned and turned his back to her, facing the club.

"It is time," he spoke so loudly that Callie cringed and clutched her ears. The club exploded into flames, and the heat waves pushed Callie back. Raphael stood facing the fire longer than he should have. Eventually, he turned on his heels and walked toward Callie.

"I should throw you in the flames, watch as the fire licks your body and melts your skin, but somehow, I still have compassion for you." Raphael caressed her cheek, then grabbed her hand to teleport back to the penthouse.

"How did you do that?" Callie asked. Raphael ignored her as he drank straight out of the decanter from the fridge.

"I called upon Hades to send hellfire to that disgusting club." He turned toward her and smeared the blood on the corner of his lips. "I can only hope you understand how lucky you are. Any other vampire who makes such public and mass murders is immediately thrown into hellfire. If he would have suggested it, I would have let him. You have shown me nothing of queen material."

"I don't know how to be a queen!" Callie wailed.

"Drop to your knees." Raphael looked straight ahead, ignoring her whimpering face. His body was rigid and tense from the anger he held.

Callie obeyed and kneeled in front of him, silently weeping. She held no remorse for the murders she had just committed but felt terrible for disappointing Raphael.

"You can start by abandoning your human ways and only pleasing me." He caught her by surprise as he shoved his cock into her mouth. She choked and continued to cry as his thickness ripped the corners of her lips.

"If you ever disobey me again, there will be no queen title for you. I will let Hades deal with you as he wishes." Raphael pulled out and gave Callie one last look of disgust as he headed toward the bedroom. "You should sleep in the bed. You don't deserve to lay next to me."

His final words made Callie wish she had never died for him.

Chapter 10

Raphael refused to speak to Callie for a week after the incident. He stayed in the penthouse to oversee her, but she had no will to commit any more murders. She begged him to say anything to her, even how much he hated her, but he wouldn't.

The problem was that he didn't hate her but began to feel a strong distrust and dissatisfaction with her. He imagined that if she never discovered the truth of the prophecy, she would never gain the tendencies of a disloyal patron.

However, she had done everything in her power to prove she was unworthy of obeying him, let alone his master, Hades. He feared she would never live up to the overwhelmingly high expectations he and all of Hell had for her. He had been naive when he first became a vampire but never experienced the inner turmoil and outward chaos Callie lived.

Their silent week dragged on like months to both of them, but Raphael knew he had to punish her, or she would never become submissive to him. Callie cried herself to sleep every night on the bed, weeping loudly enough for Raphael to hear in the coffin below. She abstained from drinking any blood, not that she needed to, as Raphael referred to her as a "bloated glutton."

He finally broke the silence one night.

"Please forgive me, mon chérie." He kissed her deeply as moonlight streamed into the living room. "I hated being stern with you, but I had to discipline you somehow."

Callie's eyes shone with tears as this had been the most affection she had received in weeks. All of the bitterness she held towards him melted away. She opened her mouth to speak but he silenced her with another kiss.

Raphael still didn't trust Callie enough to go out into the real world again, so they spent their evenings making passionate love and holding each other in the coffin. They both knew the serene nights they were experiencing wouldn't last forever.

Callie struggled to fall asleep one morning and had a

terrible thirst for blood. It had been almost two weeks since she last fed. She admired Raphael's jawline, his beautiful face glowing in the pitch-black room. Slowly, she rolled over to place her fangs on his neck. Before she could break his skin, he awoke and slammed his hand onto her throat. She stared back at him with fear in her eyes, amazed he had reacted so quickly.

"Now, now, mon chérie, what did I tell you?" he whispered seductively into her ear.

"I don't care! I need it, please. Please give me your life force. I need to feel it running through my body."

He licked slowly from her collarbone up to her ear. It sent chills down her spine and made her writhe underneath him. He slowly tightened his grip around her neck and she squirmed with excitement.

"You can have my blood when you deserve it. Do you think trying to drink from me while I sleep is a good idea? Most certainly not. If I did not know it was you, I would have killed you before you opened your mouth." His words should have terrified her, but they only made her want him more.

Her eyes widened as she arched her hips up towards him, rubbing against his hard length. Raphael narrowed his eyes as he probed around her entrance, just barely sticking his tip inside.

"Do you want me or my blood?"

"Both!" Callie yelled as he roughly thrust inside of her, slamming her head against the top of the coffin. She scratched her nails against his shoulders as he pounded her, but he wouldn't bleed. She turned her head and opened her mouth to bite his shoulder as he pulled in and out of her. Raphael slapped her, making her head fly the other direction.

Blood pounded in her ears as she stared at him, trembling slightly. He brushed a strand of hair out of her eyes and kissed her lips gently. He bit his bottom lip so it bled, and she gratefully sucked the few drops from him. "I will never hurt you, mon chérie. But you cannot feed from me without my permission. I do this for your safety, and you are always safe around me."

*

Callie awoke the following night, and her whole body ached. She had not fed the night before besides Raphael's scant blood and was irritated. She changed out of her typical nightgown and put on her seemingly eternal outfit: black boots, black jeans, and a black cropped top.

Raphael always left the keys to his sleek cars on the kitchen counter, so she walked over to grab a pair but found them gone. He had sensed her restlessness long before she awoke.

"What are you up to this fine evening?" Raphael asked, not moving from his chair. He drank a glass of blood and read a newspaper.

"I am tired of staying locked up in this small house. I'd rather be anywhere than here. All I do is please you and relive all of my murders," she mumbled.

Raphael scoffed. "Forgive me, my queen. I did not realize my exclusive penthouse was not up to your standards." He smirked, swirling the wine glass in his hand.

Callie huffed, becoming more irritated. He had never spoken to her in such a sarcastic manner.

Could he still be upset about last night?

"If I were actually your queen, things would be different. I would have an entire wardrobe and my own car, and oh, and I wouldn't be trapped in this hellhole with you."

"You are free to leave anytime," Raphael responded suavely. "But I do warn you, you cannot navigate this nightlife without me. You will be lost and make more mistakes, but please leave if you wish." Raphael tapped his finger against the newspaper. Callie read the words against his finger.

'Los Angeles Strip Club Explosion That Left Two Dozen Dead Ruled as a Gas Leak.'

Callie stood still, shocked at what she had read. Quickly, her shock turned into rage. Raphael was the one who created her for whatever damned reason; he was the one who watched her kill endlessly without intervening. All of these murders were his fault!

There was no reason to place the blame on herself as he was the one who had turned her into a killing monster.

She scowled and turned around, walking out of the penthouse. She wanted to attack him so badly, to slam him up against the window, shattering the glass and send his body flying down, but she knew he would sense this before she even tried.

"Try not to murder anyone else, hm?" Raphael called out, and Callie tried to ignore him. She stomped into the elevator and screamed once the door had shut. As much as she hated to admit it, Raphael was right. She couldn't control herself around him, let alone by herself. She needed to leave this city and go somewhere she felt she belonged. The ding of the elevator brought her back to reality, and she stepped into the parking garage.

Remembering the pair of keys at the bottom of her purse, she dug them out. A covered bike along the row of black vehicles stood out to her, so she walked over and ripped the cover off. A grin spread across her face, knowing she had found the vehicle matching the keys. She straddled the bike and smashed the helmet on the ground. A trail of smoke blazed behind her as she peeled out of the garage and set out on her journey in the night. Although she had no maps, she knew exactly where she was heading.

Two hours into her trip, she stopped at a gas station in the middle of nowhere. She fed on the attendant, making sure not to kill him, then filled up her tank and continued. After four perilous hours of driving, she finally felt her racing mind calm.

She skidded to a stop once she reached her destination, a giant yellow tent in the middle of the desert. The fluorescent lighting inside glowed, and Callie could feel the heat radiating off of it. She quickly got off the bike and stared in amazement. The buzzing of humans inside of the tent indicated a show had recently ended.

Suddenly, a girl pushed her way out of the giant tent flaps and stomped toward Callie. She had her arms crossed, and hatred radiated from her body.

"What happened, darling?" Callie asked, stepping in front of her path.

"I'm so done with the troupe! They expect us to do so many shows a night, and the men are perverts. I should have never come out here."

"Don't worry, you'll never have to see them again." Callie gracefully hugged the girl and sank her fangs into her neck. She drained her body and dragged it into the woods to bury. Afterward, she wiped the dirt off her hands and dusted off her pants. She put on a bright and cheerful smile before she entered the tent. The bustle continued only for mere seconds until everyone stopped to look at the stranger who interrupted their space.

A pale, gorgeous woman with long, silky red hair stood in front of them. She was petite with a rather large muscle build for her size. Her face glowed, and she smirked as they practically drooled over her. A tall, dark-skinned woman pushed her way to the front of the group to examine Callie fully.

"I'm afraid we are closed to the public," she spoke in a strict tone. She wore a purple turban on her head, and a yellow snake lay draped across her shoulders. The snake raised its head to stare and hiss at Callie.

"My apologies, my name is Calypso. I came rather late to the show, but I spoke to one of your past members outside. It seems there is an opening in your circus."

"'Tis true, Marielle quit tonight, but we can fare well without the additional aerialist."

Callie bent backward and touched her hands to the ground. She lowered onto her forearms and curled her legs until they touched her forehead. Callie looked up at the woman and winked. She quickly jumped up and did multiple cartwheels and front flips across the floor. Once she landed, she lowered down into splits.

A few of the troupe clapped their hands, but the woman's firm facial expression remained.

"Come on, Solange, we need another girl for the trapeze duet. Let alone Marielle was the double for the lyra performance." A tall and muscular man stepped forward to confront her.

"Yes, I am very well versed in lyra and trapeze," Callie smiled. "I grew up in Germany, and my mother pushed me into academies at a young age. I have been in America for a while, but it has always been a dream of mine to join a circus."

"Alright," Solange said. "Someone, please show her around. We will see you at practice at four pm. Our first show is at eight."

"Of course, thank you so much, ma'am," Callie replied charmingly as she turned on her heels and exited the tent.

She barely made it back to the bike before bursting out in laughter. She had never been flexible in her life and would never have dreamed of being able to perform the routine and contortion that she executed.

Raphael was right; there is much more to being a vampire than meets the eye. I can act as an equilibrist, making humans think I trained all of my life. Humans are such simple creatures; all you have to do is bend backward, and they see right past the bloodsucking fangs. Maybe I'm not a monster like he says, and I can control my urges.

Callie peeled out of the parking lot and sped off into the night. She came to a pull-off along the side of a winding mountain road. She hopped off the bike and walked to the edge of the road, looking down at the barren rocks and sand beneath her. The stars shined so bright that she had to squint to not be blinded. Although she had just fulfilled an impossible dream, she still felt empty. Her body ached for Raphael's presence, though she was still upset with him. He was the only one who could understand her, yet he made her feel like a failure.

What would he say about me being in a circus? Probably something about feasting on the entire troupe.

She stared longingly at the stars until the faintest color began to appear in the sky. Callie quickly jumped down, landing without a sound, and buried herself next to the mountain wall. By the next sunrise, she would be a star.

*

Callie dug herself to the top of the sand the following night. She shimmied out of her hole and shook the sand off her body and hair. She jumped back on top of the mountain wall and pulled herself up, surprised to find her bike still there. The engine roared to life as she sped off, spewing dust and rocks behind her.

She ignored the honks of a car she inadvertently swerved in front of and left them in the dust. She skidded to a stop in the packed parking lot and ran inside the bustling tent. Almost a hundred people in full costumes were running around, adrenaline and sweat pouring off their bodies.

Callie was mesmerized by the bright colors and sparkles of their unitards. The women had elaborate makeup painted on their faces, while most of the men sported upturned mustaches in classic circus style.

Solange grabbed Callie's arm and let go immediately, shocked at how cold her body was.

"Where have you been? It is almost thirty minutes until curtain!" Her thick Creole accent came out.

"Stuck in traffic," Callie responded coolly. She sensed Solange's distrust but knew it was too close to showtime for her to do anything.

"Fine, Karissa, come get Calypso changed. And warm up, please!"

An equally pale girl motioned for Callie to follow her to the back. She parted the way, pushing away glancing strong men and thick fur coats that blocked the path. Karissa grabbed a sparkly purple leotard identical to her own and handed it to Callie.

She looked around for someplace to change without wandering eyes but realized there were none. Everyone was too busy running around grabbing last-minute costume pieces or adding the final touches of makeup. She shrugged and started to strip, feeling no shame in her nakedness.

Karissa scowled as a few men laughed while Callie bent over to pull her outfit on.

"Don't worry about them. They don't know I'm a killer," Callie told Karissa. She stared blankly back, and Callie figured she must not speak English.

She could tell by the nearby screaming of the crowd that it was nearly showtime. The smell of their sweat and blood was intoxicating. She imagined herself walking out into the spotlight and drinking the blood of every human in the stands. She knew her fantasy was immoral, but she couldn't help the murderous thoughts from entering her mind.

Callie brought herself back to reality and began copying Karissa's stretches. She was only half focused, absorbing the excitement and energy from the nearby crowd. Eventually, Karissa moved closer toward the curtains, but Callie stayed in the shadows as the loud music and screams of the crowd were overwhelming.

She watched from the sidelines as clowns juggled bowling pins, swords, and flaming torches. She was so enthralled by the flames licking the gasoline-soaked torch that she was nearly trampled by a girl on a horse. She stepped to the side as the horse practically bucked the rider off, who gave Callie a nasty look.

The horse and rider took off at a gallop and did laps around the arena as the jugglers peeled back behind the curtain. A handsome man in a top hat and red jacket walked into the center of the arena with a whip, guiding the horse. The rider began to perform acrobatic tricks on the back of the horse while the crowd clapped and cheered in wonder.

Callie was not impressed by her flexibility, and the brief interaction with the woman was enough to make her feel murderous. She gritted her teeth and squeezed her fists together until the woman fell out of the handstand she held on top of the horse. The crowd gasped in unison as she fell face-first to the ground and barely caught herself. She managed to smile and wave at the crowd while the man brought the horse to a stop. Callie giggled, which the woman noticed as she stomped past her.

The curtain pulled, and Callie was tossed to the side again. Crew members rushed past to pull rigging ropes to lower the trapeze from the banisters. The hustle and bustle made her feel alive. She felt so unimportant and almost invisible, which was a new and incredible experience after always being the center of attention as a vampire.

Karissa grabbed Callie's hand and pointed for her to stand next to a man in a similar sparkling purple shirt. Karissa left and ran to the opposite side of the arena to stand next to her partner. Callie could feel the hot breath of her partner rolling onto her neck, and she turned toward him.

"So, how do we do this?" she asked. He laughed as he cracked his fists.

"You'll climb to the platform first, and I'll go behind you. Gabriel and I will start swinging; then I'll pick you up when I am in a knee hang. You would have known this if you came to practice?"

"I don't need practice. I just wanted to see if you knew what you were doing." Callie started her ascent up the skinny rope ladder. The thin rope shook as they both climbed to the top of the platform. Callie began to feel anxious as she hoisted herself onto the platform, which barely had enough space for the two performers. Her anxiety was something new to her as a vampire; she had always felt fearless and confident in every other obstacle.

Her partner seemed to sense her anxiety or see it in her face as he moved to stand in front of her. "Are you sure you've done this before?"

It was too late for Callie to respond. The spotlights landed on them, and Callie instantly grimaced and winced in pain. The crowd's thunderous claps and cheers were amplified to unbearable levels. She fell onto her knees and gripped the edge of the platform with her fingers, her nails leaving indentations in the steel.

What am I doing? Why am I doing this? Why do I

constantly have to prove to myself that I am capable of doing everything? I'm a vampire, for damn sake. I shouldn't have to flip off of a trapeze to prove that to myself.

The show must go on.

Callie's head shot up, and she searched the crowd. Due to the blinding lights, she was unable to focus on any faces. But she recognized the deep, husky voice in her mind—it was her Vampire King.

As Callie stood tall and proud after hearing Raphael's voice, her partner swung on the trapeze. She doubted he had even noticed her breakdown. She watched in amazement as he and Gabriel swung back and forth, almost touching each other and then nearly kicking her and Karissa as gravity brought them back to the platforms.

After swinging back and forth a few times, the men flipped upside down and hooked both of their knees onto the trapeze bar. As Gabriel swung back to the platform, Karissa jumped off with her arms above her head and connected with Gabriel's hands.

Callie was too busy watching them, so she stumbled backward as her partner's hands flew at her face.

"What the hell?" he shouted at her as the trapeze swung back toward the center.

No, the show must go on.

Callie took two steps and jumped off of the platform, hurdling herself at her partner, who screamed, "No!"

If a human had leaped, they would already be in the netting twenty feet below, but Callie's strength was unimaginable. She met her partner's hands in the middle of the swing, and Karissa gave her a shocked look. The girls met in the middle, nearly touching, and then were propelled back toward the platform. As they flew back toward the center, she felt the grip loosen between their hands and was thrown into the air as the trapeze hit its highest peak.

Callie instinctively curled into a ball as she somersaulted through the air, then straightened as she felt herself fall. Gabriel grabbed her hands this time while Karissa met with Callie's original partner.

"What the hell was that?" Gabriel yelled down to Callie. She could only grin as she felt the adrenaline speed through her veins. It was the same rush and high as if she had just drained a body. She let go of one hand to turn herself around just in time for the next jump. As Gabriel released his grip and threw Callie into the air, she propelled herself to the top of the circus tent.

The audience gasped as they watched Callie fly ten, twenty, nearly forty feet in the air. Everyone stood to their feet, watching and wondering where the aerialist had gone, while she held onto the scaffolding at the very tip of the tent. She could finally see the hundreds of people from this view, and her heart raced with excitement and hunger. She locked eyes with Raphael, the only person sitting at this point, and he shook his head in disappointment. She blew him a kiss and dove down toward the trapeze, head first.

Callie's arms were straight in front of her head. She was a flying rocket, and the crowd began to scream in fear once they spotted her speeding down. There was no way she would be able to regain her position on the trapeze, and there was no way she could have jumped that high in the first place! But Callie was a vampire, so she flew perfectly into her partner's unsuspecting hands, and the crowd roared.

The trapeze began to slow down, but Callie gladly released one hand to wave toward the crowd, which they loved. They cheered and clapped in sheer wonder at what they had witnessed. Once the trapeze was back over the platform, Callie jumped down, and her partner thudded beside her. He grabbed her shoulders and started to shake her and yell in a foreign language. She let him berate her for a few seconds, then coolly shrugged him off and did a backflip off of the platform.

By now, her act was up; all of the fellow circus crowd knew she was something supernatural. Her final backflip off the platform, landing silently and in a perfect position like a gymnast, would be impossible for a human to complete at over twenty-five feet. Acting as if nothing unusual had occurred, she sashayed past the nearly rioting crowd. The circus crew all tried to grab her, but an invisible force field kept their reaching arms far back. Solange blocked the exit of the tent, and a few tall men surrounded her.

"You blasphemous devil!" she spat. Her usual calm snake partner rattled its tail.

"Please forgive us for her rather uncalled-for show of power." Raphael appeared behind Callie, holding onto her back and trying to diffuse the situation. "I can assure you every audience member will rave over the amazing theatrics of your show. Nobody suspects anything more unnatural than a circus."

Solange was fuming, her body shook, and her nostrils flared as she exhaled deep breaths.

"You know your kind is not welcome here."

"I am well aware, ma'am, but my partner is still learning and testing her boundaries. It won't happen again. My sincerest apologies." With Raphael's final words, he grabbed Callie's hand and dragged her out of the tent, leaving the angry mob behind. She turned around to give a smart comment about how their show would have been bland without her, but Raphael read her mind and immediately silenced her. He stopped in front of a black sedan Callie had not seen in the parking garage before. He opened the passenger door for her, and she rolled her eyes as she reluctantly sat inside.

Raphael peeled out of the parking lot and slammed on the gas, throwing Callie back into the seat. They both remained silent for almost an hour as they drove through the empty, dark desert roads.

"I don't understand why you are making us sit in this stuffy car when we could just fly or teleport back," Callie huffed. She was visibly irritated with Raphael, and her goal was to make this car ride unbearable for him.

"I would rather not piss off the circus freaks any more than we already did. Speaking of circus freaks...are we going to talk about that?"

"Awe, are you afraid the strong man would beat you up?" Callie mocked him, pinching his cheek. Raphael kept his gaze forward on the winding road speeding ahead of them.

"Circus people are a tribe of their own, like we are. If word got out that vampires were messing around with them, it could end badly for other vampires in the area."

"Why does it matter? I thought Hades wanted them all dead anyway."

"Only the ones that don't support his rule." The silence was deafening and uncomfortable, so Raphael turned on music. The bass screamed out of the car's speakers and blasted them with violent lyrics. He played the Satanic Duo, Callie's favorite artist when she was a human. She couldn't help but let a wide grin spread across her cheeks.

"They were my favorite; how did you know? Oh wait, you read my mind."

"This did not come from your thoughts," Raphael chuckled and pushed harder on the gas pedal. "But from the deepest longing of your soul. Stored right next to your love and admiration for vampires and everything evil."

Callie rolled her eyes and turned to stare out of the window. There wasn't much to look at but the black night and occasional rocks and cacti. She was still mad he had taken her away from the circus. It was the only place she had felt comfortable recently. She let her head rest against the cool glass, closed her eyes, and listened to the music. The lyrics penetrated her soul with talk of murder and demons.

Callie began to hyperventilate, and her chest felt hard again, like when the demons had entered her. When she had listened to these songs as a human, it was no issue to hear lyrics of killing and dying. Now, they were telling the misery of her life. She *had* killed people.

Oh God, what have I done?! I am a demon now. I don't have a soul. Or it sits in the hands of Hades. I am no longer human. I no longer have any morality. I've killed hundreds of people! Probably more...I kill with no thinking of what their families or friends feel...

"Snap out of it, Calypso," Raphael growled. He listened to the inner turmoil inside her mind. "You can't go back and relive all your kills; it will make you crazy."

But the memories already flooded her mind.

The frat boy.

The dozens of men at the club.

The single mom.

The ex-circus performer.

Half of the people she couldn't even recall their faces; they were just a means to an end that would never be fulfilled. Her hunger would never stop, and she would always be a murderer.

"We can go see them, you know," Raphael continued, trying to pull her out of the abyss she was falling deep into. "The Satanic Duo are playing a concert in Los Angeles for Halloween. It's only a few days away. I'm sure you would love to meet them up close and personal."

Callie was about to respond with questions and excuses before remembering they were vampires who could do anything. They could bend any human's will to their own and then feed from them.

"I had my share of celebrities as well," Raphael continued. "I took a hiatus in the early years of American stars. Marilyn Monroe, of course, was a beauty everyone adored. Stevie Nicks, Jimmie Hendrix." He paused, looking over to find Callie still ignoring him and staring out the window. She was the epitome of angst. "The names don't mean anything once you become an immortal God."

Those words got her attention, and she whipped her head around, the tears streaming down her face. "God, you're talking about celebrities, and I am reliving every death I have caused."

"You can't fall into that hole of despair, Callie," Raphael was stern but spoke her human name, attempting to comfort her.

"You'll never come out of it. You can't focus on death; you must focus on your power and how good it feels. You can't afford to have morality and empathy for the human race."

Callie was done listening, so she turned the stereo as loud as possible, deafening them with the unholy lyrics. The speakers exploded, causing sparks to fly out of the sides of the doors. Raphael's attention was on the speakers, so she grabbed the wheel and pulled down as hard as she could. Raphael flew out of the window instinctively, but Callie purposely remained in the car.

The sharp and fast turn made the car spin and then flip onto its side, rolling over multiple times before finally crashing against a large boulder. The car was indented and smashed everywhere, and glass littered the sand. Smoke came out of the crunched hood of the car. Raphael stood a few feet away from the terrible wreck.

Any human would have died, if not instantly, then from blood loss, but Callie remained unharmed. She bled from deep gashes in her face, neck, chest, and arms. Her face had smashed against the dash, making her lose a few teeth. She was upside down, still buckled in, taking in the adrenaline from the crash. She stayed in for a few more moments before shimmying out of the seatbelt and smashing open the window. She stood up, brushed the glass shards off her, and pulled a few larger pieces out of her hair.

"Callie would have died in that crash." Her voice faltered, still regaining her strength. "Don't you get it? I AM the monster! I am the hole of despair."

"Why did you have to crash?" Raphael took her into his arms and kissed her bloody forehead. "Did you need to feel something?"

"I need to feel pain, to feel fear. But I don't feel anything," she sobbed. "Nothing but guilt for everyone I killed. I try to kill myself to make it right, and I can't even do that."

Raphael sensed another car approaching on the road, and

they needed to leave. Callie was motionless in his arms and felt heavy. She weighed on him and had given up all her fight. They teleported away, leaving no trace but the wrecked car.

Chapter 11

The following nights leading up to the concert were uneventful. Callie stayed in the coffin most of the night, refusing to drink and instead wallowing in self-pity. Raphael knew it was Halloween night when he awoke to Callie blasting music upstairs.

As Callie put on eyeliner and lipstick, she couldn't help but feel jittery and nauseous, like she was a teenager again. She decided to put her wallowing aside, at least for one night. She hadn't been this excited in what felt like a lifetime. Going to a concert as a vampire would be an out-of-body experience, let alone seeing and meeting some of her favorite musicians.

Callie fitted herself in a red tube top, black skinny jeans, and her prized black boots, while Raphael wore a partially unbuttoned white blouse.

"Do you have to stick out?" Callie groaned as she tossed her hair in front of the mirror.

"What do you mean? It's Halloween! I plan on getting this shirt bloodstained; we'll fit right in." He grinned and wrapped his hands around Callie's waist. She smiled as he kissed her neck, endorphins rushing throughout her body. She nodded, signaling that she was ready and wouldn't take no for an answer.

"Do you at least want a drink first?" Raphael asked.

"It's Halloween! I plan on getting this shirt bloodstained," she mocked in a low tone. Raphael grabbed her hand and teleported to the venue.

They appeared in the middle of a large crowd that pushed toward the front of the stage. Callie took a moment to regain her bearings. Teleporting perpetually made her feel disoriented as it took a few seconds for her sense of vision and touch to return to their normal heightened state. Raphael followed behind Callie as she cleared through the crowd and approached the stage.

She stopped behind the mosh pit, and the crowd roared as an opening act appeared on stage. The artist screamed into the microphone, which made Callie grimace and cover her ears.

Raphael comforted her by wrapping his arms around her waist and pulling her back into him.

She melted into his chest and swayed with the pounding music. Callie grinned, revealing her fangs, as he licked and kissed her neck, making her body jolt with erotic electricity. She couldn't control herself any longer so she grabbed the man in front of her and bit into his neck. She moaned loudly as it had been days since she tasted sweet, hot blood on her tongue.

"Not too much, mon chérie, save some for the rest of us." Raphael grabbed the man and sank his fangs into the wound she had made.

Over the past few weeks, Callie had become more powerful in her mind-controlling abilities. With little effort, she could now put a human in a trance and completely erase their memory of the feeding. The man was pushed to the side, and the vampire couple continued moving forward in the crowd.

They both squirmed past the thick bodies and fed every few feet. Their plan was almost too easy, as the majority of the concert-goers were drunk or drugged. Any human who was lost in the music or their own intoxication was immediately dragged into their fangs.

Callie could tell the artist was almost finished with their set when a group of photographers came out and began to fill the night with bright flashes. She looked over toward Raphael, who was feeding on a girl a few feet away from her.

"It's almost time," She spoke of meeting her favorite artists.

"Do you have enough blood in your system to control yourself?" His words spoke only to her, blocking out the noisy crowd and bass from the speakers.

"Hardly," she cooed. "I could do this all night." Callie took one last drink from the man she held and shoved him away.

She turned back toward Raphael, who disappeared. She glanced around quickly, scanning the crowd for his tall frame and blond hair, but there was no sight of him. She hovered off of the ground, only a few inches to not draw attention, and finally spotted him on the left side of the venue toward the exit.

Raphael had his back turned toward her and was talking to a man. Callie squinted as Raphael stepped aside, and she was able to view the man he spoke with. He was taller and more muscular than Raphael but had a dark complexion, with curly black hair, and a beard. Callie swore she saw him grin at her, and they both vanished before her eyes.

"What the hell, Raphael?" She spoke out loud and into his mind. She waited a few seconds before he finally responded.

I have to take care of business. Wait for me.

"Fuck that," Callie was furious he had abandoned her in the middle of their special night. She pushed her way out of the crowd, wiping the blood off her mouth and throwing a few humans to the ground in the process. She spotted a door toward the stage that security guards surrounded. Assuming the artist area would be behind the heavily guarded area, she walked over like she owned the venue.

She made the few security guards step aside with only a mean glance and the willpower of her mind. Once inside the dimly lit hallway, she began to feel anxiety rise in her chest again. A stressed-out man walked past, hardly noticing her since he was so engulfed in his cell phone and multiple clipboards he carried. She was drawn toward a door at the end of the hallway, knowing her victims were inside. She took a deep breath before twisting the door handle and stepping inside.

Two men in their thirties sat on a couch, staring at their unexpected visitor. Noah, the main singer of the group, sat with a cigarette half-smoked in his hand. He had multiple face tattoos and dark, soulless eyes. Elijah, the music producer and backup vocalist, wore a baseball cap covering his equally empty eyes.

"I thought I told you no hoes tonight." Noah scoffed, flicking ash onto the ground.

"I didn't order her. You know she's not my type," Elijah responded. They were both too calm and unphased, being in the presence of the dead.

"I'm actually a fan of yours, or I was." Callie rolled her eyes at their unintelligent conversation. "I wanted to ask you a few questions before your show tonight."

"How did you get back here? Bro, we need better security." Noah reached for his cell phone, which was on a coffee table in front of them, but it slid onto the ground.

"I wouldn't do that. If I was able to get back here unphased, imagine what I could do to whatever little manager you'd have run in here."

Both men still looked unphased, but Noah sank back into the couch. "Why do the weird bitches always come out on Halloween? What do you want to know? Make it quick."

Callie laughed as she extracted the previous year's memory from Noah's mind. He had taken a fan to the back of the tour bus after their show. While on her knees to pleasure him, she had pulled out a knife from in between her large breasts and tried to hand it to Noah. 'Please sacrifice me,' she had begged him. He stepped back in confusion as she continued to plead with him. 'Sacrifice me to the devil. I want to be famous like you!'

"Unfortunately, I am not like your big bosom friend. I don't need to be sacrificed to the devil," Callie sat down in a chair across from them. Her words finally piqued an interest in Noah, who flailed his nostrils.

"I want to know when you would like to die. Would it be tonight or another night? Either way, I would love to have the honor of dragging you both to Hell to meet your maker," Callie continued. The scant yellow lighting in the room flickered.

"What the fuck are you talking about?" Elijah practically yelled.

"Oh, excuse me, I didn't properly introduce myself! I am Calypso, the Queen of Vampires. Well, soon to be, but that doesn't matter."

"The only thing you are sucking is dick," Noah laughed, trying to play off his worry. He readjusted himself in the peeling leather couch.

"So, are you scared to go to Hell? Probably not, since you worship him. I'm sure he can't wait to see you," Callie ignored Noah's sexual comment.

"We don't worship anyone," Elijah harshly responded.

"We both know that is a lie," Callie laughed. "Ninety-five percent of your songs mention the devil, lucifer, satan, but you claim not to worship him?"

"The devil is a lie anyway," Noah interrupted. "It's just part of our genre, part of these characters we created. Rappers from Hell. We don't believe in that shit. It just gets our ratings up."

"Wow," Callie shook her head in disbelief. "So you made this all up? Your depression, drug abuse, killings, and devil worshiping? You both are a bunch of frauds! Some of us have actually killed..." She trailed off and tried to calm herself after raising her voice.

"It's not that it's made up. We've been artists for over ten years. Sure, we struggled with a lot of that in the beginning. Yeah, we still make songs about dying, but that doesn't mean we are begging or waiting for death," Elijah muttered and pulled his cap down.

"Making money is all that matters now, huh?"

Noah flicked his cigarette and glanced towards the door, ready to finish the conversation. He unzipped his pants and motioned for Callie to come to him. This infuriated her, so she leaped out of her chair, knocking it to the ground, and clung to him. She ripped into his neck while Elijah screamed. Noah was too shocked to make a sound.

Callie felt nauseated as soon as she took the first sip from his neck. She jolted back and stumbled off of him, falling onto the coffee table. Her vision faded in and out, and a fire raced through her throat.

"You lied to me!" she screamed, making a lightbulb burst. "You have the blood of Hades inside of you!" She grabbed her forehead as it exploded with pain. She sank to the ground as she was too weak to stand. She had to struggle to keep herself conscious.

Callie knew what was happening to her, as Raphael had explained it one night. She was dying. He had cut his wrist with a knife and let the blood drip onto an ant hill while they trained in the desert. The hoard of ants climbed over each other to be the first to the decadent blood. Within seconds, they all convulsed and died rapidly.

"You see," Raphael explained, "You can only drink the blood of Hades if you are allowed to. If a stray vampire were to attack and drink my blood, they would die a quick and painful death like these ants. The same would happen if you decided to drink from a demon. Hades infuses his blood into his demons to prevent any vampire from feeding and trying to take their power."

"How come I don't die when I drink from you then?" Callie had questioned him.

"First, you were a human, so you were able to. Since then, it has been very minimal. You have been able to tolerate it only because you are my queen."

Callie returned to the present, and the two men stood up, staring at her from afar. Noah held a shirt to his bleeding neck, and they both looked strung out.

"Tell me," Callie struggled to push herself up to a sitting position. "The devil's blood is inside of you."

"I already told you, the devil isn't real! If he were, he would have already dragged me down to Hell," Noah cried. Elijah made a noise, and Noah shook his head.

"I think we saw him one night," Elijah spoke quietly.

"Do tell quickly!" Callie clenched her jaw as another agonizing pain shot through her veins.

"It was when we first started to blow up during one of our first tours. We had just finished performing in...I don't remember where. We were so fucked up. But this guy was staring at us from the bar the whole time. We figured he was from a record label, so we went up and talked to him after our show. He offered it all:

fame, money, endless fans, and power. But Noah didn't like him. He said if we were going to be famous, we would do it on our own; we didn't need help from anyone. The guy was disappointed but asked us to have a drink with him at least."

"How does this story translate into seeing the devil?" Callie rubbed her temples, trying to make sense of the jumbled story she heard.

"That's what I'm saying," Noah said. "Elijah is convinced this guy is the devil because of a look he has. So what? We've seen so many weirdos over the past few years."

"What did he look like?"

"It's not just that," Elijah shook his head. "Yeah, he looked dark and evil, but I've seen him again! He's been to other shows too. I've seen him wearing the same clothes and watching us in the same weird way. I saw him tonight, too! I looked out behind the curtain earlier, and I swear I saw him."

"What did he look like?" Callie spoke louder this time.

"Tall, black hair and beard. Dark eyes. But he is always wearing the same Fuck The Population bomber jacket."

Callie shot up to standing and held her chest as it became hard to breathe. She saw the image of him in her mind, the devil, Hades, she had seen him earlier! He was the man Raphael had been talking to. Her head began to swirl, and she became extremely dizzy; she knew it wasn't from the poison. She felt a fire rise in her body, this time in her intestines, and she knew she had to leave.

"Hades is here," were the only words she managed to say before she bolted out of the room, leaving the two men dazed and confused. She ran down the hallway at human speed, unable to reach her full potential. The red glowing exit sign was her light at the end of the tunnel, which seemed to move farther away as she ran. The door was heavier to push open than she expected, and it took a few shoves to wedge herself out.

A security guard yelled at her, but she ignored him and continued running out of the venue. By the time she was outside of the sweaty mess of bodies, she was profusely sweating herself. She knew this was not a good sign as she had never perspired as a vampire. Once she was more out of sight of the venue, she vomited. Her bile was black and gritty, and she collapsed next to it.

Callie had no strength to call out to Raphael. She rolled onto her back to receive comfort from the stars, something beautiful to look at while she perished, but they hid behind the clouds and light pollution that night. The full moon did little to arouse her.

"Well, well, what do we have here? A dying vampire. Could this be your queen?" a deep and poignant voice cut through the night. Callie didn't have to look to see who it came from. Her body began to feel warm. She felt Raphael drop to her side and stroke her face.

"Mon chérie, what did you do?" Raphael's voice was full of hurt and betrayal. "I told you to wait."

"You...you left me." She struggled to spit out the words and rolled over to vomit again. "You spoke to Hades and couldn't even tell me."

"Look at me when you say my name." Hades squatted down to Callie's level and grabbed her chin in his hand. Her entire face lit up with pain and heat as his fingertips connected with her skin. He forced her head upward to meet his eyes. They were as dark and empty as Elijah had described. Callie felt as if she was instantly spiraling into a black hole as she stared into his pupils. The smell of death and cedarwood rolled off of him and filled her nostrils. His perfect complexion and muscle build made her nipples hard, which she despised. He had an aura of power around him that she could almost see as if it were a faint glowing halo surrounding his frame.

"They don't believe in you, you know." Callie spat the lingering vomit in her mouth onto the ground next to Hades' feet. He smiled as he stood back up to his full height. "You tricked them! Giving them your blood in a drink."

"You are a smart girl, Callie. By the way, I meant to congratulate you on your horrific club murders." Callie hated the way he spoke, as if he was mocking her.

"Hades, you have to do something! She is dying!" Raphael insisted.

"No, I have offered you one too many favors regarding your queens. Shall I remind you of your last one?"

Callie's head swam in confusion, and she curled into a ball as another wave of pain crashed over her body.

"If she is to perish, she was never meant to be. If you want to cure her, she can drink my blood at her ceremony in Hell," Hades continued.

"Callie's not ready!" Raphael hissed.

She began to swim in and out of consciousness as they continued to argue. Their words and her pain lost all meaning. The only thing she clung to was Raphael's face, she would do anything to stay with him. Even if that meant sacrificing her soul.

"Stop!" Callie finally yelled. They both stared down at her in surprise. "My name is Calypso. Callie died when you killed her." She grimaced at Raphael. "That's why I have been struggling so much; I've been trying to be someone I am no longer. Callie is dead. I am ready to become Queen."

A malicious smile spread across Hades' face, and he rubbed his hands together. "Finally stepping into your destiny, I see."

"Great, let's go. She doesn't have much time!" Raphael helped Calypso to her feet, throwing her arm over his shoulder to prop her up.

"I'm afraid she still has some unfinished human attachments to take care of," Hades responded coolly.

"What do you mean? I am an orphan," Calypso meekly chuckled. Each laugh felt like it shattered her ribs and punctured her lungs.

"You forget, I have briefly seen your soul. I felt your love for that human boy; what is his insignificant name?"

"Justin? You can't be serious."

"I'm afraid I am. You still love him. Get rid of that attachment to your human life and meet me in Hell. If you are meant to be Queen, you will survive." Hades turned on his heels and then paused, glancing back at Calypso. "And if not, don't fear. I have a special place for you in my kingdom." He disappeared after his last words. Calypso gasped in shock and hardly noticed Raphael throw her into his arms as they teleported away.

*

They landed on a dark street in Tampa, over a thousand miles away from where they had been only seconds before. Calypso opened her eyes to see her and Justin's old house and immediately vomited.

"I can't do this," She moaned and turned away from the painful memory.

"You have to, mon chérie. Here, have some of my blood and see if it helps." Raphael bit into his wrist and pushed it into Calypso's mouth. She forced herself to take a few sips, but it did nothing to cease the immense pain.

"What did Hades mean back there? About the last queen?"

"You are delusional and hearing things," Raphael spoke gently, but she could tell by his stiff and off-putting body language that he was lying.

"I know what I heard!" Calypso yelled, her voice echoing off of the nearby houses.

"We don't have time for this; please go make your amends."

"I have to know what I am getting myself into! You at least owe me that."

Raphael sighed and glanced away before meeting her eyes. He had hoped to keep his past a permanent secret.

"There was another woman I thought was my queen before I met you. It was almost a hundred years ago and should not concern you. I met her when she was human and instantly fell in love. Her father was a preacher and hated me at first sight. That didn't stop her; we both fell for each other and spent every night together. Her father threatened to take her away, away from me, so she begged me to turn her that night. I did, and she was an excellent companion.

"She exceeded in all her powers and was always obedient and submissive, so naturally, I assumed she was my Vampire Queen. I took her to Hell and to Hades and immediately felt something was off. She wasn't the same; she was terrified. As she drank the cup of Hades' blood, she collapsed to the ground and began convulsing and vomiting like you. I begged Hades to spare her, to let her go and punish me instead. It was my fault for bringing her to him; I had made the mistake, not her. After I pleaded and cried to him, he finally granted me the favor. He had a witch restore her, undoing the curse to her body, and she was sent away."

Calypso swayed as miniature spasms rolled through her body. She squinted her eyes closed, and she received Raphael's memories of his previous love. "What happened to her?"

"I don't know. Hades restored her but promised if she went against him or his rule in any way, he would kill and throw her into hellfire. I haven't seen her since that night."

"So that's it? Do you still love her?"

"I suppose I love her as much as you love Justin," Raphael shrugged. "We never lose feelings for our first love, do we?"

"What happens to me now? What if I am just another mistake?" Calypso whimpered.

"You are not. From the moment I saw you, it was different. I was basing my assumption on the love I had for her, but I sensed the power in you, Calypso. You are so strong; I know you are my queen. I have no doubts this time. Now, make haste. We want to bring you to Hell still alive."

Calypso trudged to the backyard fence and sighed before she started to climb the chain links. She reached the top and fell over, crashing hard onto her side. She vomited and coughed profusely as dirt filled her nose and mouth.

"Callie?" Justin walked around the corner of the house to find his ex-fiance sitting clumsily in the dirt. His face was shocked, and he held an unlit cigarette in his hand. He kept his distance, not wanting to help her up, and she meekly smiled at him.

"Hey, Justin. Sorry for my crazy entrance. I just, uh, wanted to talk to you." She awkwardly stood up and brushed the dirt off of her pants.

"You know phones still exist, right?"

"Yeah, I know that," she laughed. "But I got a new number, so I couldn't call."

"So you decided to fly from California back to Florida just to climb over my fence in the middle of the night to talk to me?" Justin was unconvinced of her story.

"That sounds pretty crazy," Calypso turned around to vomit and cursed herself for not preparing what to say to him beforehand.

"Have you been drinking? You look like shit."

"I definitely drank the wrong poison tonight." She laughed. "Look, Justin, I'm sorry. I'm sorry for barging in like this, but I can't stand this bad blood between us. I know I hurt you and wanted to come here face-to-face to apologize. I never meant to hurt you."

"God, that is such bullshit!" he yelled. His face began to turn red, and she could see a few veins pop out around his forehead. "If you never meant to hurt me, you would have never cheated on me! You would have never allowed me to plan a trip for us and then leave with another man two days in."

"I swear I didn't mean for it to happen that way! I didn't even know Raphael lived in Santa Monica." She nervously glanced around the empty yard that held so many memories for them. Visions of picnics and gardening flooded her mind.

"Raphael." Justin scoffed. "What a great name."

"I promise you, Justin, I didn't know he was there! I just saw him when we were at the restaurant, and..." Calypso trailed off.

"Whatever. I'm over it." Justin shook his head and flicked the cigarette in his hand, though it remained unlit. "How did you meet him anyway?"

"We met one night in Tampa. It was a long time ago. We talked for a while, but nothing happened because I was with you. It was like...if we ever meet again, it was meant to be. Then I saw him in California, and...it was meant to be." Calypso hated lying to him. But she knew it was easier than trying to explain Raphael was a vampire who had stalked her over a period of time.

"Where is he now? Does he know you came to see me?"

"I don't know where he is," she looked over her shoulder. "Yes, he knows; he actually encouraged me to come see you."

"Again, we could have done this over the phone. Besides, how do you not know where he is?"

"Oh, you know, luxury businessmen are always jetting off to somewhere new. I can hardly keep up," Calypso waved her hands around, and Justin rolled his eyes.

"Is that why you left me? To live a new exclusive life of a rich housewife or something?"

"No, Justin," Calypso reached out to touch him, but he stepped back. It was probably a good idea since her skin was ice cold yet on fire simultaneously. "I loved you. I still do love you. But...I guess our love was just old and comfortable. Raphael was new and exciting. We had an instant connection, and it felt like fate seeing him again. I never should have left you the way I did. That's one of my biggest regrets. But I hope you are doing okay now, and you know it's okay to move on."

"Don't worry, I moved on the second my plane touched down. It's hard to trust people now. I can't get close to anyone anymore. I have this gut-wrenching feeling they're going to tear my heart out like you did."

"I am sorry, Justin. Do you think you can forgive me?"

"I already have," he sighed. "You seem like you are living your perfect life, and I am happy for you. I'm not going to be the one to hold you down."

Calypso sighed in relief and grabbed her stomach as she began to feel nauseated again.

"You really should go to the hospital; you look so pale and dead. I've never seen you so fucked up before," Justin hinted with a smile, which made Calypso smile in return.

"Oh, I'm fine. I should get going, though."

"At least walk through my house this time, and don't jump the fence like a psycho?"

Calypso almost nodded but sensed the presence of other humans in the house and didn't want to draw more attention to herself. "It's fine, really. I don't need to catch up with any of the boys. Could you actually not tell anyone about this? Trying to keep a low profile and all."

Justin opened his mouth to object, but one of his friends opened the sliding glass door, and he heard.

"Yo Justin, are you ever going to get back in here?" His friend Tyler called out into the night. Justin walked around the corner to respond, and Calypso took this moment to climb back over the fence. She landed in Raphael's arms, who appeared out of thin air, and teleported to the underworld.

Justin looked over his shoulder, and Calypso was nowhere to be seen, which shocked him. There was no way she could have climbed the fence and disappeared so quickly and quietly, especially since she was visibly drunk in his eyes.

"Yeah, sorry," Justin shook his head. "I was just talking to Callie."

"No way; she finally called you after all these months? What did she say?" Tyler asked enthusiastically.

"I really don't want to talk about it right now. I'm gonna go for a walk and clear my head."

Tyler patted Justin on the back as he walked back inside his house. A few other friends sat in the dark living room playing video games. They hardly noticed Justin walk in front of the television and grab a lighter for his cigarette. He walked a few houses down when he became acutely aware of two crows with beady red eyes watching him.

He took a long drag of the cigarette and exhaled, his mind still swirling from seeing Callie again. Nothing made sense to him for her to show up unannounced in the middle of the night. As he was lost in his thoughts, he felt a cold breeze surround and constrict him. He struggled to breathe and couldn't scream out for help. His hands were thrust behind him, and he felt immense pain in his chest.

Justin vanished from the night, leaving behind only the burning cigarette.

Chapter 12

Calypso refused to open her eyes, realizing she was terrified of entering Hell and observing Hades in his natural habitat. She would gladly avoid him but knew it was impossible as he was her soon-to-be master. She would have to worship him as a God; she knew this, but her soul hated it. She despised how Hades had looked at her and could only imagine his evil thoughts.

"Come on, Callie," Raphael whispered into her ear, gently placing her on the ground. She slowly opened one eye at a time while still holding onto him for balance and support.

As her body adjusted to the new environment, she became acutely aware of the heat and humidity that clung to her skin. She knew they were in Hades' castle, as Raphael had previously described. The room was so enormous it could have been a vast dining hall or ballroom but was strikingly empty except for two large chairs. One chair sat in the direct middle of the room and was much larger than the other, which was placed off to the side. The larger chair was much more ornate, laid with swirls of gold and gemstones around the entire wooden frame and a seat of rich and luscious red silk. A heavy scent of fire and cedar filled the air.

As Calypso pondered her surroundings, she realized everything was crafted out of golden stone; the floors, walls, and ceiling were all covered with chryselephantine. She grazed her palm across the cold floor which felt incredible on her feverish body.

There appeared to be only one exit out of the grand room. To the right, from what her blurred vision could make out, lay an equally impressive hallway.

A piercing scream snapped her attention to the hallway, and she saw a monster, the only way she could describe or perceive the horrid beast, dragging a young male. The chains scraping against the stones screeched almost as loud as the human, which sent shivers deep into her soul. She couldn't imagine what horrible deed the man could have done to deserve such an ending.

"He was a nonbeliever," Hades stepped into the room, looking much different than he had on Earth.

His shorter black hair was now shoulder length, and his curls were more defined. His beard was also longer and seemed to fall in perfect smooth waves. His forehead was wider, and the bridge of his nose was more defined, but he still had a perfect complexion and features.

"To believe in God is righteous," Hades boomed.

"To believe in Hell is wise, but to believe in nothing is pure foolishness. To believe that he, a mere mortal, is his own creator of life and death is an atrocity. When he died of a car accident, his soul thought it would dissolve into oblivion or rejoin the stars," he laughed. "So I make sure his naive soul will always believe in Hell."

Calypso was shocked at his words. To Raphael, this came as no surprise. He had witnessed thousands of souls receiving punishment in Hell, and nothing affected him anymore. He couldn't afford to have any sympathy or empathy for others, especially humans.

"She is ready, my Lord," Raphael spoke in a loud and confident voice, slightly pushing Calypso forward to Hades.

She longed to turn around and glare at him for his submission but knew it would only create problems. As Hades walked closer, she shrank to her knees out of pure terror or of his powers she did not know.

"Are you willing to accept me as your Lord and savior? To obey all of my commands and to never stray from the dark path? To serve Hell and rule over the entirety of the vampire race?"

Calypso took a deep, shaky breath before she nodded and forced herself to look into his eyes. "Yes, I do."

Master, Raphael spoke into her mind.

"Master," she choked out.

"Very good." Hades smiled and walked to his grand throne to retrieve a dagger and a small bowl. Calypso nervously peaked at Raphael, who stood afar with his hands folded in front of him. He was confident the blood of Hades would heal his queen.

As Hades returned to stand in front of Calypso, he quickly sliced the palm of his hand and squeezed a few drops of blood into the black onyx bowl. He handed it to her, and she took it, slowly holding the bowl to her lips. She continued to maintain eye contact with him as she tilted her head back, and the blood touched her tongue. Fire rose inside of her again, but it was not tortuous this time. Heat raced throughout her limbs and veins, and she sighed in relief as every pain disappeared. The blood was so sweet and intense that she found herself licking the bowl, trying to swallow every drop.

"How do you feel?" Hades questioned once she lowered the bowl from her mouth.

"More." She stunned herself and Raphael by uttering the sole word. Hades' grin spread to his ears, and his furrowed eyebrows gave him the authentic look of a devil. He ripped open his shirt and ran the dagger from the tip of his collarbone to just above his navel. As the blood began to bead at his skin's surface, Calypso couldn't contain herself.

With adrenaline pounding through her body, she jumped forward, attaching her fangs to the top of Hades' chest as she sucked the blood from his wound. She clutched his ripped shirt and hardly noticed as he placed his hands on her back, pulling her closer. His erection throbbed against her chest, and the bloodlust made her rub against it.

Raphael struggled to keep a straight face as he watched Calypso drink from Hades while he tenderly held her and threw his head back in ecstasy. She dropped to her knees to finish drinking at his navel, which was too much for him to handle.

"She's had enough, don't you think?" He tried to keep his voice level with no tone of hatred, though that could only describe his feelings.

Hades smirked at him, knowing he had overstepped a boundary and struck a chord with his subservient. Raphael would do nothing, though, as he was loyal almost to a fault.

He stepped back from Calypso and pulled his shirt together.

"Don't worry, she is still plenty thirsty," Hades spoke in a low tone. Raphael stepped forward and grabbed the dagger from his hand.

"Calypso," Hades continued. "You have pledged your loyalty to me. Now, you must do the same to Raphael. Do you accept him as your partner and teacher, to submit to him and keep him faithful?"

"I do." She briefly made eye contact with Raphael. He cut his palm the same way Hades did, and she gingerly drank from his cut, embarrassed at how she had thrown herself at Hades.

Hades raised his arms to the side and began to make an announcement.

"Legions of Hell! Demons, mortals, and vampires, you have a new ranking to obey. The Queen of Vampires was born on this day. Let it be known that Raphael and Calypso are the king and queen, the rulers of your bloodsucking race. Anyone who disobeys will receive a swift and painful death." The words echoed through the castle and in Calypso's mind. She realized that he spoke through the minds of every living vampire.

She stood up to rejoin Raphael, but Hades stopped her.

"You have one last task before I set you free. Your sacrifice to me."

Calypso squinted in confusion and gasped when she saw two demons dragging a blond man into the room.

"C-C-Callie?" Justin screamed. "What's happening?"

Tears instantly filled her eyes, and she shook her head.

No! NO! This can't be happening. This can't be real!

She turned to look at Raphael, who dropped his head, confirming that this was indeed Justin, whom she had just seen only an hour prior.

"You told me he would be fine, that I just had to release my attachment to him." She glared at Hades as tears filled her eyes and spilled onto her cheeks.

"I told you to release your attachment to him, and you did. So you should have no problem sacrificing him for me." The last two words were spoken with a deep growl.

She turned her head away from him and met Justin's wide eyes. He looked so frightened, and her body trembled for him.

"Release him." She scowled at the demons as she approached Justin. They stood back, and she hugged him quickly. "I'm so sorry," she cried. "I'll make it quick, I promise." She bit her tongue hard, then grabbed Justin's cheeks in her hands and kissed him. She shoved her tongue as deep into his mouth as she could, praying that he would swallow the scant blood on her tongue.

She pulled away and ripped into his neck with her fangs. She immediately popped his carotid vein, giving him a swift death, and his body fell heavy in her arms. Having no desire to drink the blood of her ex-fiancé, she let his body smack against the stone floor and bleed out.

"I was not expecting that." Hades laughed from his grand seat.

"I had to give him comfort before death. He didn't understand any of this."

"Very well," Hades responded. Calypso ran to Raphael, buried her head in his chest, and wiped away her remaining tears. "Now, join me as guests of honor for a royal banquet."

Calypso looked into Raphael's eyes and pleaded with him. He frowned at her sadness but was not interested in having Hades spend any more time with her.

"We are honored, really, but this has been such a long and exciting night. I'm afraid neither of us could entertain or bring anything useful to the table."

"I insist! Everything has been prepared for this special occasion." The words trailed off of Hades' lips like sweet wine.

"We'll make it to another one, I swear," Calypso answered. "I was not expecting my Halloween night to go this way. I need some time to adjust to my new power. I can't wrap my head around it."

Hades looked displeased as he began to walk toward the hallway. "Very well. I'll enjoy the virgin myself." He snapped his fingers at the demons as he walked past the cold, bleeding corpse.

"Wait!" Calypso called out. "May I please take his body with us back to Earth? To give him a proper burial."

Hades paused as he considered her words. He made no remark but nodded and flicked his hand, and the demons disappeared into the hallway with him. Once they were sure Hades was out of sight, Calypso walked over to Justin's body and threw him over her shoulder.

"That was a rather bold request," Raphael hissed at her.

She rolled her eyes and grabbed his hand, implying she wanted to leave immediately.

"You have the power of teleportation now. This is the last time I will do it for you."

In the blink of an eye, the three made their way through another dimension.

*

Calypso felt she could finally breathe again once they appeared in the penthouse. She gently laid Justin's corpse on top of their bed and stroked his ice-cold cheek. His eyelids were stuck half open, so she was able to see his yellowing sclera. She rushed out of the bedroom and into the living room, where Raphael grabbed a decanter from the fridge.

"If you can't celebrate in Hell, we should here at least," he murmured as he poured two glasses. Calypso heard the hint of hurt in his voice, and she looked at him sharply.

"We could have stayed if you wanted to party with Hades so bad. I figured you wanted to leave after that spectacle."

Raphael bit his tongue and shut his mind so she couldn't read it. Watching Calypso yearn and drink from Hades had agonized him more than he was willing to admit.

"Once you've been to one royal banquet, you've been to

them all." He swirled his glass lazily, then finished it in one gulp.

A sudden knock at the door made both of their bodies freeze in response to the unwelcome noise. Raphael was at the door immediately, ready to strike down the enemy on the other side. He peered out of the peephole, something that had to be installed due to the building code, and was shocked to see who stood on the other side.

He opened the door to Calypso's astonishment. A small-framed, beautiful woman stepped inside, her long black hair trailing behind her. She was petite and had glowing tan skin, while her brown eyes held flecks of gold that Calypso could make out from across the room. She was dressed simply, in only a long white dress and bare feet.

"I apologize for coming unannounced. But I heard the news, and I wanted to congratulate you both." Her voice was more profound than expected.

"And you are?" Calypso asked rudely.

"Pardon me; my name is Ahyoka; you can call me Ayai."

Calypso looked toward Raphael, who was close behind Ayai. She realized this was his former love, his failed queen. She shook her head and smirked, appalled she had the nerve to visit them.

"How have you been? What have you been up to?" Raphael asked awkwardly.

"Oh, nothing special. Hiding out in the desert, trying to avoid other vampires and demons. I did not mean to barge in. But I needed to tell you that I am happy you finally found her."

A sharp scream pierced the air and made all three of them wince. Raphael and Ayai were stuck in horror while Calypso ran to the bedroom. She recognized the bloodcurdling scream; her victim had been reborn.

"Oh, Justin." She sat on the edge of the bed and wiped strands of hair from his face. "It's okay now," she whispered.

He stared back at her, terrified, and gripped his neck where she had bitten him. It was healed now, but the memory still lingered with him.

"Get away from me," he shouted. "You're a vampire! You killed me!" he screamed, not aware of the power of his voice, and winced in pain.

Raphael and Ayai appeared in the room. Raphael's eyes were wide and red; he was ready to kill the freshly born vampire. Calypso stood up and blocked Justin's body.

"Don't make me hurt you." She scowled at him.

"What the fuck did you do?" he snarled back at her.

"What is happening?" Ayai asked, unaware of the betrayal that unfolded before her eyes.

"This," Raphael pointed at Justin, who curled in a ball, slowly rocking back and forth, "was Calypso's human sacrifice."

Ayai's face turned with concern, and she stepped out of the room, knowing this battle was not for her to fight.

"You never told me I would have to kill for Hades!" Calypso shouted at Raphael.

"You are ignorant if you thought you would never have to kill for him! This was your first test of loyalty, and you betrayed him. You betrayed me!"

"I didn't betray anyone! It's not fair that Justin had to die for some stupid rule! I did kill him. But I brought him back to life."

"Hades won't see it that way," Ayai interjected from the hallway.

"Nobody asked you. Aren't you supposed to be dead anyway?" Calypso sneered.

"Raphael begged for Hades' forgiveness, and the favor was granted to him. From the sounds of it, you attempted to trick him, pretending to do his bidding but getting what you wanted in the end." Ayai was calm and collected in her response, which infuriated Calypso.

"You—you all are vampires. You." Justin pointed to Raphael with a crazed look in his eyes. "Raphael." He laughed. "You took my fiancé away from me. She said she had met you before and fell in love, but I knew she was lying to me. You took her from me!"

Justin jumped off of the bed and flew at Raphael.

He pushed him aside, and Justin crashed onto the floor. The thick carpet was the only thing protecting him from breaking his spine. Calypso ran over and pulled his arms behind his back, keeping him from rushing Raphael again.

"Enough!" she shouted. "Raphael turned me, but I wanted to be a vampire. Now I am bound to him and Hades."

"Hades." Justin paused. "The devil. He took me from my home."

"I'm sorry, I didn't think he would do anything to you. He only told me I had to release my attachment to you."

"Which you clearly did not," Raphael boomed.

"You kissed him, filling his mouth with your blood, knowing he would die and knowing he would become a vampire. Did I not speak of the de rigueur, to not make another vampire without *his* permission?"

"It doesn't matter how or why it happened." Ayai walked back into the room. "You both need to decide quickly what is to be done. He will know soon enough that a soul is missing."

"I doubt it," Calypso responded. "He has enough souls in Hell to keep himself busy."

"He will go searching for him one day."

"Send me back to Hell." Justin pulled out of Calypso's grip. "I'm not living like this. I refuse to become a monster like all of you."

"Justin, no, how could you say that?" Calypso grabbed his hand, trying to reason with him.

"I'm already dead. Send me back."

"I don't know if that would be a good idea."

Raphael began to pace and rub his temples. "If we return him, Hades will know that you betrayed him immediately after swearing your loyalty to him. He will kill you. Perhaps even me for bringing you to Hell in the first place."

"What if Ayai takes him?" Calypso asked. "She's been hiding out for over a century."

"No, absolutely not. I am not getting in any more trouble with the devil."

"Ayai, this may be our only option," Raphael approached her and grabbed both of her hands, staring longingly into her eyes. "She has a point. You've been able to allude to his demons for this long. Another body can't be too much to hide."

"I have only just been able to be comfortable, not having to look over my shoulder every few seconds. I cannot trust or help him understand our way of life. That is too much to ask of me."

"Why don't you just kill me again, Callie?" Justin faced her. "You did it fine the first time. Just rip my neck apart and send my soul back to Hell. It will be like nothing ever happened."

"I'm not losing you again!" she cried.

"You lost me the night you left with him."

"It won't work that way, Justin," Raphael intervened. "Once you become a vampire, your soul leaves you. If you were to die right now, that would be the end of you. Hades would never find your soul as it ceased to exist once you were reborn."

"What if Calypso brings him back?" Ayai asked. "She begs for mercy, apologizing for the terrible mistake she made. Says she wasn't thinking clearly."

Raphael shook his head. "I'm afraid he has taken a liking to her. He would love a reason to keep her in a torture chamber to fall right into his hands."

Calypso stepped back in disgust. She couldn't believe the words that had come out of his mouth. The four vampires stood in silence for a while, all staring at each other while each and every scenario and outcome played in their minds. Finally, Justin stepped forward and broke the silence.

"If you won't let me die, I will go with her."

"No, Justin, wouldn't he be better protected with us?" Calypso grabbed his arm, trying to stop him.

"No, he needs to leave. Hades could very well send a

demon to follow or spy on us. He can't know we were in contact with Justin. Some souls are so scared and confused when they die that they travel through the endless depths of Hell and are never judged by Hades. We will have to pray he assumes this is what happened to Justin's soul."

"I am doing this for you," Ayai looked to Raphael. "Because I owe you for saving my life. But do not think this is for her. She is trouble." Ayai grabbed Justin's arm, and they disappeared.

Calypso whimpered as Justin disappeared. She feared she would never see him again, and she had just brought him back into this life. Raphael had already kicked back the carpet and stomped downstairs to the coffin as dawn approached quickly. Calypso followed him and began to strip off her now-soiled clothes. Raphael stood in a corner, his hands folded behind his back.

"What you did today was a total lack of respect for me and Hades. You took an oath to him, to both of us, and you don't understand its severity. Just because you are now queen, that does not entitle you to choose what rules to follow and break. You are bound to even stricter scrutiny than the average vampire because you are supposed to be above them. I hope I am not dethroned and punished due to your ignorance and lack of submission."

The painful words stung like a thousand lashes, and she turned away to hide her tears.

"I never want to see you disobey him again or even have the thought pass through your mind. My loyalty lies with him, not with you, Calypso. If you ever step out of line again, I will gladly drag you by your hair to Hades' feet myself."

Calypso dropped to her knees and wiped her tears on his feet, trying to plead for forgiveness, but Raphael kicked her off. She let out a loud cry, which he immediately silenced.

"No, you don't get to cry. If Hades asks you to kill a human, you shall ask him how he would like you to do it. If he asks you to murder an entire village, you shall bring death upon them with the swiftness of a breath. If he asked you to end my life, you shall watch the light leave my eyes as you rip my heart out."

Calypso whimpered and crawled backwards until she reached a wall. Raphael stomped toward her, nostrils flaring and a vein throbbing in his forehead.

"Do you know what happened to me after I drank the blood of Hades and swore my loyalty to him?" Raphael continued. "He took me back to my home village, to my home, to be exact. He stood back while he commanded me to prove my loyalty to him. First, I asked him to set the barn on fire—the barn where my father had mercilessly beaten me. Hades did as I asked, and I went into my house while I smelled the livestock and hay burning. My mother was the only one in the house; she was in her bed, very ill. She reached out to my face and told me she always knew I would return, her angel. I gently ripped into her neck, but I killed her."

Calypso began to tremble in fear as Raphael sent the images into her mind. She was paralyzed as she watched Raphael's beautiful mother reach her hand up to him, touching his cold cheek one last time before he ripped into her neck and drank her blood. Once her body was drained, Raphael carried her in his arms out of the house, which had begun to catch fire. Although he had just murdered her, he couldn't bear the thought of her perfect face being melted away by the flames. By now, his oldest brother and father had come running to the house; they had both been out drinking. His father held a pitchfork and attempted to stab Raphael, who stepped aside effortlessly.

"I always knew you were a devil!" His father shouted. Raphael gently lowered his mother to the ground and pushed his father aside. He leaped onto the back of his brother, tackling him to the ground and snapping his neck in the process. Raphael's father backed up in horror as he watched his eldest son guzzle the blood that spewed out of his middle son's neck. Raphael turned back to his father, a crazed animal with blood dripping down his face onto his shirt. His father was paralyzed in terror as Raphael approached him.

He fantasized about making this kill as slow and agonizing as possible. Raphael grabbed the pitchfork out of his hand and stabbed the sharp metal into his foot. His father howled in pain, but this was only the beginning. He kicked both of his kneecaps, sending them backward and instantly shattering the bones in his legs. His father fell forward; the only thing holding him up was the pitchfork placed in front of him. Raphael grabbed both of his arms and yanked them outward, pulling the shoulder bones out of his body, then he stabbed his hand through his chest cavity, just barely caressing his heart.

"Please, son." His father could barely get out the words due to his immense trauma and blood loss. His eyes closed as he faded in and out of consciousness. Raphael forced them open.

"No, I am going to be the last thing you see before I send you to Hell," he articulated each word slowly, squeezing the heart harder with each syllable until it finally exploded. Raphael pulled out the now shriveled organ and slammed it onto the ground.

Hades appeared from behind a nearby thicket, clapping and marveling at the destruction his king had brought about to his own flesh and blood. A sudden rustle made both of them turn to see a young boy who ran to his father's corpse before dropping to the ground in horror. Raphael approached him slowly. He had never seen his younger brother as a person; he was still swaddled to his mother's breast when he left home. Raphael called him into his arms, and the young boy walked into them in a trance.

"That's enough," Hades called out. "You have more than proven your loyalty to me. Spare the child."

Raphael hugged his brother, quickly erasing the memory of the horror he had just witnessed. He put him in another trance and set him on his way down the rocky dirt road. He was sure he would be found soon enough as neighbors would flock to the burning house eventually.

Calypso came back into her body and was soaked with tears. She was appalled at the terror she had just witnessed, the terror her partner had committed to his family. Raphael dragged her into the coffin, throwing her in roughly.

"That is what undying loyalty looks like, Calypso. No questions asked." Raphael joined her in the coffin, turning away from her, and immediately put himself in a deep sleep.

Calypso curled up into a ball, still crying and shaking. Though she had committed brutal murders herself, she could have never imagined Raphael's monstrous actions. She now wondered who he was and what this meant for her, now being sworn to his loyalty in blood.

Chapter 13

Cold wind stung Calypso's face, and she tried not to breathe as the ice-cold air burned her lungs like fire. The snow and frigid temperatures otherwise did not bother her. She wore only a thin turtleneck and jeans; she would rather feel the frostbite form on her fingers than be weighed down by unnecessarily heavy clothes.

Raphael was the complete opposite; harsh winters reminded him too clearly of his childhood, so he took any precaution to protect his body from cold temperatures. He wore a thick black wolf-lined fur coat. His long blond hair was covered in icicles, resembling an ancient Viking.

Calypso wiped a strand of blood from her nose; her enemy had head-butted her before she broke its cervical vertebrae. The pain from her broken nose was only momentary as her bones began to rejoin almost immediately. She noticed her body healed even quicker now that Hades' blood flowed through her veins. A severed head dangled in her hands, and she tossed it aside.

Snow-covered mountains in front of them would have been awe-inducing to any human, but Calypso was too focused on the mission in front of them. Blood was spilled everywhere, staining the innocent snow. Steam rose from the blood as it melted the snow below it, the bodily fluids still hot from the recent kills.

At least a dozen bodies lay decapitated with their limbs broken and strewn throughout the top of the mountain peak. If any human ventured to this mountaintop, the bodies would be unrecognizable once frost settled into the rotting skin. Calypso assumed wolves would find their next meal here; she had smelled their pulsing blood once they had teleported to the middle of the Switzerland Alps.

Only days after being metaphorically crowned Queen, Calypso and Raphael had both received a message from Hades. They were instructed to go to Europe to eliminate a steadily growing colony of vampires who disobeyed Hades. Raphael had made Calypso teleport herself, which took much of her strength.

She was exhausted once she appeared in the mountains, far behind Raphael. He continued to give her the cold shoulder after she betrayed her loyalty to Hades. If she knew it would have given her so much hurt to save Justin, she may have had second thoughts in the moment. Her problem was she never thought of the future but only how she felt in the present.

"Where are you, Calypso?" Raphael was twenty feet in front of her, kicking aside a thick-bodied corpse. Calypso was surprised at how large these vampires were. She was not expecting them to be a struggle to kill. "They are gluttonous and filled with the blood of all the humans of the local mountain villages," he explained to her.

"I'm here with you," she panted. She wanted to feed, although she did not need to. But she knew she was forbidden to drink the blood of an enemy of Hades.

"Are you sure? You haven't been killing up to your normal speed and standards." A fierce wind ripped through the mountains, blowing his hair and fur coat behind him.

"I feel guilty for killing vampires," she admitted. "They are one of us, and we are in charge of them. It's a betrayal to our species."

Raphael laughed, and his booming voice caused the snow and rocks to shift underneath their feet. "We are not the same species; we are much more powerful. As the king and queen, our loyalty resides only in Hades and the vampires who are loyal to him. Anyone else is scum beneath our feet and shall be treated as such."

A hideous scream erupted from behind a nearby pine tree, and a large woman bolted toward them. Calypso pounced on top of her, slamming her back into the snow. She gnashed her fangs at the queen, who stuck her hand into her chest and ripped the heart out in a swift blow. The rage disappeared from her eyes as the life left her body while Calypso squeezed the heart, letting the pumping blood fall onto the corpse.

Before Raphael could comment on her kill, a small child peeked out from behind the tree. "Mama!" she cried out.

Calypso reached the child before Raphael and scooped her into her arms. She held the child to her chest and could feel its small body shaking with fear.

"Calypso," Raphael warned. "You know what we have to do."

"No, please!" she cried, tears freezing as they rolled down her face. "She's only a child! She didn't decide to be brought into a world of darkness."

"No, she didn't, but she will suffer the consequences of those who decided to go against their master and create her."

"Raphael," Calypso begged and stepped away from him. "Please, I'll go to Hades myself and beg him! We will raise her as our own, teaching her the rules and to worship him."

"Will you tell him about your betrayal before or after?" Raphael struck Calypso across the face with the back of his hand, and she dropped the child out of shock. She placed her hand over her swollen cheek and let out a loud cry as Raphael picked up the child by her hair and sliced her neck with a long knife.

"Watch," he demanded while the child gurgled out blood as Raphael stabbed the knife deeper into her neck. "This is what happens to those who disobey him."

Calypso cried violently as she watched the fear in the child's eyes. She didn't deserve to die such a painful death, but Raphael was ruthless to Hades' enemies. He ran the blade along her neck, then yanked her head backward, severing the neck from the rest of the body. He dropped the body and cleaned the blade in the snow, leaving the angelic blood spilled next to the body.

"Get up," Raphael called to her as he walked away. "We have more ground to cover before we can go home."

*

Thousands of miles away, Justin and Ayai lay under a star-filled sky. After the chaotic events, Ayai teleported them to the

Mojave desert. She had spent her years alone, wandering and seeking shelter throughout the deserts of the southwest.

The first night was rough for both of them. Ayai was paranoid about being discovered by a demon of Hades. Although she had eluded them for almost a hundred years, she now harbored a fugitive. Justin was uncooperative and refused to drink any blood, though he already desiccated from the rapid shifts through the universe. Ayai forced him to drink her blood, only giving in as she held him down and pinned her forearm to his mouth.

They were able to find shelter in an empty foxhole, a tight squeeze for two. The following night, Justin woke up in a panic, surrounded by dirt and sand, and caused the hole to collapse on top of them. Ayai was able to quickly dig her way out of the ground while Justin struggled, making too much noise and not having total control over his limbs.

Once they were out of the ground, they discovered a group of humans had set up camp not too far away. Justin was almost frozen by the nearby flicker of a campfire, so Ayai quickly grabbed his arm and started running away. Justin had no choice but to keep pace with her and found his flow in the rapid movements.

By now, Ayai was exhausted from teleporting twice in one night, not to mention she had not drunk blood in days. This was normal for her as she stretched out her feedings as long as possible, but the recent use of power had depleted her.

She suddenly stopped once they reached southern Nevada. Although dark, she recognized the landscape as she had passed through this area hundreds of times in her lifetime.

"I need to feed." She gripped her knees and hurled over, spitting up a small amount of blood.

"Uh, what do you usually do?" he asked, unsure of how to comfort her.

"I usually keep blood in my home in the Black Rock. I was too afraid to take us there last night. I will have to find a human to feed on; I am too weak to make it back."

"Do you mean the Black Rock desert?" Justin exclaimed. "That must be hundreds of miles from here!"

"Don't worry, we'll make it there before dawn. We have already covered as much, and you barely noticed." Ayai took off walking at a much slower pace. She could hear the nearby sounds of a highway, so she followed the noise. Justin followed far behind her, ready to give her space in case she decided to feed off of him.

Ayai dropped to her heels and slid down the large sandy hill, stopping a few feet from the edge of the highway. She closed her eyes and exhaled slowly, willing anyone to stop and help her.

A few cars sped by before one finally pulled onto the shoulder a few yards ahead of her. She limped toward the car, and Justin stayed hidden in the shadows at the base of the hill.

"Can you please step out and help me?" Ayai called to the driver as they rolled their window down. "I got lost hiking and injured my leg."

A middle-aged man stepped out of the vehicle, and Ayai collapsed into his unsuspecting arms. She bit into his neck gently and gratefully swallowed his thick blood. After feeding for a few seconds, she covered the wound with her hand and turned her head back to Justin.

"Come here! We don't have much time!"

"I'm not feeding from another person! I told you, I don't want to be a vampire!"

"Your life is my responsibility. If you don't feed, I will drag his lifeless body into the road; then his death will be in your hands."

Justin begrudgingly walked over to Ayai and closed his mouth around the bleeding wound. He grimaced and closed his eyes tightly, pulling the blood into his mouth.

The hot and salty blood flowed down his throat, bringing life back into his body. He became lost in the ecstasy of drinking, only brought back by Ayai physically pulling him off of the man.

"That's enough. You don't want to kill him." Ayai pushed Justin a safe distance away. "Get back into the car and continue your drive. Hold pressure on your neck until it is done bleeding." The man followed her instructions and drove away without hesitation.

Justin was shocked. The man did not question what had happened or attempt to stop the feeding. He followed Ayai back up the hill, who now looked much better.

"I want you to hop onto my back," she instructed him. "Hurry up, we don't have all night. This will be faster than running."

Justin laughed and shook his head, then hopped onto her back like he was a young child again. He expected her to take off at a full run but was taken by surprise when she rose into the air and took off, flying like a jet. The stream of wind pushed him back, and he had to grip onto her shoulders to stay on.

"Vampires can fly?" he yelled into her ear. Ayai was so concentrated on her mission that she barely heard the words he spoke to her. She had to get them both to safety and was worried flying would attract notice from any vampires or demons in the area. She would have teleported them to her safe house if she had enough strength, but she was still too weak even after feeding. For her entirety of being a vampire, she had only teleported on three separate occasions, with two of them being her most recent journeys.

After almost an hour of flying, Ayai lowered from the clouds, and Justin could make out the faint outlines of nearby mountains. Soon enough, they were hurdling into them, so he thought, but Ayai skidded to a stop in the middle of a tall peak. There was a flat ledge with enough room for them to stand comfortably on.

"That was incredible!" Justin exclaimed. Ayai laughed and sat on the ground, picking rocks out of her heels that had been embedded in the harsh landing.

"Yes, vampires can technically fly. I was given that gift from Hades; otherwise, I wouldn't have enough strength to fly for another hundred years or so."

Justin cleared his throat and sat down next to her, his legs dangling off the edge of the mountain.

"So this is your home?" Justin motioned to the small cave, opening up against the wall of rocks.

"Yes, this has been my shelter for a while. I don't refer to any place as my home. I am a wanderer. I stay in one location as long as it provides shelter. I move on when I feel my time is done. But this is a very safe, remote location, inaccessible by humans, so I have stayed here."

Justin stayed quiet for a while, picking at his fingernails as he felt reality crashing into him. This would be his life now. Living in a cave with a stranger, drinking blood to survive while resisting the urge to kill whoever he fed on. Longing for someone he could never have, longing for a life he could never return to.

Ayai sensed his feelings and placed her hand on top of his. "I cannot imagine how difficult this must be for you, especially since you did not choose this." Justin looked away, not wanting to acknowledge the truth. "But you need to decide what you are going to do about your human life."

"What am I going to do about it?" Justin scoffed. "I'm not doing anything! I'm dead."

"There have to be people that care about you. Friends and family, I know it is hard, but you should give them some sort of explanation. I did not when I was turned, and it is one of my biggest regrets. My father did not even recognize me when I visited him years later. He said that I was a spirit tricking him because his daughter had died! It could have been different if I had just left a note or seen him one last time."

Justin pondered her words while the stars twinkled in the otherwise empty night.

"What am I supposed to do? Show up back home looking like death and tell them I'll never see them again?"

"You can come up with something. I know you are smart and creative."

They sat silently for a while longer before Justin finally

reached into his pocket and pulled out his cell phone. He wasn't expecting it to be there, let alone working, after shifting through dimensions and flying through the night. His phone battery was low, and he had almost a hundred notifications of messages and missed calls.

"Come on, it's only been two nights," he muttered as he selected Tyler's number. The phone dialed through, and his heart began to pound.

"Justin?" Tyler sounded groggy on the other end.

"Hey, bro."

"Hey, bro? You disappear on us, and that's all you have to say?" Tyler laughed. "Where are you? It's like six am."

"I'm sorry. I didn't mean to worry you. After talking to Calypso, uh, Callie, I had to get out of there."

"Okay, so where are you?"

"Um, I'm actually on a layover flight to Budapest."

Tyler erupted with laughter on the other line. Ayai couldn't help but crack a small smile as well. She swung her legs off the side of the ledge as Justin talked.

"I decided I'm going to be a monk. I was so caught up in her and our relationship, and it was too toxic. I didn't see that until I talked to her again. I saw how good she was doing and how I was still stuck in Florida doing nothing with my life. So I said fuck it, I'm going to the airport and getting out of here."

"You didn't even take anything with you! All of your stuff is still here at the crib."

"I don't need material objects to be happy. Just put it in storage or give it to my mom."

"This doesn't sound like you. Oh, your mom! You better call her and tell her your crazy plan. She's about to set up a missing person alert."

"Can't you just call her? I'm about to board my next flight."

"Bro, she's your mom! She deserves to hear this craziness from you."

"You're right," Justin sighed. "I'm sorry I left like this. I wasn't planning it, but it felt like something I had to do. Now, there is no going back."

"I get it, but I wish you would have said bye. When are you gonna come back and visit?"

"I don't know..." Justin trailed off. "I don't even know how this monk stuff works. I probably won't have communication with the outside world. But I'll reach out when I can. See you, brother."

Justin ended the call and began to dial his mom without taking a breath in between. Tears started to well in his eyes before she answered the call.

"Justin? Honey, where are you?" His mother sounded frantic.

"I'm okay, Mom. I'm sorry I didn't have any service the past few days."

"What happened? Are you alright? Tyler called me and said you never came home! That Callie called you, and you just walked out of the house!"

"I know, it sounds bad. I just decided that I had to move on with my life."

"Well, you know you can move on and still call your mother and tell her you are alright! Your dad and I have been worried sick! I better call the police back and tell them not to put out the report. I still had to wait a few more hours before they would call it anyway."

"Mom, I don't know if I will see you again. I'm sorry, I decided to give up everything and go live as a monk."

Anne stayed quiet on the other end of the line, processing what her son had just told her. He had never been one to consider meditation or Buddhist practices.

"I went to the airport after talking to Callie. I used the rest of my money to get a flight to Budapest, and I'm going to join a monk ministry over there. I need a change in my life, something bigger than myself, and this is it. I'm sorry I didn't come to see you guys beforehand."

Justin could hear his mother begin to cry. He felt so far

away from her, although he was only a few hundred miles away. But over the past few nights, he had become a new species, a creature of the night. He hated lying and hurting her but couldn't imagine looking into her eyes ever again. She would know he wasn't the same person anymore.

"I, I just don't understand any of this, honey."

"I know you don't, but this is what I'm being called to do with my life. Look, I'll talk to you soon, okay? I know it's late at home."

"Justin, just please be safe. Did you even look into vaccinations or anything you need to do on that side of the world? Well, I guess you had to; you didn't go waltzing into the airport with no passport," Anne laughed to hide the pain she felt from her heart breaking.

"I'll be fine, Mom. I love you, and Dad too."

Justin ended the call and debated throwing his cell phone off the mountain edge, then decided against it. He wiped the tears from his eyes and stood up as Ayai tried to comfort him.

"I know that was hard, Justin, but you made the right choice. Great story about the monk, too."

Justin shrugged his shoulders. It was the only reasonable excuse for disappearing from their lives. Maybe he would eventually die on a mountain retreat or whatever monks do.

"Why don't you tell me about your life? I need to get my mind off of this."

Ayai motioned for him to come inside the cave. The area was surprisingly large; the ceiling was tall enough for them to stand under, and it went deeper than Justin could focus on. Ayai picked up a shard of rock from the ground and quickly scraped it alongside the mountain wall. A spark jumped from the friction and lit a vintage lantern that hung against the wall. As the light from the fire began to brighten the cave's interior, Justin noticed the scratches next to the lantern; this wasn't her first time.

"Wow, that looks ancient." Justin laughed.

"It is a fond memory from my childhood." Ayai forced a

smile. They sat down on colorful woven rugs, and Justin leaned back against the cold stone.

"How many hundreds of years ago was that?"

"I am not that old." Ayai threw a piece of rock at him, purposefully missing. "I was only born about a hundred years ago, in the year nineteen hundred."

"Only a hundred years ago." Justin rolled his eyes. He couldn't imagine living that long.

"That is nothing! Raphael is seven hundred years old. Hades and the other Gods are timeless; they have existed from the first breath." Ayai shook her head as she saw and felt the noticeable changes from Justin. "I'm sorry. I know you don't want to think about either of them. But they are both the reality of why we are here."

"Why are we here?" Justin shouted angrily. "Because Callie couldn't bear to see me die, yet she murdered me!"

"It is more than that. She has such a deep love for you. I could sense it. I know you do not understand yet, but she risked her life to keep you alive. Hades created the vampire race, so they are all loyal to him. Or they should be, but we are all still humans or have human tendencies. Everyone has a mind of their own, so not every vampire is loyal to Hades. That is why he chose Raphael and gave him his blood so that he could become more powerful than the others and control them. But it was too much for just one person, so he needed to find another. Hades made him the King of Vampires, so he needed to find a queen.

"That is how we met," she continued. "I was living in Georgia at the time with my father. We, that is, my ancestors, used to be members of the Cherokee tribe. My true name is Ahyoka, but my father shortened it to Ayai since it sounds more white. I was my mother's true happiness; that is the meaning of my name. She was very ill during my young childhood and passed from influenza. Our tribe was already transforming, but after her death, my father fully jumped into white America. We all had to change our names, our dress, how we spoke, and how we lived.

He became a pastor and held a church service every Sunday. I would help him, of course; I had no choice.

"One night, I stood in the back as my father preached to us. Raphael walked in, which was not unusual. By now, plenty of white people had come into our ministry. But he was different; he watched me the whole time, and I felt flattered as no other man had ever looked at me with such admiration. He asked me to join him afterward and even asked for my father's permission. I thought he was such a gentleman. We walked in the night, hand in hand, talking until the sun began to rise. He was so eloquent and romantic that we connected immediately over the death of our mothers. He kissed me before he left, stating that he had work and would return the following night.

"I was head over heels for him. He came to me most nights, which I did not question. My father, on the other hand, sensed something evil in him." Ayai's voice hardened. "He forbade me from seeing him. I disobeyed, of course, as any other teenager would. I would sneak out until my father put locks on the outside of my door. Raphael somehow still found his way into my room to just lay next to me as I fell asleep, begging him to take me away. One night, my father said I would be moving; he was sending me away to family out west. I cried and screamed, yelling terrible things at him. I remember running out of the church and into Raphael's arms. He finally said he would take me away, that we could be together.

"I did not even return to my house to apologize to my father or grab any of my belongings. We ran off in the night together. That was when I found out he was a vampire. He confessed to me under the moonlight, but I was so in love with him that I didn't care! I begged him to turn me so we could be together for all of time. I couldn't bear the idea of being without him during the daytime. He did not hesitate; he fed me his blood and snapped my neck."

"Oh my God," Justin whispered. "How old are you, Ayai?"

"Nineteen," she dragged her fingers in the sand.

"I hate him," Justin seethed. "He is a monster, praying on innocent young women."

"Justin, he did not pray on me. I saw him for who he was and asked to be transformed like he was. He taught me everything: how to kill, how not to kill, how to run, and how to read minds. It was the best few weeks of my life. Up until this point, I did not know he had an ulterior motive. I thought it was just the two of us until the end of time. But no matter how hard Raphael loves, and he did love me, he has another love first. The dark God." Ayai sighed, and her chest began to burn.

"He took me in his arms one night and told me he loved me more than any words could describe. He asked if I trusted him with my life, and I said yes. He told me that I was to become a queen, his queen and that I would rule over the entire race of vampires. Before I could question him, he teleported me to Hell, to Hades' castle, where you were taken.

"I instantly knew something was wrong. I couldn't breathe, and I was frozen in fear. When I saw him...I dropped to my knees. He was the most frightening thing I had ever laid eyes on, and I watched my mother die!" Ayai tried not to cry but could no longer hold back her emotions.

"We were told about this spirit as a child, of evilness, and I learned about the devil as a teenager. Nothing I was told or read could have prepared me for this moment. It was as if my spirit had abandoned my body when I was in Hell. I tried to close my eyes as Hades approached me, but he forced them open. I looked to Raphael for help. I begged him in my mind, but he was as still as a statue. It was at that moment I realized who he loved the most. I did not realize that all of his powers and greatness came from Hades. Raphael is his most loyal soldier, demon, or vampire, whatever you wish to refer to him as. He brought me to be next, his great Vampire Queen.

"Hades fed me his blood, and I instantly began to vomit and convulse. I knew I was dying, and I begged for it to come quickly. I don't remember much; I was in and out of consciousness as the pain was so great. The next thing I knew, a powerful spirit was taking my pain and sickness away. Hades informed me that I was saved from death but would never be welcome in his kingdom. That I had to hide from him and his demons, or I would be cursed to torment in Hell.

"After that, I teleported back to my hometown, which I did not know I had the power to do. I ran for nights on end, burying myself in the ground, and as soon as the sun set, I was running away. This went on for months. I could never stay in one place; I barely fed as I was too afraid that every person I saw would be a demon of Hades. After years of doing this, I was exhausted and finally gave up. If he wants me dead, he will find me, I thought. I have been fine since, of course, but sometimes the fear still crawls in at dawn."

Justin was speechless at Ayai's life story. He still hated Raphael, but the new fire ignited was for Hades. He was the creator of all the chaos.

"So Callie is his queen then?" Justin spoke after a long period of silence. He picked at the fraying edges of the rug they sat on.

"It seems as if. Her body accepted Hades' blood, unlike mine. But she took an oath of loyalty to him and has already broken it with the death and creation of you."

"What do you think will happen?"

"I dunno," Ayai's improper grammar took Justin by surprise. "I suppose anything could happen now, but we shall take it one night at a time. If he wants us dead, we will die. Now we can only hope that Calypso stays loyal and keeps him happy so we go unnoticed."

"Do you think...Could he..." Justin trailed off, not wanting to speak the words out loud. He swallowed deeply and noticed the faint change in light; the lantern was dimming as dawn began to break in the early morning sky.

"Do you think Raphael will stay loyal to her? Could he betray her and tell Hades what happened?"

"I could see the fear in his eyes last night. He wants to tell Hades because of his loyalty. But he would be implicated in the creation of her as Queen. I don't think he would betray her because Hades would look down on him. Come, let us move further back."

Ayai and Justin moved toward the back of the cave, crawling on their hands and knees as the space became more compact. Once they had reached the furthest end of the cave, they were surrounded by total darkness. Justin could barely make out her figure anymore.

"This cave is perfect because the sun never reaches back here. I prefer it to burying myself in the ground."

"Aren't vampires supposed to sleep in coffins?" Justin asked. His mind began to trail off as he felt the weariness take over his body.

"Not us; we aren't the chosen ones." Ayai stroked his cheek before they both fell into a deep slumber as the sun climbed the horizon.

Chapter 14

After a month of climbing through the Alps and destroying rouge vampire colonies, Calypso was exhausted. She hated burying herself in the freezing snow each dawn but had no other choice. Raphael was prepared for their freezing adventure, having already lived through seasons of rough winters. Calypso let the frost turn her fingers red and brittle. She was not concerned as any time she received fresh blood, her impurities disappeared.

Raphael was still harsh, making her prove herself endlessly by taking on the worst kills. She brutally murdered each vampire as he instructed her but was still not forgiven for creating Justin or wanting to save the innocent child vampire.

Calypso now operated in a haze, barely speaking and feeling as if she were a robot, waking and killing on repeat. Once they finally reached the end of the mountain range, she breathed a sigh of relief and stripped her tattered and blood-stained clothes. They had come to the edge of a lake, and she jumped in, feeling the freezing glacier water cleanse her body.

She surfaced and motioned for Raphael to join her.

"Join me; the water is exquisite!"

"We don't have time for your nonsense; we still have more ground to cover." Raphael barely glanced at her naked body as he responded.

"No!" Calypso walked out of the lake and stood in front of him, dripping wet. "What are you trying to prove? Enough is enough! We have completed our mission. There will always be rogue vampires. Does he really expect us to travel the whole world, killing vampires for the rest of our lives?"

"How dare you question me," Raphael growled and approached her with force. Before he could grab her, they were both thrown to the ground by a sudden wind. Sand and rocks blew up into a spiral, and Calypso groaned as she knew a demon was forming between them.

"You have both been excellent soldiers," Hades' deep voice

boomed from the shadowy figure. "You must return to Hell to receive your next mission."

"Already?" Calypso moaned as she turned to dress herself. Once fully clothed, she noticed more demons had appeared and surrounded them. Before she could plan to escape, they rushed into Raphael and her, causing immense pain.

Calypso could only imagine they were forcibly teleported to Hell, as her body and soul felt they were being stretched across time and space. She tried to scream, but no voice came out.

They landed harshly on the cold, gold-lined stones of Hades' grand room. She looked up, and her body began to shake in terror. Hades sat with one leg crossed on his enormous throne. Ayai and Justin were chained next to him.

Ayai was suspended from the ceiling by her braids while a heavy ball and chain wrapped around her neck, pulling her toward the ground. Justin was shackled to the ground with barely enough room to move his head. Barbed wire wrapped around his entire body and cut deep with every movement and breath he made.

"My Lord, please forgive me," Raphael bowed down to him.

"How dare you make a mockery of me!" Hades screamed. Calypso lay frozen in fear on her knees.

"Raphael, my most loyal servant, now lays with the Queen of Disobedience."

"I'm sorry," Calypso cried.

"You are sorry?" Hades climbed off his throne and towered over her. She could smell the anger pounding off of his body. Heat radiated off of his body, and she broke into a sweat.

"I, I didn't know there had to be a human sacrifice," she stuttered. "If I had known, I would have never turned him into a vampire!"

"You both are a disgrace," Hades turned on his heels and began to pace in front of Ayai and Justin. "I was looking forward to devouring Justin's soul. To learn more about you, Calypso. But

I could never find him. After a few days, I became suspicious; no soul could avoid me for that long. Especially a mere weak human." Hades paused to kick Justin's chest, shattering his ribs and causing him to howl in pain.

"So I sent you both away. I knew you would be distracted by your mission; those glutinous bastards were never my concern. I sent my demons searching every inch of Hell to no avail. It was then I knew what you did; my slave disobeyed my commandments."

"I am not your slave," Calypso growled under her breath. Hades turned swiftly and kicked her across the room. She slammed up against a far wall and dropped to the ground.

"Your attitude is not well received."

"I should have told you," Raphael spoke, still laying prostrate on the ground. "I could not admit failure to you."

"Get up," Hades commanded both of them. Raphael rose instantly, avoiding his eyes while Calypso barely managed to stand.

"This must be a trying time for you," Hades grabbed Raphael's chin and forced his eyes upward. "You swore your undying loyalty to me, then she comes into the picture. You don't know who to choose, who to protect, who to serve."

"No, my undying loyalty is for you," Raphael whimpered. "Please, forgive me. I was only trying to protect her from her mistake. She understands the gravity of it."

"Does she? She seems not to understand her place. Let her act on her own accord."

Hades released Raphael and motioned for Calypso to walk forward. She refused, but demons grabbed her wrists and dragged her to Hades. She was forcibly pushed onto her knees, and her head pulled back to look at him. He towered over her, heaving with anger. His black eyes swallowed her, and she opened her mouth to beg for forgiveness, but nothing came out.

"I knew you would be a problem, but I gave Raphael a chance to submit you. I see now this was a mistake."

"Please, I'll do anything!"

"I have already made up my mind. Your immediate betrayal shows that your loyalty only lies with yourself. Now, you pull my greatest soldier into your lies. But I am a God of fairness, and I will give you both a second chance."

Raphael dropped and began to kiss Hades' feet. He ignored him and stared at Calypso.

"You kill the original vampires tonight. I want them both dead, the ones who first betrayed me. If you fail, your friends will become my victims. If you succeed, I may have mercy on all of your souls."

"Where are they?" Calypso asked.

"Last I heard, they were making a nuisance back home in Greece. I would hurry; you don't have much time."

Raphael grabbed Calypso and pulled her away. She stared at Justin and Ayai, who both had hopelessness and fear in their eyes.

"I'm so sorry," she mouthed to them before Raphael teleported them both away.

The color of the sky told her it was a few hours past midnight. She had become an expert at telling the time based on the sky's color and the appearance of the stars. Tonight, there was no moon to wonder in, only a bleak darkness that felt heavy and suffocating.

Raphael had taken them to a random countryside so they could think. He slammed his fists on the ground and let out a long cry.

"Raphael, please forgive me," Calypso tried to touch him, but he avoided her. "I didn't think they would be discovered."

"It was only a matter of time," he muttered. "He's the God of the underworld; why did I ever think we could outsmart him?"

"I really am sorry. I know how much your relationship with him means to you. I never meant to cause any harm."

"You should feel the same way." He sneered. "You should feel sorrow for hurting him, not me! You are supposed to be equally devoted to him."

"My devotion lies with you," she whispered. "I am doing all of this for you! I gave myself to Hades so we could be everlasting together."

Raphael shook his head in disbelief.

"I'm going to make it up to the both of you. We're going to find them. Come, I smell humans this way." Calypso took off running, and Raphael followed behind.

After a few minutes, they stopped outside of a busy city. The street ahead appeared to be a main section of town, with colorful architecture resembling the area's classic heritage mixed with more modern buildings. Most storefronts were closed for the night, but many vendors had tables set up in the street selling their handmade jewelry and trinkets. They began to walk down the street, investigating the sellers and their tables.

"I don't know what you think you are looking for," Raphael grumbled behind her. She ignored him and instead focused on the sounds of the bustle around them. She almost missed moments like these, immersing herself in the human world and feeling a sense of belonging.

A nearby woman at a table grabbed her attention. She was loudly asking anyone to come and have their cards read. Calypso decided to take the bit. She walked over and could immediately tell the woman was a con artist. If her fake crystal ball and head scarf weren't enough of a giveaway, Calypso could sense the desperation reeking off her body.

"Beautiful woman, what are you seeking tonight?" The woman asked as she shuffled her tarot deck.

"I'm looking for someone," Calypso answered her. "A beautiful woman, similar to myself. She is ancient, ageless almost. And feeds off of the blood of humans."

The woman began to cackle, and Raphael shifted uncomfortably. He hated revealing any part of themselves to humans, even if they didn't believe. She started rambling about the death card she conveniently pulled while Calypso's attention was pulled toward an elderly lady who peeked out of a nearby alleyway. They met each other's eyes, and Raphael nodded in confirmation.

The old woman stepped into the shadows and was met by two vampiric figures. She was tattered, and her wrinkles were filled with dirt. One eye was slightly larger than the other, although it could have been from disease.

"You two ought to be careful, lots of thieves around Thessaloniki at night," the woman finally said.

"You should be careful, too," Raphael grabbed her hand and brought it to his lips for a kiss. "The vampires come out at night."

The woman blushed and shook her head. "Those dun exist no more. I haven't heard tales of the Vorvolakos since Nana was tellin' me stories. Carolin won't tell you that, though; she'll tell ya all the lies you wanna hear for a shiny penny."

"Is Carolin the tarot reader?" Calypso asked. She glanced around to ensure they were alone. Not a soul passed by the dirty, empty alleyway.

"I'm Carolin! They used to respect me 'round here, you know? I had my own shop and everything, Nana's baked goods, after my Nana. But strange stuff started happenin'." The old woman began to accelerate her hand gestures and speed.

"People started missing then showin up real mean. Like Sophia! Real nice gal. Sweet as could be. I'd walk past her window on my way to the shop. She'd smile and talk with me. One day, she was gone. I didn't see her for a long time, started asking about her, and nobody knew nothin. One night at the market, I bump into her, and she doesn't know me!"

"Did this happen to anyone else?" Raphael asked.

"Sure, tons of folks started going missin'. Nobody cares, though, not about us ol folk. The new generation wants us to die off, so they can buy our shops and turn them into new hoity fashion wear! That's when it all went down; I lost my shop cause everyone stopped comin. The streets empty during the day and busy at night! I tried to tell everyone, something not right goin on. Now they call me crazy Carolin. There goes crazy Carolin, telling her story to strangers again!"

"The Vorvolakos, they are here, standing right in front of you." Calypso grinned as her words changed Carolin's countenance.

"We don't want to hurt you; we just want to know where the one causing all this trouble is," Raphael reassured her. "White skin, blonde hair. Have you seen her around?"

Carolin started to stutter, but Raphael looked into her eyes, which gave her confidence.

"I ain't seen nothin' of your type. But if I were to point yous in a direction, it would be to the cave at the base of the mount. I heard some tourists talkin a few days ago about a disappearance over there. No body, only a hat and a pile of blood, was found."

"What mountain do you mean?"

"Mount Olympus!" Carolin exclaimed. Raphael flicked a shiny coin in the air, and Carolin caught it, turned, and started hopping and singing down the alleyway.

"The crazy ones are always attracted to you." Calypso snickered.

"We've got to head south. The clouds are rolling in, but the sun will be here soon enough." Raphael began to sprint away, leaving her behind. She caught up quickly, and they made it out of the city and back into the countryside in no time. The terrain shifted from sparse grass and rocks to uphill and large boulders. After a few minutes, they both spotted the famed Mount Olympus. Calypso stopped to marvel at the beauty.

The mountain range was thousands of feet above the lush hillside they stood on. The peaks of the mountains were covered in snow, which she still found beautiful even after their miserable month in the Alps. She knew the highest peak was Olympus itself, though it was covered by noctilucent clouds. The wispy clouds shined bright in the night, and although water vapor caused the phenomenon, it felt magical all the same.

"Do you think they are up there, the other Gods?" Calypso wondered.

"We'll never know if you don't stop daydreaming back there." Raphael continued walking at a brisk pace until Calypso cut him off.

"What have I done for you to be so cruel? I know I disobeyed Hades, but you have become so distant since you created me! From the moment your blood touched my lips, you've hated me! I've tried so hard to please you, but I always fall short. I can't honor you, let alone your master.

"I've done everything you ask of me, and the one thing I try to do for myself, I ruin. Turning Justin was a mistake I will always regret, but I can't take it back. Either forgive me or kill me now!"

Tears streamed down her face, glowing in the faint brightness of the sky. Raphael wiped her tears with his thumb and kissed her forehead, resting his on top of hers. The bridges of their noses came together, and she could finally feel his heartbeat next to hers. The tender moment brought tears to her eyes again, but he shushed them away.

"You are right; I have been extremely unfair and demanding of you," he whispered. "I know how hard it is to find your place in the world, and I have forgotten how I struggled. I always knew you were my queen, so I expected everything to come naturally to you. Don't ever doubt my love for you, mon chérie. I have searched millions of souls for even a glimpse of your breath, and I finally have you in my arms."

Their lips met, and Calypso stifled her urge to jump on top of him ravenously. He sensed her lust but ended the kiss abruptly as a bat flew overhead.

"Let's follow him; I'm sure we aren't far from the cave."

The bat flitted through the darkness, drawing closer to a nearby mountain wall. Its loud screech penetrated their eardrums, but the pain was meaningless as they focused on the task ahead of them. As they approached the cave, they smelled the overwhelmingly nauseating stench of death and decaying bodies. Knowing this was the home of the original vampires, the betrayers of Hades, they stopped to embrace each other one last time.

"If this is our last moment together, it's been one hell of a ride with you," Calypso whispered into his collarbone.

"Don't say that. We are the King and Queen of Vampires and this is child's play for us." He pushed the memories of his first and failed attempt to kill the enemies out of his mind. This time would be different; he had a secret weapon.

They held hands as they entered the black opening. Bones littered the ground; some were obviously ancient, while others were fresh, with skin still attached. A few human bodies lay thrown against the sides of the cave walls, trespassers perhaps or enemies of the vampires; anyone who had become a meal was ripped to shreds.

As they walked into a large opening of the cave, fire shot up from the sides of the walls. Skins soaked in alcohol, Calypso could tell by the lingering smell, burst into flames, which illuminated the scene in front of them. Blood was etched into the cave walls in ancient Greek scripture. Though she could not translate the symbols, she knew it was ominous. Bats lined the top of the cave so thick they could not see the rocks behind their slender bodies.

A thin and tall blonde woman stood on a high ledge, with an equally crafted blond man sitting at her side. Each of their features was exquisite and perfect, made in the image of their God. Although there were no grand thrones, the image was reminiscent of Hades' grand room.

"You, the one who turned me!" Raphael called out.

"Such a pitiful remark from you, the one I called a king." The woman sneered. She jumped down to eye level, and both Calypso and Raphael hardened their bodies, ready to attack.

"Calm down; I just want to have a little chat." She seductively moved her hips as she sashayed around Raphael, reaching her fingertips to rub against the hairs on his neck. "I was in hiding last time, or did you forget? Let me remind you: my brother and a handful of vampires crushed you and your legion of demons. You would have died had I chosen, but I decided to spare your life so we could have this final battle."

Calypso examined Raphael's twisted face and realized the words she spoke were true. She entered his mind and saw the scene of vampires ripping into every limb. His arms were broken, and his legs were torn to shreds. They held him down as the blond man approached him, a vicious look in his eyes and blood scattered across his face and chest. Just as he was about to plunge his hand into Raphael's chest, he stopped and retreated. Raphael could barely teleport out of the carnage and back to Hell.

"You've brought the queen, I see," she continued and stopped in front of Calypso to examine her. "I always thought that prophecy referred to us, that we would be the King and Queen of Vampires. Imagine King Adamantios and Queen Demostrate ruling over the entire race."

Adamantios let out a booming laugh from up above that caused the bats to shift overhead. Demostrate tried to touch Calypso's face, but she interjected with her arm.

"What did you do to make Hades hate you so brutally?"

Demostrate's face immediately lost her smirk, and she clenched her fists together.

"How dare you say his name in my house!" Her scream shook the rocks above them.

"Did you forget about your ruler already? Let me remind you, he burned you and your brother at the stake."

Calypso's words were interrupted as Demostrate flung her against the cave wall. Calypso caught herself and skidded on her feet. "What's that? Did I strike a cord?"

Easy now, Raphael spoke into her mind.

"He came to us, promising eternal wealth and power! Of course, we agreed; our family was the poorest in the town. We didn't know what we were sacrificing; how could we? He bound us to a stake and slit his wrist over our mouths so we could consume his blood. The fire was so agonizingly painful that I screamed and prayed for it to end. Finally, it did; we had new bodies and an undying loyalty to him. Adamantios and I did everything he asked of us! Killed anyone without hesitation, performed wicked and vile acts on others and each other if he asked us to." She paused, taking a deep breath as her emotions welled up.

"We did not question anything he did to us. He gave us these names and made us forget our human life. We were kept in a cage, with no interaction besides the demons that constantly tormented us. After hundreds of years of pain and torture, I began to question it all. Why were we kept in a cage, so he let us roam his castle. Why weren't we allowed in this room? Why weren't we allowed out of the castle? Why weren't we allowed on Earth? Please, master, make us another companion. Not just one, but two, ten! When we discovered we could create them ourselves..."

We need to attack now while she is off guard.

But Calypso paid Raphael no attention. She was enthralled in their story, just as Demostrate had planned.

"Hades had a favorite virgin around before Persephone. His glorified human virgin who we murdered and turned into a vampire. He should have killed us then if he were smart. But he continued to trust us and let us push the boundaries of Hell. Before he knew it, we had created our own army on Earth. He was too busy stealing the heroine that he didn't notice if we slipped into the human world to kill. We were ready to kill him and overthrow that beast from Hell, but he found out somehow. Someone betrayed us, and our whole army was wiped out. He banned us from Hell, so we couldn't return and finish the job. Now he hides there, never leaving the underworld for fear we will kill him."

"What a charming story," Raphael stepped forward. "But the lies you tell are inadequate. None of your so-called army betrayed you; Hades is an all-powerful God. He knew you were planning on overthrowing him before the thought entered your mind. He let you both escape with a purpose so that we could slaughter you on this eve."

"Please." Demostrate scoffed. "If he were so smart, why would he ever bring the queen to existence if she is to kill him?"

Raphael leaped and slammed her onto the ground. She narrowly escaped from underneath him, and a swarm of bats descended on them. They clawed and nipped at their arms and faces, distracting them so Demostrate could escape to the top of the cave ledge.

They tried to push the bats away and move forward, but the swarm was so tight they could barely breathe.

"We need to get up to them!" Calypso yelled over the screeching and flapping wings.

Raphael pushed her forward and let the bats obliterate him. Once she was out of the thicket, she had to overcome two vampires who were waiting to kill her. They were slow, almost zombie-like, and she could kick their heads off easily. With every step she took, more vampires appeared out of nowhere to attack her. All of them were the same: mechanical movements and weak, nothing like any other vampire she had fought.

Calypso continued to rip the heads off of the zombie vampires, but they started to overcome her. For every one she would kill, two more would take its place.

She was slammed onto her back, and the breath rushed out of her lungs. The vampires began to stomp on her, shattering her forearms and ribcage. She let them mutilate her body and stifled her cries of pain as her bones were constantly broken and healed.

Raphael was still trying to escape the bat swarm. The continuous biting and smacking of the bats caused him to scream in frustration. His voice was so high-pitched and piercing that it caused the bats to retreat momentarily. He took his chance and leaped at the herd of vampires that crushed his queen.

Calypso used every force of power in her body to raise herself and, in the process, slammed five vampires against the cave wall. She heard cackling from up above and jumped up to the ledge, leaving Raphael to deal with the swarm of vampires below.

More vampires surrounded Demostrate and Adamantios; these exceeded in agility and alertness compared to those below. Calypso was eager to slay the traitors, so she matched every blow and threw one after another off the ledge, knowing Raphael would finish the job below her.

Finally, they were alone on the small ledge, with only feet between them. Calypso was exhausted but refused to show her enemies. She wiped sweat and blood off her face and clenched her fists.

Adamantios sat in a stupor while Demostrate had a giant smile across her face. Calypso rushed forward, but the enemies didn't move, which caught her off guard.

"You and me, we can destroy him," Demostrate whispered as she stepped closer. "With our powers combined, nothing can stop us from ruling over Hell!"

"I'm not interested," she growled back. Her body was on high alert, every hair standing, and electricity pulsed through her veins.

"You know you want to," Demostrate appeared behind her, kissing the back of her neck. "Your purpose is to disobey him, create chaos, and kill him. If you don't do it, he will kill you!"

Calypso's feet left the ground, and she slammed into Adamantios. A faint glimmer of consciousness shined into his empty pupils before she ripped the heart out of his chest. The roar from Demostrate was deafening, but she ignored it as she raised the postmortem organ over her head and crushed it, dripping his blood onto her tongue and chest.

Raphael managed to escape the hoard of vampires, who all collapsed as Adamantios was killed. Demostrate flew into the air to kill Calypso, but Raphael appeared in front of her. He withdrew a small sword he had retrieved from Hades, and her chest punctured the blade as she flew into him. He watched as the look of pure rage and hatred transformed to fear, then emptiness, as her body fully reached the handle. Her body continued to fly into him, smacking against the guard of the sword, her ribs shattering with every millimeter she moved. Her head lay against his, and it took a moment for him to compose himself enough to throw her and the sword onto the ground. He quickly removed the blade from her chest and sliced her neck in one swift movement. He had to be certain of her death before he could check on his queen.

With the task finished, he rushed over to Calypso, whose hair, face, and chest were stained with the blood of a traitor. Her face was blank, unsurprising for the grueling fight they had just endured, but it was empty enough to concern him.

"Are you alright?"

Calypso sat frozen as she received an image in her mind of her ripping Hades' heart out of his chest. It filled her with horror, and Raphael picked up on her fear. He shook her shoulders, which brought her back to life.

"Yeah, but what did she mean?" She smiled faintly, and he could tell it was forced. The words of Hades killing her echoed in her mind.

"I don't quite understand it myself. Come, we must hurry now." Raphael grabbed the severed head and tucked the sword back underneath his shirt. Calypso met him with the now flattened heart, and they teleported back to the underworld.

Hades sat carelessly on his throne, flicking his fingers as he rested his heavy feet on Justin's back. He barely looked up as the two vampires appeared in front of him.

"Although you completed your task, I must say I am disappointed. I was looking forward to endlessly torturing these two."

Ayai fought against the chains holding her back, while Justin had no fight left in him. He had given up the moment they had been captured by demons back on Earth.

Hades slowly approached them and examined the head and heart offered to him. He grabbed the heart, squeezing the little remaining blood out of it. Calypso was mesmerized by the thick red drops that lined the gold and ivory floor. A twisted complexion spread across Hades' face as he gazed into the glossed eyes of his nemesis. He had once loved and cared for her like a daughter, and she took his trust and powers and used them against him. Nobody could ever return from such a betrayal, but here she was, as a corpse. Raphael released her hair, and Hades held the head at eye view. He twisted it around, studying the frozen countenance.

"How will you torture them now that they are dead?" Calypso broke the silence.

"There is no afterlife for a vampire. I thought you would have been told that." Hades took a moment to give Raphael an unforgiving glare. "You die once and are reborn into a vampire. Once you die in that form, there is no coming back. Your soul has already died once and disappeared. You only earn life back into your body."

This newfound knowledge terrified Calypso for some reason. She had never thought about her life after a vampire; she felt invincible like nothing could ever kill her. Deep in her heart, she knew death was inevitable. Perhaps this is why she had always despised Hades, her subconscious hating him for the future torture she would have to endure. But this changed everything; there was no afterlife for her.

She dropped to her knees, and her body felt powerless. A single tear rolled down her face. Raphael and Hades spoke in a hushed tone, discussing the fight assumably.

"Please forgive me for sinning against you."

Calypso's words grabbed both of their attention, and they turned to stare at her sullen body. Hades kneeled down next to her, and she automatically made eye contact with him. This time, his eyes were not unpleasant to look at and were full of curiosity.

"I have never fully devoted myself to you, but I swear on my life that changes today. I have always been absorbed with my ego. That's why I turned Justin; my ego couldn't handle the fact that I had to sacrifice someone so important to you. But I've realized that you are more important than him, more important than me! You are an all-powerful God, the creator and the destroyer, the beginning and the end. Never again will I doubt or disobey you. I see my purpose now, and it is to be a devout servant to you."

Hades' eyes shone at the unforeseen proclamation. He grabbed her chin and wiped away the tear with his thumb, letting it trail down her smooth cheeks and over her lips.

"Good girl," he spoke in a low, seductive tone. With her debt settled, he stood up to continue the interrogation with Raphael.

"As I was saying, the vampires were under a trance. Once Calypso killed Adamantios, they all ceased to exist."

"It seems as if he was under a trance as well." Calypso stood up to give her input. "He just sat there in a stupor. She was the one who talked the whole time and had any movement."

"Although I demanded Raphael and my demons to eradicate the witches a long time ago, it does not come as a surprise that a few managed to slip through their fingers. Demostrate must have found one to channel his power into the other vampires. The witch failed at their job, as you two saw, which I am grateful for."

"Your friends are free to go. You both completed your task, so my qualms with them are over." He turned to face Justin and Ayai, who were now huddled together and shaking. "You may not be of my concern anymore; however, if any of my demons or vampires stumbled across you on Earth, it is fair game."

Hades walked out of the room with two amorphous demons trailing behind him with the decapitated head and heart. Raphael immediately ran over to Ayai to make sure she was okay. He smoothed her hair and examined her throat where the chains had been. Calypso was slower to the scene; watching Raphael show so much care infuriated her.

"Justin, are you alright?" she questioned in an overly friendly tone.

"No, stay the hell away from me!" he shouted and crawled away from her. He watched her face crumble in response and bared his fangs at her. "You have caused me nothing but pain! I have been dragged to Hell not once but twice because of you and these stupid games you play."

"What are you talking about? I just saved your life!" Calypso became defensive and looked toward Raphael, who didn't back her up as expected.

"The torture he put us through will stay with me for a lifetime. Then you just defended him, begging him for mercy. First, you betrayed him, and now you betrayed us."

Calypso's mouth dropped open; she was at a loss for words. Justin flared with anger while Ayai's head was downcast, refusing to make eye contact. He wrapped his arms around her, and she glanced at Raphael, then teleported back to Earth.

Calypso shook her head after they disappeared and teleported herself back to Raphael's penthouse. She couldn't bear to stay in Hell any longer.

Faint daylight streamed through the tall windows, so she quickly headed downstairs to the coffin. There was no time to remove the disgusting fluids of the night off of her body, but she didn't care. Justin's flagrant remarks hurt her; how could he think she betrayed him? Showing her loyalty to Hades had helped them in her eyes. He could have gone back on his words to release them if he had sensed more distrust of her.

"He's pissed and has the right to be." Raphael's grandeur voice echoed behind her. "He did not agree to be brought into the darkness to become a pawn between you and Hades." He paused, biting his tongue before speaking again. "I have to say, I was shocked at your sudden change in heart."

"What was I supposed to do?" She whipped around, and the ends of her hair smacked him in the face. "You told me I need to be loyal to him! It finally hit me after the fight; I need to take this seriously."

"Very well, come." Raphael seated himself in the coffin and

motioned for her to join.

"I still have one question. Demostrate told me that it was my purpose to kill Hades."

"Do you feel that way?"

"No..." Calypso trailed off. She was firm in her loyalty toward him now. But she couldn't help but feel something unexpected was brewing, especially after the image that flooded her mind. She was too afraid to tell Raphael what she saw.

"Then there is no question. Demostrate was a liar; she would say anything to deceive others for her own gain."

As Calypso lay beside him, Raphael had to calm and steady his breathing. He couldn't let her know his fear over what she revealed to him. She couldn't know the truth but was coming ever so close.

Chapter 15

The subsequent days were spent in each other's arms. Calypso was terrified at what the future held for them. The next fight or mission could end in one of them dying permanently, and she couldn't imagine life without him. She was still torn over Justin, whom Raphael assured her was safe.

Raphael was pleasantly surprised by Calypso's calmness. He preferred her to stay close rather than chase her all over town to clean up her messes. He constantly buried his uneasiness and clouded his mind so she could not enter it.

On this particular night, they lay on the elegant Persian rug that covered the living room. Calypso lay naked on his chest, and he stroked her back as the moonlight streamed in. The world was quiet and peaceful, with no other sounds besides their hearts beating together and the waves that lapped below.

Soft kisses echoed in the still room, slowly turning more passionate and hungry. Calypso straddled Raphael and he moaned as she rode his thick length. He bit her bottom lip and she arched her back in response. He grabbed her hips to keep her pressed into him.

"Calypso," a voice whispered, and she shot straight up, her heart racing.

"What's the matter, mon chérie?" Raphael whispered drunkenly, continuing to rock her hips against the motion of his thrusts.

"I heard my name." Her bare chest heaved as she tried to calm herself. The room returned to silence, and she pressed herself back onto him, her nipples brushing across his pectorals. Her tongue slid into his mouth, and she melted into ecstasy momentarily.

"Calypso, your presence is requested." She groaned and rolled off of him, laying on her back to collect herself.

"I think Hades is calling me," she whispered.

Raphael turned and propped himself up with one elbow.

The moonlight accentuated his muscles, and the sight made it impossible for her to leave.

"I knew this day would come soon. He'll send you on a solo mission to ensure he can trust you."

"You think he still doesn't trust me?" Callie's mind raced with horrific possibilities as well as the image of her ripping Hades' heart out.

"He does. If not, he would have told me by now. But he has reason to doubt, with your sudden devotion to him. He wants to make sure it is pure."

Calypso nodded and took a shallow breath before standing up to dress herself. For once, she decided on something modest: long, flowing pants with a top that had the shoulders cut out but the neck covered. She pulled her sparkling red necklace on top of the blouse, squeezing it in her hand for comfort.

"You'll be alright." Raphael appeared behind her and kissed her bare shoulder.

"I've never been without you before."

"Please," he laughed. "You are not required to bring a soul to Hell since you were summoned. But if you ever show up unannounced, make sure you bring someone he will like."

Calypso nodded and gave him a final kiss before she closed her eyes and sent herself to the underworld.

She felt she would never get over the eerie sensation that always crept over her body as she appeared inside Hades' castle. Her anxiety was more heightened for this trip as she suspected she was still untrustworthy. Hades grinned at her arrival and rose from his throne. He held his arms out as he stepped down the stairs and approached her. She curtsied in response, mentally shaking her head at herself for the embarrassment.

"This meeting has no time restraints. However, when I summon you in the future, I hope you will be more prompt."

"My apologies, I was indecent."

"As you are now," Hades chortled. "Dressed very modestly compared to your normal attire."

"I wasn't sure what I would get myself into this evening. I wanted to make sure I was dressed for any occasion."

Hades nodded and turned toward the hallway. He held his arm at a crook, implying that she should hook her arm around his. Calypso swallowed deeply as she jogged to catch up with him and intertwine her arm with his. She kept her body facing forward so he wouldn't see her blush, and she tried not to focus on how his biceps rippled with every step he took.

Since he was so much taller than her, he had to significantly slow his stride for Calypso to keep up with him. They walked silently through the empty hallway, and the footsteps echoed around them.

After a few strides, they came to a split in the hallway. Hades led to the left, but Calypso managed to peek and see a large frame hanging on the wall toward the right. As they entered the new section, the roof vastly opened up and reached a point many feet above them. The intricate gold designs previously on the floor and wall stones had disappeared, leaving plain gray rocks. Windows lined only the right side of the hallway, and Calypso turned her head to observe the surroundings.

She gasped and released his arm, rushing toward the glass. Outside of the castle, an enormous fire burned. She had never seen one so large in her lifetime. The flames started at the ground and reached above the castle, farther than she could view. Bright hues of red, orange, and purple waved as the flames burned. If she focused her hearing, she could hear the subdued crackle of the fire outside.

"Is this the hellfire Raphael told me about?"

"This is for protection. No souls burn in this flame; the hellfire you speak of is much more wicked."

"Protection?" Calypso laughed.

"There are many creatures and demons in Hell that I do not wish to enter my sanctuary. It protects me from having to pay them any thought."

Calypso was surprised by his answer. She felt herself linger but couldn't pull away from the flames.

"So beautiful," she whispered.

Hades tucked a strand of fallen hair behind her ear. He gently stroked her bare shoulder with his thumb, which caused her body to tremble and turn toward him.

"I have been pondering on the subject of beauty myself. Every time you are in my presence, I can't help but feel drawn toward you."

Calypso wanted to belt out for him to stop, but she couldn't. Her heart beat profusely in her throat, and her cheeks turned as red as the flames.

"Do you know why I've called you here?"

"To test my loyalty." Calypso pushed herself against the window, trying to create space between their bodies.

"I need to be certain you will never disobey me again."

"I've sworn my loyalty to you."

"Yes, but would you ever break it? What if Raphael and I gave you contradictory orders?" Hades placed both hands on the window, closing the distance between them and sending heat to Calypso's body.

"I, I don't think that would ever happen. We are both loyal to you; we'll do whatever you command us." Calypso tried not to meet his eyes.

Hades forced his knee in between her legs, causing the heat to spread to her inner thighs. She gasped and quickly bit her lips, cursing herself for making a sound. He grinned as he watched her squirm for a moment, then took a step back, and she sighed heavily.

"I've realized how lonely I have been once I saw the love you and Raphael share. It reminds me of my lovely affair with the most beautiful woman."

"Persephone," she choked out.

"Indeed." Hades smiled fondly, and the flames cast a shadow upon his face, accentuating his jawline. His curls hung down to his chin, creating a fiery halo around his head. "She has been gone for so long that I have forgotten how nice it is to have a companion. Someone to rule with, to share the loneliness of this eternal castle."

"What happened to her?"

"Raphael hasn't mentioned her?" The corner of his lip twitched, threatening a smirk.

"Not at all. He has left me in the dark about many things surrounding you and Hell."

Hades stepped in again, lessening the space between their bodies. His eyes opened wide, and Calypso met his dark iris. She had fallen into Raphael's gorgeous blue eyes before, but they didn't compare to this darkness. She felt her body pull toward him, and she couldn't help it. Her soul was reaching for him, anything to enter his exquisite eyes. She stood on her tiptoes and placed her hands against his chest to balance. Hades held one hand around her back, pulling her closer. Heat flared on her chest, and she wanted nothing more than to fully give herself to him. Anything to be in his presence, in his powerful and warm embrace.

She was almost to his eyes, nearly entering his body. His beautiful, midnight black eyes. They swallowed her entire being and she saw the reflection of her dazed countenance in his pupils.

Calypso jerked back as her lips brushed against his beard. She slammed herself into the cold stone wall, realizing they had almost kissed.

"What did you do to me?" Calypso asked, keeping her eyes downcast so as not to meet his again. She was terrified, having momentarily lost control of her body.

"I was searching your soul; I have to make sure you are honest with me," Hades' response was too cool for the body heat they created together.

"I told you I am your loyal servant," she growled. "Do you really have such distrust for me, or is it all women?"

"My distrust of women started with Persephone and Demostrate. They broke my heart in unimaginable ways."

"What did Persephone do to you?" Calypso wanted to add that he was the one who kidnapped her but decided against it.

"She can tell you herself once you fetch her."

"Excuse me?"

Hades breached the space between them again. This time, he rested his forehead against hers, holding her close as she attempted to struggle away. Calypso gasped as a precious image entered her mind. It was an Egyptian temple, or what was left of one. The outside was covered in sand, with a small entrance that could be made out.

"She's in a temple?" Calypso asked.

"Yes, she'll be waiting for you inside. Now that you have the location, you should leave quickly as daylight approaches." Hades turned and began to walk away from her, his hands clasped behind his back.

"Wait, I must return to Raphael first."

"That won't be necessary. This is a mission for you to complete yourself."

"I won't let him know the details. But if I am gone for too much longer, he may begin to worry."

"I'd close off your mind when you see him. We wouldn't want to make him jealous, would we?" Hades' smug grin was the last thing she saw before she was forcibly sent back to Earth.

Calypso landed on the polished floors abruptly, still shocked at the final words that came out of his mouth.

Raphael stood in the kitchen, pouring blood out of the decanter. He immediately finished his task to help her up.

"I've been waiting for you, mon chérie." He kissed her passionately, then pulled away as she did not reciprocate with her usual full intensity. "Is something wrong?"

"Not at all, still adjusting to being back here. I didn't teleport myself; Hades sent me here on his own accord."

"Did you do anything to upset him?"

"Not at all." Calypso gave a cheerful grin and made sure her mind was inaccessible to him. She didn't want to reveal her close encounters with their ruler. "He just wanted to make sure I am prompt in going to my mission."

"A solo mission, what a big night for you." Raphael handed her a glass of blood, which she eagerly gulped down. He refilled it, and she drank it just as fast. "I hope you won't be gone for too long."

"It shouldn't be too long. It's just a simple retrieval mission. I would tell you more, but I must keep it a secret for now, you know, because of trust and all."

"Of course." Raphael nodded curtly, his eyebrows coming together.

"Don't worry, my soul will ache for you every moment I am away." Calypso stood on her tiptoes to kiss him and placed her empty glass on the counter. She took a few steps away from him, turned, and gave him one last smile before she teleported herself to the image in her mind.

Raphael gave a small grunt as she disappeared. He kept himself momentarily busy with cleaning up the glasses and decanter, typical house husband duties. He tried not to fret over Calypso but couldn't help it. He was suspicious of her closed-off mind, ignoring the fact that he had been closed off to her from the moment she became a vampire, but with reason. What could she be hiding from him?

A retrieval mission, what could that mean? I'm sure he is sending her to grab something mildly unimportant from the depths of Hell. After all, I have fetched everything with any sort of meaning or power to him. But could he really send her into Hell's bowels without the proper knowledge or protection? No, he wouldn't, or would he? Is he that selfish, that cruel? No, Raphael, get it together.

Lost in his thoughts, he scrubbed so anxiously that a glass shattered, impaling his palm. The pain was minuscule and temporary, but it sent a new thought into his mind. He gasped and became weak in his legs at the thought. He knew where Hades had sent her and needed to get there fast before he never saw her again.

*

Calypso appeared in the Egyptian desert, the sun soon to rise on the horizon. She squinted, although it was still relatively dusky. The image Hades had put into her mind was quite different from what stood in front of her. The crumbling temple was now little more than a large sand dune. It had an odd shape, so she knew the temple was buried underneath.

Knowing she had a short window until dawn, she began to dig like a crazed woman. Sand flew behind her and piled at her feet. Her mouth and eyes became victims to the coarse granules, but she continued, spitting and partially blinded. Finally, her nails scraped against something hard, and she pushed the sand away with furiosity. She was able to dig a small hole, barely wide enough to fit her body, that led to the stones she felt.

Calypso lengthened her arms out in front of her and squeezed her shoulders through the narrow sand tunnel. She wiggled herself forward enough to place her palms on the stones completely. Her heart pounded as she connected with the cold stone, but nothing happened. She was mildly disappointed after the work she endured to get here. Pausing for a moment to breathe and think, she bit her thumb harshly and then smeared the blood across the stones.

A low grinding sound was emitted, and the stones slid to the sides, leaving just enough room for her to continue crawling inside. As soon as she was inside the structure, the sand tunnel collapsed, and the stones slid back into place. She frowned, not knowing how she was going to get out, but that was not her present concern. She stood up slowly, not sure of how much space there would be.

As her eyes adjusted to the darkness, torches along the walls burst into flames. This wasn't her first time seeing this spectacle, but it made her uneasy nonetheless. The floor, walls, and ceiling were all covered with a thick layer of dust, indicating how long it had been since anyone had entered the temple. A strong smell of death, decay, and stale air penetrated her nostrils. A narrow hallway lay ahead of her, and she set forth on her quest.

The hallway itself was short, only a few feet long, before it opened into another room. This next room was larger, completed by another span of hallway that opened up into another expansive room. She was able to make out drawings in the third room, faint brown pictures she somehow knew were etched in blood. They were poorly drawn stick figures and unintelligible, meaningless to her. As she walked through the next hallway, her hair began to stand up on her arms. She knew she was close to Persephone as her aura of power was electric in the air.

This area was the largest and seemingly final room inside the temple. The torches illuminated the highly decorated walls and singular sarcophagus that lay in the center.

Calypso had viewed pictures of these when she was a human in grade school, but it did little to prepare her to come face-to-face with one. The coffin-like structure was massive compared to her own and much more vibrant. It was fully made out of gold, or encrusted at least, with generous human-like detail. She was enthralled with the detail of it all; the face seemed to really be staring back at her. She wondered if Persephone looked similar to the rather plain woman's face she gazed at.

A first attempt to pry open the sarcophagus failed. The gold was extremely heavy, more than her vampiric strength could lift. After a brief moment of thought, she concluded that it must be opened with blood, just like the doors of the temple. This time, she bit her palm and squeezed the blood onto the face of the coffin. Crimson dropped and splashed against the pursed golden lips.

Immediately, a loud groan was released from the coffin. Calypso jumped back in surprise, just in time, as the lid was thrown open. A long and ghostly cry sounded as a frail arm reached up, barely having the strength to pull its body out of the deep pit. Lucious brown hair appeared first; time and solitude had done nothing to destroy its beauty.

Curls swept down her face, her eyes still closed, as she slowly rose to standing. The woman was tall but very skinny. Calypso could easily spot blue veins running past her jawline to her chest. Dainty, soulful eyes blinked, with eyelashes long enough to make even the gorgeous vampire jealous. Her lips were a pale pink, plump and soft, while her nose was a prominent feature but nonetheless a beauty.

The woman held eye contact while Calypso waited for her to say something. After so long, she must have something to say. All she did was bat her eyes, looking like a lost doe.

"My name is Calypso, the Queen of Vampires. I was summoned to rescue you from this chamber and bring you back home."

Persephone emitted another painfully noisy sound, not moving her lips.

"Ah, I don't have any water with me. Perhaps I can find some condensation by the rocks." Calypso doubted her words but was prepared to do anything to please this God. She took a few steps toward the entrance of the room, scanning along the walls and ground for any signs of dampness. As Calypso examined the stones, she failed to notice the tall woman move behind her, holding a small, jagged rock overhead.

Calypso turned to ask for help but was thrown to the ground as Persephone gashed the rock against her. She made a flimsy cut into her neck, and she dropped down and sucked ravenously. Calypso was frozen with shock; why was the Goddess of fertility drinking her blood?

Persephone slowly pulled away, her mouth slightly agape and eyes as wide as ever. She still held the rock in her hand and slashed it against her own wrist. Calypso tried to scoot away from her but was held down.

"No, I can't," she turned her face away from the blood. Persephone didn't accept her answer and forced her wrist into her mouth. Calypso could only stomach a few drops of blood; it was as delicious as Hades', but she knew it was forbidden.

Now I can speak with you.

Calypso's eyes widened as the woman's voice entered her mind.

Who sent you? Persephone demanded.

"Hades."

Persephone tried to laugh, but it came out as a harsh gurgling sound.

Hades wants nothing to do with me. Who really sent you?

"I speak no lies." Calypso stood back up and dusted herself off. "Hades sent me here to bring you back to him. He spoke eloquently of your beauty and how he longs for it after being alone for so long."

Persephone's face turned dark and distraught, but Calypso didn't have much time to process the change as the temple shook. It felt like an earthquake as the ground trembled beneath them, and the ceiling threatened to cave in. Persephone grabbed Calypso's hand and began to rush toward the hallway.

Quickly, we need to hurry! It has smelled your blood; there won't be much time now.

"Time for what? Who smelled my blood?" Calypso demanded as she jogged behind her. The question was never answered as a piercing scream echoed through the air. The sound could only be described as animalistic, a mix between a lion and something of a dinosaur.

Don't turn around. We're almost at the door!

Calypso couldn't hear her footsteps or shallow breaths as the loud booming sound followed her. She could feel the heat of the monster's breath on her back. She wanted to turn around to catch a glimpse of her foe and try to size them up but decided to listen to Persephone due to the allegory of Orpheus.

As they reached the entrance of the temple, both women slammed their fists against the stones. They desperately pummeled against the unmoving bricks.

Calypso ripped her forearms open with her fangs and slathered her blood against the walls, to no avail. The pounding of the beast came closer, and she knew they were out of time.

"Raphael! Help us!" she cried out loud and in her mind, praying he received her message.

Drink more of my blood! Persephone commanded.

The beast had entered the room; they were out of time. Calypso caught a glimpse of the giant, reptilian-like creature as she ripped into Persephone's dress. Her fangs penetrated the breast, knowing she needed the strongest blood pumping from her heart. This time, she drank deeply, almost unable to stop, but not knowing how much she would need to consume. When Persephone became weak in her arms and fainted, she let her fall slowly to the ground.

The beast was steps away, ready to strike.

Calypso let out a loud cry as she pushed against the stone wall with all of her might. Her muscles popped out of her arms and back as she continued to exert her power and will against them. A small crack appeared, and she continued to press against it, finally breaking through. Persephone had come to but was still depleted, barely able to hold her head up. She muttered something in Latin, which caused the beast to roar in response. Calypso picked up Persephone and shoved her through the small entrance she had made.

The beast grabbed Calypso as she slid her head and shoulders into the passage. She shouted as claws punctured her sides. She was pulled back into the temple and desperately clawed the sides of the stones. A muscular white hand appeared before her, and she took hold, knowing it was her king. He struggled to pull her into the tunnel as the beast refused to remove its grip. Calypso screamed in pain as her body was clawed and stretched, but Raphael finally pulled her into the tunnel.

Calypso's eyes closed as the sand collapsed around them, and she waited for imminent death. It was impossible to avoid the wrath of the beast, but somehow they did. She suddenly felt cold stones underneath her palms and opened her eyes to find herself in Hades' grand hall.

Persephone lay prostrate and silent next to her, refusing to look at her or Hades. Raphael approached him with a bloodthirst in his eyes while Hades stood looking the scene before him.

"How dare you!" Raphael shouted in his face. Hades slapped him for his disobedience, which infuriated him more.

"How dare you question me! I sent my servant on a mission alone."

"I didn't tell him," Calypso panted, adrenaline still rushing through her veins. "He was there as we exited the temple."

"You knew what you were doing," Raphael said, his fangs bared and ready to strike. Hades knew he never would and ignored him, instead walking to Persephone. He stopped in front of her hands and turned his head to examine her. Her fingers slowly covered his feet, their first connection in hundreds of years.

"My wife, you have returned to me," he spoke in quiet adoration. Raphael returned to Calypso to help her up, although she didn't need it. They watched as Hades helped Persephone to stand. Calypso noticed she still refused to look him in the eyes.

"Oh my, what has happened to your dress?" Hades felt underneath her garment, caressing her breasts to check for any punctures, which were now healed.

"The beast. She fell and tore her dress as we were escaping from it," Calypso said too loudly. Hades nodded, not looking at her, instead marveling at the glory of his wife.

"We are finished here." Hades wrapped his arm around Persephone's waist, leading her forlorn spirit out of the room.

"That's it?" Raphael exclaimed. "You sent her there to die and give me no explanation?"

Hades paused before exiting and turned around to face him. "Calypso completed her mission, as was expected. Her powers are truly remarkable."

Raphael sneered as Hades and Persephone left the room. Calypso felt disgusted and insisted they return home immediately.

"Raphael, what happened?" She asked once they were back in their lair. She gave him time to pace and slam his fists against the wall. She had never seen him this angry, even after she had turned Justin.

"Hades lied! He lied about sending you to bring Persephone back."

"I don't see how. She was there and she is back with him. The only thing he didn't tell me was about the beast."

"Do you know how I knew where you were?" He stopped, pushing his sweaty hair back over his forehead.

"I assumed you heard my cry for help."

"No, the temple was created to block any connection from the inside. Even through our blood-mind connection, it could not be heard."

Calypso's eyes welled with tears as the realization of her fate set in.

"I was the one who took Persephone to the temple five hundred years ago. He commanded me to trap her there after suspecting betrayal from her. He created a vampire-eating beast to ensure anyone who tried to rescue her would perish. Hades did not mean for you to come back from the temple. He wanted you to die."

Calypso tried to make sense of what she heard. She felt betrayed by Raphael, who never told her he had committed such a terrible deed, and by Hades, who just hours ago was making her swoon.

Is that why he touched me? Calypso unintentionally opened her mind as she tried to understand.

"He touched you?" Raphael grabbed her arms and shook her, filled with rage and jealousy.

"He rubbed my shoulder, touched my back, small things just to make me trust him. Nothing else happened." Calypso felt ashamed, and tears rolled down her cheeks.

"You trusted him because he enticed you?" Raphael's voice hardened.

"I trusted him because I thought that was my duty. Because you told me I had to trust him!" she yelled.

Raphael released her and began to pace again.

"She wouldn't talk to me," Calypso sniffed. "Is that because of what you did to her?"

"What I did to her?" Raphael turned and screamed. "I followed my commandment. Persephone did not speak to you because Hades cut her tongue out! She talked with his demons, trying to change Hell to suit her own needs. When he discovered her blasphemy, he cut her tongue out so she would never speak falseness against him. Her wrongdoings tormented him, so he summoned me to dispose of her, away from him and far away from Hell."

Calypso was shocked and shook her head in disbelief. The complexity of the situation she endured crashed down on her like the weight of the world.

"What happens now?"

Raphael continued to pace and ignore her. Now that she had somehow evaded the trap, he knew her fate was nearing. Hades tried to kill her once, and this wouldn't be the last time. Their time remaining together would be brief unless he could convince Hades the prophecy was false.

"Raphael?" Calypso stood up and touched his arm as he stomped past her. "Please forgive me if I have done something wrong." She was too afraid to reveal she had drunk Persephone's blood.

"No, mon chérie." He stopped and kissed her forehead. "It is not you but I who have made a mistake. I--" His throat closed up and refused to let him speak. He placed his head against hers and held her close. His chest heaved with sadness, knowing this could be their final night together.

"Raphael, please tell me what is happening. I have never seen you so worried." Calypso could barely keep her eyes open due to exhaustion and the rising sun.

"I made the mistake of creating you, my queen. You would

have been better off without me and without this darkness encapsulating your life."

Calypso began to cry silently as they lay down in the coffin. Raphael held her as she cried, letting his own tears flow onto her angelic cheeks.

Chapter 16

Persephone blacked out after Calypso drained most of her blood. She was thankful her Goddess powers restored her injuries quickly so Hades would never know about the blood-sharing that occurred. If he were to discover, they would both be killed immediately, and she couldn't let that happen, not when she had come so far. Hades had made a mockery of her and her lineage, and revenge was the only option.

She had dreamt of the day of escaping her tomb prison for hundreds of years but never expected a pale, beautiful woman to be her savior. At first, she doubted this vampire could be the *one*, but after tasting the power in her blood, she felt confident.

Hades was disappointed to see her, of course, since his plan was to trap the vampire in the tomb with her. But he was oh so friendly as he led her down the endless, winding hallway toward his bedroom. He chatted incessantly about the work he had done since she left him, as if she had a choice or cared.

As she entered his room, the old feeling of disgust crept over her body. Nothing had changed in the past five hundred years. His bed was positioned in the same place, in the middle of the wall, surrounded by bone fragments and gemstones. She always hated how gaudy it looked. He was the God of death; everyone knew and respected him, and there was no need to entertain the fact in his sanctuary. Aside from his wall centerpiece, the room was dark and drab, without a single carpet or anything to give the room comfort.

She automatically dropped to her knees as Hades turned to face her. She knew the ritual, it was all too familiar for her.

When she had first been kidnapped and entered Hell, she fought it with every fiber of her being. After thousands of years, she discovered the secret to pleasing him and her sanity. She had to obey him, no matter what. Anything else would cause catastrophe to her life and others. Only in private could she turn her genuine feelings of hatred on, but not for long.

She could only allow herself to feel malignance for a few moments. Otherwise, it would consume her and cause rash decisions to be made, like last time. Her emotions had gotten the best of her, and her punishment was to lay alone in a rotting tomb without a tongue to swallow her pride.

Persephone kept her eyes downcast, and her shoulders slumped forward. Her palms faced open on her knees, indicating he was in charge of what happened next. They both knew what would consume the next few hours; the air practically sparked with anticipation and tension, but Hades wasn't ready for that yet.

"Oh, how I've missed you." Hades cupped her chin in his hand, forcing her gaze upward.

Her expression was forlorn but still receptive to his touch.

"I apologize for keeping you tucked away for so long, though you must understand why. I cannot tolerate any disrespect against my authority over Hell, and you minimized it, to say the least. How could you betray me after all I had done for you? But that was in the past, and we are both here now. I am a forgiving soul, as you shall remember." He released her chin, and she kept her gaze locked on him as he paced slowly in front of her.

"I was waiting for this exact moment for the supposed Vampire Queen to emerge to test her powers and send her to you. To see if she was indeed a lesson from the Fates, which has been confirmed up to this point. Sending Calypso to you only increased my suspicion. Can you blame me after not speaking to you for centuries? You have every reason to be furious with me, with your extraneous female emotions. However, this situation has proved to turn my suspicions toward her, which I'm sure you agree with." He paused, waiting for her to nod, which she performed hastily.

"I have continuously pondered how exactly you two managed to escape the temple I specifically created to keep vampires trapped. The walls were sealed with witchcraft and blood, even a monster to feast on her soul, but my grandiosity proved to be nothing to her. Raphael fled to her rescue, expecting to be doomed. Perhaps you can shed some light onto my darkness."

Hades turned and opened the footrest against the end of his bed. He pulled out a small wooden box, and Persephone's eyes lit up. She couldn't believe he kept it after all this time. Of course, he had. Hades pulled back the lid slightly so she could gaze upon her fleshy organ that lay inside.

"Of course, I kept it after all these years. The question is if you deserve it."

Persephone scooted forward toward him and continued to nod at him. She tried to speak, but only jumbled, gargled, and moaning sounds escaped from her mouth. Hades removed her tongue from the box, still as pink and moist as the day he cut it out, and dangled it in front of her.

"I will give you all you desire if you tell the truth. Will you actually honor your vows to me this time around?"

Persephone could wait no longer and reached for her tongue. She pulled gently to remove it from his hands, not wanting to seem too eager and opened her mouth wide. Her tongue slid into the back of her throat and automatically began to regrow to its muscles. She breathed deeply as she adjusted to losing space in her mouth, wiggling it profusely to confirm it still worked.

"You are right about Calypso," Persephone spoke after swallowing. "She is the one the Fates warned you of and cannot be trusted."

"How do I know you tell the truth?"

"She knew what she was doing in the temple. She used her own blood to enter the walls and to open my coffin. Once I had risen, she ambushed me and drank my blood. I was so feeble after being trapped in that damn box. I couldn't fight her off. She forced me to drink her blood. I fought against her but eventually gave in."

Hades studied her closely for any signs of deception but found none. Her story sounded truthful, as Persephone was a very prideful woman and would be deeply moved by a subservient stealing from her life force.

"If this is true, if you share the blood connection with her, I need you to summon her. I will send her a sleep demon. You shall call out to Calypso and bring her to me. I will end this battle once and for all. Then, we will focus on rekindling our flame. But until then..." Hades didn't have to finish his sentence for Persephone to understand his meaning.

"I will prove my loyalty to you." She swallowed one last time before opening her mouth wide and extending her tongue. Hades swiftly sliced it off, and it fell into his hands. She flinched, expecting the pain and blood that filled her mouth. The tongue was placed in the box, which he kept partially open as he placed it on top of the footrest. It seemed to watch and tease her as she opened her mouth again, eager to please her master.

*

Calypso was tormented by nightmares throughout her daytime sleep. She had visions of herself burning in eternal hellfire, her skin constantly melting and regrowing, causing endless suffering. When the hellfire ended, she was lost in darkness. Demons taunted her, calling out to follow them, but every step disoriented her.

Finally, she stumbled into a dark room, with only a spotlight hanging above captive Persephone. Her jaw was bloody and broken, her lower mandible hanging by only a bone. The large gaping hole where her tongue was missing was swollen and bruised.

Calypso, help me.

She jerked awake from the agonizing images, breathing heavily and covered in sweat. A slight tremble in her arms disturbed Raphael, who still slept. He placed a reassuring hand on her thigh.

"What has you up this early, mon chérie?"

"I can't stop thinking about Persephone." She didn't want to lie to him, so this was the closest she could get without revealing her nightmares. She knew it would cause him more distress.

"Why? She isn't our concern anymore." Raphael's tone was stern, indicating that she should leave the matter alone.

"That doesn't stop me from thinking about her. How do we know she is safe? After everything he did to her."

"What Hades chooses to do to his wife is private and will be kept as such."

"Wife?" Calypso felt hurt by the sentiment and then immediately felt guilty. "Sorry, I can't imagine anyone treating their wife so poorly. We aren't married, and you treat me as a queen should be." She wrapped her arms around him and kissed him deeply, hoping he didn't sense her discomfort.

"We are married in blood," He whispered into her lips. "You are my queen, my wife, my breath." He kissed her neck passionately, rubbing his fangs across her collarbone like he knew she loved.

"Please, let me go check on her."

Raphael sighed; his seduction had done nothing to change the situation. "Seeing as you refuse to give this up, I will accompany you."

"Do you think he will take it as an ambush if we both show up?"

Raphael pulled back and broke their embrace. He knew Hades would be more vigilant, and the both of them showing up unannounced would make him even more suspicious.

"I cannot allow you to go alone." He wanted to scream, chain her, and refuse to let her leave their lair, but there was no point. It was over; Hades had won, and poor Calypso would never know the battle she existed in.

"I'll bring him a soul like you said I must when I enter Hell on my own accord. I'll make sure it's a soul he will like, that will put him in my favor, right? And I'll tell him exactly what I am telling you: that I want to see Persephone to make sure she is alright. Which is the truth; she's been through so much trauma. I don't have any friends, and I want to make sure she is alright."

"Don't seem so friendly. He knows you aren't that cordial, and if you act differently, he will know you are lying. Please, don't stay too long. Check on her if you must and come straight back here." He kissed her forehead, and his heart raced. He stepped back to admire her beautiful face and adjusted her necklace. The stone shined as bright as ever, almost casting a glow under her face.

Calypso gave him a brief smile before she disappeared. She pushed the anxiety out of her chest as she appeared in a low-lit motel just outside of the city. The singular streetlight buzzed annoyingly, indicating it would go out at any second. She snorted as she fondly remembered the night Raphael caused a streetlight to burst out of jealousy for her.

Moving her attention back to the slim pickings in front of her, she focused on a young girl who was severely out of place. The motel was a beacon to the poor drug abusers on the outskirts of town. Anyone who rented a room barely inhabited it, as there was more fun to be found standing outside. Multiple people smoked cigarettes, a few drank cheap beer, and one lady was passed out underneath a faded ice machine sign.

The girl appeared to be in her late teens, almost ready to be alone in the world, but not quite yet. She had to have run away from home; her clothes were too clean compared to those of anyone around her. She stood beside a room door, anxiously stepping from one foot to another. Any loud sound made her startle. She looked around quickly and returned her gaze downward like a deer.

Calypso stayed in the shadows underneath the motel sign as she called out to the girl. Her mind was easily penetrated, and she began to walk forward immediately, although she didn't know why. She left the muffled chaos behind her as she continued toward the shadows. She stopped in her tracks as Calypso appeared behind her, wrapping her arm around her neck and muffling her bloodcurdling scream with her hands.

She had never teleported with another soul before, so she was unaware it would be so painful. Every atom felt as if it were being ripped apart as she desperately clung to her victim. She would be worried about choking her but didn't care since she was bringing her to death.

They both dropped onto the cold stones in Hades' grand room, which caused an echo of their fall. The girl jumped up quickly, but Calypso held her back in a chokehold in a second.

Hades sat on his throne, overlooking the empty room as usual. Calypso briefly wondered if he had been expecting her, then pushed the thought out of her mind.

"Hades, uh, my Lord," Calypso stumbled, unsure how to address him.

"Calypso, you shouldn't have come unannounced if you wanted to devour my presence. You must prepare a man for that sort of matter." His white teeth sparkled as he smiled, revealing two sharp incisors she hadn't noticed previously.

"No, I have a purpose for my visit, and it is not to indulge in you."

Though you make it hard not to.

She hated herself for her lustrous thoughts.

"I see you brought me a gift." His response was curt and stiff, unlike his usually too-friendly and drawn-out tone. "Usually, you kill her first."

"I thought I should save the fun part for you." She dragged the girl forward, who balked, attempting to dig her heels into the ground. Calypso choked her harder and threw her onto the ground in front of Hades. He stepped down from his throne to examine her. He was monstrous in size compared to her. She fainted as soon as she saw his face.

A hunchbacked and wrinkled human appeared from the hallway and threw the girl over his shoulder.

"I don't enjoy killing unless it is an enemy or a soul who deserves it." Calypso's face dropped. She thought she had chosen the perfect soul for him. "However, I'll take my time with this one.

Perhaps we could enjoy her together. Her body is esculent." The corner of his lip threatened to smile.

Calypso gave him a weak smile in return.

"Have you done so with your partner?"

"Done what?" she asked.

"Take an innocent soul and feast as one. To feel a virgin squirm under your touch as you play with their skin. Teasing them as you rub your fangs over their neck. Letting passion overtake your body as you watch your partner rip into them. Feeling their hot blood cover your body as you climax together."

Calypso's mouth drooled and her legs trembled as Hades described the temptation to her. His dark and sultry voice did oh so well to paint the picture for her. Her heart raced as she imagined the two of them tangled together after feasting on the girl.

Hades licked his lower lip and Calypso shook her head quickly.

Damn it, get out of my head!

"Ah no," she responded. "Raphael and I prefer to keep our passions contained to the privacy of our home."

"You vampires are no fun anymore," he sighed.

Calypso wrung her hands awkwardly while he stared at her. She opened her mouth to explain her visit, but he beat her to it.

"I know you did not come here to feast on an innocent virgin with me. So, to what do I owe this honor?"

"I wanted to make sure Persephone was doing alright. I imagine adjusting to being here after residing in the temple for so long could be difficult."

Hades had begun to walk back to his throne, but her words made him stop and turn around to face her. His eyes emitted a new radiance that Calypso had not been privy to before.

"You are here for Persephone?"

"Yes, if it is alright with you, I would like to see her. I know we exchanged no words and only met briefly, but I felt I shared a connection with her."

"Of course. She is resting, but I will take you to her chambers."

Calypso followed Hades into the hallway and struggled to keep up with his long strides. Her heart nearly caught in her throat as they passed the windows encased by hellfire. Their intimate moment was not lost on him either, who glanced back at her knowingly.

Hades took a sharp left, and the demeanor of the castle seemed to change. The walls were damp, and the air felt heavy. Calypso noticed a few spiders hiding in the corners of the ceiling. This didn't concern her as Persephone had been away for hundreds of years. She was sure she had a whole wing to herself. Hades stopped suddenly outside of a pair of tall wooden doors. Both handles were rings made out of metal, with a lion's head at the bottom.

"Go ahead, she's waiting for you inside," Hades urged her to open the door.

Calypso nodded and pulled against one of the rings. She jerked her hand away as the lion burned her. The door swung open, and Hades pushed Calypso inside. Persephone sat chained against the wall. She lifted her head, and her eyes widened once she made out Calypso's face in the darkness.

Calypso's head burst with pain as she was slammed onto the ground. Demons swarmed in from the hallway, holding her down as Hades stepped on her hands. Once he had broken all of her phalanges, he gouged his heel into the center of her palm, crushing her veins and carpal bones.

She screamed in agony, but it only fueled his anger toward her. The demons peeled her body off of the ground so he could kick her ribs. One blow sent her hurdling backward, surrounded by demons who pushed her back to him. They cackled and whispered in her ear, but she couldn't make out any of the words. The second kick made her vision disappear for a few seconds as she projectile vomited onto the floor. Hades went to kick her again but stopped when she flinched before the strike.

"Please," she coughed out blood clots onto her chest.

"You betray me and expect mercy?" Hades grabbed a handful of her hair and dangled her in the air, her feet far above the ground. He examined her bruised and bloody face, which showed only confusion.

"Betray you? I've done everything you have asked of me," She said feebly.

"As the Fates had it, you betrayed me before you were even conceived." He threw her against the wall, causing the air to leave her lungs. As her wounded body crumpled against the floor, Hades picked up Persephone and carried her out of the room. Demons rushed forward to attach the chains to Calypso, who had no strength to move.

I am sorry.

Persephone spoke into her mind upon exiting the room with Hades. Once the room was empty, Calypso let out one long sob, which was all her body could manage. She was in so much pain that she gave in and floated into unconsciousness.

*

Raphael tried to keep himself occupied throughout the night, but nothing kept his mind from worrying over his counterpart. He paced the entirety of the penthouse until he felt sick, adjusting every painting and book, though they were already aligned.

As the time crawled well past midnight, he decided to head into the city and feed. She would have to be back by then, as dawn was right around the corner. Raphael hated leaving the house without her; his life felt empty and meaningless. He had spent hundreds of years without her, but since their first contact, his purpose in life had become her: finding her, seducing her, loving her, protecting her. Raphael walked along the cold, empty street and dug his hands into his pockets.

The slightly chilled wind made him reminisce about the months he and Calypso had spent in the Alps. He wished he could go back and rewrite their history; he was so enraged at her that they could never take in the beauty surrounding them. They could visit again; he would make a romantic trip out of it this time.

He imagined her naked body covered in blood from their victim, strewn across a large king bed inside of a cozy cabin. A fire crackled in the background, and a blizzard fell around them. There were no worries in the world; it was just the two of them with no objectives except making love until the sun rose.

A grunt brought him back to the bleak sidewalk. A heavyset man sat on a bench ahead of him and struggled to get comfortable. Raphael took a quick look around and confirmed they were alone. The man barely noticed as Raphael approached, sat next to him on the bench, and ripped into his neck.

Raphael stifled a moan as the thick, gelatinous blood entered his throat. He sucked greedily, not worrying about overdrinking. The man had more than enough to spare for him. He stopped only when he felt glutinous himself. Detaching his fangs from the man's rolls, he leaned against the cold bench rails and slung his arm across his shoulders. Imaginably, they were friends in a past life.

He stayed until the man's wound closed itself, leaving a trail of dried blood stained to his skin. Raphael stood up slowly and continued his early morning walk as the mist cascaded around him.

Head down, hands in his pocket. He was just another insomniac taking on the streets before the sun rose. He continued his stroll until the sky started to turn a faint shade of blue, then headed back to his apartment building. He took the stairs this time, no need to rush, but was immensely disappointed to find the penthouse empty.

He hurried down to their coffin, hoping she would be waiting for him. The stale silence smacked him, and his nostrils flared with rage. He screamed as he grabbed the coffin and flung it against the wall. It was made of unbreakable material, so it was undamaged other than scraping loudly against the wall and floor.

He smoothed his hair back and sighed before dragging the coffin back over to its stand. He placed it back in its usual position and laid inside. Calypso would be returning to him any second; he knew it. If not, she probably didn't want to risk teleporting during the sunlight. He would descend to Hell immediately when he woke and would ensure a safe travel back. He would call Maria to take care of the house while they traveled to a romantic, isolated cabin.

Everything would be alright; he just needed to rest now. Even as he repeated this, he knew in his soul that she was gone. Her frightened face was the last image he saw before he fell unconscious.

Chapter 17

Calypso regained consciousness hours, days, or weeks later, she did not know. Her lip was still swollen from the beating. She was surprised that her body healed slower than usual. Due to being in Hell or the strength of Hades, she couldn't determine.

The door creaked open, and a faint light shone in, making her squint. She stayed prostrate on the ground, afraid any move would result in pain.

"Get up," a crackled voice spoke. Calypso turned her head to see the voice came from the hunchback she had seen previously. She turned her head away and lay her cheek against the damp ground. The coolness was the only thing that gave her comfort.

"Get up now." He whacked her side with a long stick. It was a wise decision for him not to get too close.

"Hades requests your presence."

Calypso scowled as she rolled into a sitting position. She detested his name and would rather rot in the cell than have to face him again. But she figured she didn't have much of a choice and should confront death sooner rather than later.

The hunchback grabbed her chains, and they walked into the hallway together. He led the way, and she stayed far behind him, letting the chains pull to their limit.

She kept her face downcast as they passed plenty of monsters, vampires, and demons. They all cackled as she passed in chains. She was the new victim, the latest torment entering Hell. Once the Queen of Vampires, now demoted to a lowly slave.

The hunchback pushed open a large golden door, and they entered the grand feasting hall.

Calypso tried to keep her head down but was so taken aback by the intricate details that she was forced to look. Like everything in the castle, the table was enormous and made out of solid gold. The legs were flaked with gemstones, and designs encrusted with silver flakes adorned the bottom of the table. A large variety of food handsomely decorated the top. Although almost a hundred chairs were placed around the table, they were only occupied by Hades and Persephone.

The hunchback pushed Calypso into a chair facing opposite of the Gods. He fastened the chains around her waist so she was unable to move her body except for her arms. He took his place along the wall beside a few other burley vampires. She bared her fangs at them, traitors.

Hades sat unbothered, sipping out of a chalice. Persephone sat next to him, now changed and wearing a blue silk dress. Her curls were perfected, and her body was adorned with elaborate jewelry. She smugly smiled at Calypso as if to say, 'This is *my* throne.'

"Why the fuck am I here?" Calypso finally broke the silence. Her body trembled from anger and hatred.

"I thought we should honor this moment that the queen has fallen," Hades retorted. "I'm gracious enough to extend an invitation to your last supper. Besides that, I figured you would like to partake in our main course, seeing you were kind enough to bring her."

Calypso's eyes focused on the mass in front of her, and she nearly vomited again. The young girl she stole from Earth lay naked on the table. Her subcutaneous layer was cut from between her legs up to the middle of her chest. The skin and muscles of her stomach were peeled back with small forks stabbed into her vital organs. Her nipples were purple and swollen, matching the bruises encircling her neck and lips. Her eyelids were open and focused on Calypso, asking why she let this happen to her.

It was too much to view, and she turned away, crying silently.

"Don't feel guilty now. You are a murderous monster and brought this upon yourself." Persephone rose from her seat and floated across the floor, grabbing the girl's liver. She ate it slowly, making sure Calypso watched as she chewed.

"She was a fine specimen, a great choice. I have to admit, I rarely get a physical body to play with down here. They all appear as souls. I was sure to take my time with her, making sure she felt every inch of pain." Hades had never looked as evil as he did at that moment. His soulless eyes sparkled as he reveled in his latest kill.

Calypso thrashed against the chains and screamed. She tried to close off her mind, but Hades had already sent the gruesome images of him abusing the girl. She died only when her body gave up; she had been conscious of the rape until he sliced her open.

"Is that what you want to do to me? Kill me, then! Get it over with." Calypso's nails stabbed into the wooden arms of the chair.

"What would be the fun in that?" Hades flicked his hand in the air. "I have overcome the prophecy, defeated the Vampire Queen. If I kill you now, then all of these years waiting have been wasted."

"I don't understand."

"She really doesn't know," Persephone whispered to Hades. "Raphael must have not told her."

"That doesn't surprise me. He has fallen short of his duties to train her."

"Raphael," Calypso closed her eyes and imagined his face. He couldn't have lied to her. "He told me about the prophecy. He said you were told upon the creation of vampires that the first two would betray you. And that a king and queen would rise up to defeat them."

Both Hades and Persephone erupted into laughter. Their boisterous noise infuriated her even more.

"You stupid girl." Persephone sneered at her.

"Such a bold lie from the one who supposedly loved you." Hades said.

"He was trying to protect her, poor thing."

"He cannot stop fate."

"Tell me the truth," Calypso's voice cracked as she spoke.

"I created vampires against the opposition of many, on the claims that it was unnatural, going against our nature and human nature. The Fates tried to stop me with claims that my creation would overthrow me. Not only would my firstborns betray me, but the Queen of Vampires further down the line." Hades gestured with his hands as he spoke. Persephone stared at him intently.

"I paid the prophecy no mind until Raphael was crowned King. I never questioned his loyalty. He has always begged to be suckled to greatness. I knew his first queen was not the one. I knew before my blood poisoned her. You, however, have changed everything."

Hades paused to drink from his chalice and Calypso pulled against her chains. The smell of the rotting flesh before her made her nauseous.

"First, he kept you from me. He followed you for months before I caught on to him. He claimed he was studying you before bringing it to my attention, but we both knew the real reason. He knew you would be the one to betray me, to try to kill me and take my crown and the throne of Hell. I knew it when I entered your soul the first time when you were still a human."

Calypso stayed silent as she processed his words. It couldn't be true that Raphael lied to her, that he knew she would end up in chains or dead in Hell.

"I don't want to kill you, and I don't want to rule over Hell. Please, can't you let me go? I have shown my loyalty to you." She begged.

"When you turned your blood sacrifice, blasphemed my name, or when you shared blood with my wife?"

"She drank my blood first!" Calypso exclaimed and pressed against the chains.

"You lying bitch." Persephone twisted her lips and shook her head.

"You lied to me! Calling for help, just to have me enslaved."

"I think we've had enough fun here." Hades walked over to

Calypso's chair. He towered over her, and she scowled at him. She hated him with every fiber of her being. For every sweet word and image he had ever placed in her mind, it was all fake. He had played with her, waiting for this moment where she was enslaved.

"You can't keep me here forever! Raphael will never allow it."

"Your king has no say in the matter. Now, what shall we do with you?"

An elderly vampire stood behind her to gather the chains. He pulled her out of the chair and slammed her onto the ground. He forced his heel into her back, so she kneeled at Hades' feet.

"Take her back to isolation. I'll send in my demons to entertain her."

"You don't want to leave her out in the open, sir?"

"Not yet. I don't want anyone getting ideas of rescuing her. Besides, I have underestimated her powers before, which is not a mistake I will make again."

The chains pulled Calypso back up to standing, and she was dragged out of the room. She watched as Persephone sat in Hades' lap and gave her one last evil grin before the door slammed in her face.

She struggled against the chains and dug her heels into the ground to no avail.

"How does it feel to betray your own kind?" she yelled at the vampire ahead of her. He suddenly stopped, and she grinned. She had struck a nerve. He slammed her up against the wall and stared into her eyes.

"You are the one who has betrayed our kind. You were never meant to exist! I pleaded with Hades to forbid Raphael from bringing you here, but his will is my way. I will give my life to ensure you stay in these chains for all of eternity." His eyes almost popped out of his head with anger. Calypso spit in his face, and he smiled back at her, throwing her to the ground and continuing to drag her back to the dark hallway.

She was chained to the wall again, this time with her arms

held over her head. Before the door shut, she saw three demons slinking into the room. Darkness surrounded her, but she had no fear. Her hatred of Hades and now Raphael fueled her inner fire to keep burning.

*

Raphael awoke in the evening with a hole in his gut. He was still alone, so he prepared himself to visit Hell. He made sure he was dressed properly in a suit and found a random sucker in the city to sacrifice to Hades.

His victim was a man smoking a cigarette on their balcony, not too far from Raphael's penthouse. He quickly ripped his heart out and watched as the body somersaulted to the ground. Once it smacked against the pavement, he teleported to Hell.

Persephone sat alone on a throne, twirling her finger. Raphael was surprised to see her but didn't let it show. He extended his hand to reveal the bleeding heart, and she smiled at him.

"Hades will be most pleased with your offering."

"Ah, I see he has given your voice back," Raphael spoke curtly as he handed off the heart to a servant.

"He is generous to his most loyal, as you know." She slowly walked down the stairs, swaying her hips and batting her lashes at him.

"I believe you know why I am here."

"Hades!" Her voice echoed throughout the empty room. He entered the room shortly after, and she walked over to him, placing her hand on his shoulder, and leaned into his ear. "He has come to retrieve his pet."

Her words infuriated Raphael, but he kept calm and extended his hand toward Hades.

"Come with me," Hades motioned for him to follow. Their footsteps echoed in the unusually empty hallway. "You have been my most loyal servant for generations now. I've been pondering the definition of loyalty recently. To some people, it may be only having faith in their master, but you have far exceeded my expectations. No matter what I ask of you, you complete the task with no questions asked. I told you to offer a blood sacrifice to confirm your loyalty, and you gave me your entire family. I would have been happy with just one, but you kept giving. I know you, Raphael, and you would have kept giving until I commanded you to stop."

"I have always been loyal to you from the moment I was brought to Hell. Although I had not yet learned of your greatness, I bowed in awe of your presence."

"Indeed. But I want to ensure your loyalty does not falter during these trying times. That you will continue to give to me without your emotions getting in the way."

There was a moment of silence between them as Raphael feared his following words.

"You lied to her about the prophecy."

"I thought if she didn't know, then it would never happen. If she didn't know of betraying you, then it wouldn't be an option for her."

"Sweet boy." Hades kissed his forehead, bringing tears to Raphael's eyes. "You should know better than that. I knew love clouded your eyes, but you have been blinded."

"Please, Hades, I have done everything you have asked of me. You asked for a queen, and I brought her to you. I sacrificed her for you. She is the one thing that has made me feel joy again in this dark world."

"You knew this was the finality; don't be foolish. I haven't decided yet what will be done with her. But I am planning on keeping her around for the foreseeable future. I'll allow you to come and visit as long as it doesn't interfere with your duties."

Hades opened the door, and Raphael stifled a gasp when he saw Calypso chained to the wall. Her hair was disheveled, and her clothes were torn to shreds. She had a crazed look on her face, as she had been tormented by demons for hours.

They made her watch her parents' death over and over until she sobbed and begged for mercy. Then she was placed inside the car with them, her body crumpling as the car tumbled down a cliff. Although she was still chained to the wall, the pain was real. The demons made her relive every painful moment of her life. She was two years old, drowning in the ocean and unable to breathe. She was in a drug comatose, unable to move and suffering in her mind. Lastly, she was being drained by Raphael on the beach.

"Calypso?" Raphael kneeled down a few feet away from her. Hades stood in the hallway to give them space but still eavesdropped on their conversation.

Her eyes blinked rapidly, and the cloudiness disappeared. She lunged at him, but the chains held her back.

"Why are you here? To make sure your sacrifice is safe?"

"Mon chérie." He struggled to speak without crying. "I never meant for this to happen to you."

"Bullshit! You knew this was going to happen! You knew, and you still turned me." Calypso sobbed; she hated him but wanted nothing more than to be in his arms again.

"I had no choice. I told you not to come here," he whispered, reaching out to touch her cheek. She let him wipe away her tears.

"This would have happened eventually, right? We would have only been prolonging the inevitable."

"I'm going to get you out of here. I'll find a way."

"Stop lying to me!" Calypso yelled. "There is no way out of this! What are you going to do, exchange your soul for mine? He doesn't want it; he's coveted me since the prophecy was born. Get out of here!"

Raphael stood and left hesitantly. She was right; there was no way out of this. He took a final look as she kicked her legs and screamed wildly before the door closed.

"She'll come around eventually; they always do," Hades spoke, but Raphael rushed past him. If he stayed any longer, he may take his anger out on him, which was forbidden. Raphael ran past the lingering souls in the hallway and threw open the castle doors.

He stepped down the stairs, and Cerberus, the three-headed monster, growled at him. The beast did its job well, not allowing anyone to enter or leave the castle. However, Hades had given Raphael special privileges to wander through the lands of Hell, and the beast respected that.

Raphael followed a narrow path away from the castle, which was not covered in hellfire. He walked for miles until he reached the Forest of Dread. Here, souls were trapped in the torment of their own making. Destined to repeat their worst moments for eternity, with guilt eating away at their bones.

The hellfire ended at the beginning of the charred trees. The forest was sparse, with little more than the occasional black tree and a few rocks, but mostly moaning souls.

Raphael ignored their cries for help. They had fated their souls by the decisions they made during their lifetime.

The forest became more thin as he entered the next layer of Hell. This landscape was dark and eerie. Large vultures swarmed the sky, which was a deep red hue from the nearby hellfire. The smell of putrid burning flesh tingled Raphael's nose, but he continued.

He found the man lying in a ditch, letting a vulture feed on his flesh. His skin was mostly boils, filled with pus, from the constant eating and regrowing.

"Do you ever learn, old man?" Raphael grabbed the man by his bare shoulders and slung him onto the ground.

The bird flew away with a loud caw.

The man tried to laugh, but it came out as a pained cough. He attempted to stand but was thrown to the ground again by Raphael. Upon a second attempt, he was met by a blow to his ribs, shattering them and puncturing his lungs. As he rolled on the ground, gripping his side in pain, he bared a toothy grin.

"It's been too long, son. I haven't seen you in hundreds of years; I almost thought you forgot about me."

Raphael screamed and kicked his jaw. His head turned

sideways, but sure enough, his body regenerated itself, which was equally painful as the beating.

"You must be real mad about somethin'. Usually, you don't get right to the point," he spat out a mouthful of blood and a few teeth.

"This is your fault!" Raphael screamed as he rammed his foot into his chest, sending him flying into the air and landing with a harsh thud.

"You turned me into a monster! I hated you so much that I sacrificed my soul to the devil! So that I could kill you and ensure your eternal suffering. Now he has the love of my life, the woman who was made for me." Tears streamed down his face, covered in dirt from their tussle. He lunged at his father again, choking him until his eyes began to bleed.

"Enough!" A voice so clear rang through the air. Raphael stopped immediately and slowly got off of his father. No, it couldn't be her; she didn't belong here.

He turned around slowly, then dropped to his knees and wept when he saw his mother. She was as pale and beautiful as the day he drained her body. Two fang marks still resided on the side of her neck.

"No, my angel, why are you here?" Raphael continued to weep as he took her hands into his and adorned them with kisses. He had never seen her soul in Hell, attributing it to her resting peacefully in the Elysian Fields.

"You blame your father for your hatred, but it is I who is to blame."

"No, you were always so kind and loving to us. He yelled at you, hit you; how can you defend him?"

"Raphael, my sweet boy. Your father was harsh with us because I bore you out of wedlock."

Raphael dropped her hands and stared at her fiercely. He turned to stare at the man who raised him, but he avoided eye contact.

"How could you keep this from me?"

"I was ashamed." His mother wiped away a tear with the sleeve of her stained white dress. "Ashamed of myself, not of you. Your father, my husband, agreed to take me back if we never spoke of it again. He had resentment in his heart toward me and to you, but he gave us a home! If he hadn't taken me back, I would have been alone with nobody to turn to. We would have died in the streets."

"I would have rather died in your womb than grow under his daily torment," Raphael spoke between gritted teeth. The tears continued to flow, and his mother held him close to her thighs.

"This is why I am here. I broke my vows to him, which caused hatred in your heart. My sweet boy, oh, the terror you have caused. But I still love you."

Raphael felt her begin to fade away, as all souls do eventually. He hated that she stayed with him after all these years. She should be resting peacefully in a field of flowers with the sun on her skin. Instead, she was paying the price, which was dealt to her from her own guilty conscience.

Once he was alone, he dried his tears and headed back toward Hades' castle. He could only teleport out of Hell from the structure. He stormed up the stairs with a fire burning in his heart. He was bloodthirsty and ready to kill.

Chapter 18

Justin and Ayai lounged across a couch together as they drank wine and watched television. They both used alcohol to curb their cravings for blood. Ayai had control over herself but drank in solidarity with Justin.

After being entrapped in Hell, she decided to move them to a more comfortable area. They had fled from cave to cave since she was paired with Justin. She figured they would die any day now, so they might as well be comfortable and provide Justin with a human experience.

Ayai found a modern house in the middle of Joshua Tree, California. It was built in a desolate area with only a gravel path leading to and from the main road. She had scoped out the area from above to see that one man was the house's sole occupant. She convinced him to rent the house to them indefinitely as long as he kept any other humans away. He had no choice since she used her mind-changing abilities, and he abandoned his rental property the same night.

Though it was secluded, they were still cautious about living in the house. Every morning, they walked toward the mountains and buried themselves feet below the sand. In the evening, they would dig themselves out of their graves and walk back to the house, checking the surroundings to make sure no humans, vampires, or other entities occupied the space.

Ayai laughed at a cartoon commercial on the television, and Justin smiled at her. She enjoyed watching anything they could find, as it took her away from the ever-present fear of death.

"I haven't heard from Raphael in a few days." She stretched her feet out and lay them across Justin's thighs. He put his empty glass down on the coffee table and rubbed his thumb absentmindedly against her shin. Their intimacy was friendly as they both held lingering feelings for their former loves.

"I didn't know you still talked to him."

"Our capture had nothing to do with him. He checks in

with me every few days to make sure we are both safe."

"I'm sure he does." Justin was jealous of the blood-mind connection Ayai and Raphael shared. He hated being kept out of her mind.

Ayai, not sensing his emotions, laid her head back and closed her eyes as she called out to him. As usual, for the past week, there was no response. She was worried but refused to let her anxieties transfer to Justin.

His hand reached her inner thigh, and they made eye contact before a loud noise made them jump. A shattering sound came from outside, which put them both on edge, hairs raised and fangs bared, ready to fight.

The front door opened slowly, and their eyes widened as Raphael bowed his head and stepped through the doorway.

"My apologies. I hope that plant wasn't of much significance to you." He shuffled his feet and slicked his hair back awkwardly. He was met with blank stares.

"Raphael, what are you doing here?" Ayai asked gently. Justin glared at him as he squirmed, which he enjoyed watching.

"It's been a while; I figured I should check on both of you. Especially after everything that happened. It looks as if you've made the place cozy." He examined the immediate surroundings of red-stained wine glasses, blankets strewn on the ground, and the light buzz of television in the background. He sensed Ayai's calmness in the human comforts, which he was never able to provide for her, though he wished he could have.

"You mean after we were dragged down to Hell and tortured? Oh yeah, we are doing just great. Ayai thinks any night could be our last, so we might as well slow down and enjoy ourselves instead of living on the run. What about Callie? She didn't care enough to come check on us?" Justin scoffed. He finished his glass of wine and slammed it too hard on the coffee table, breaking the stem.

Raphael's face twitched at her name and he clenched his fists together, imagining her in chains.

"We both apologize for what happened and are extremely grateful you both escaped with relatively no harm. That is also why I wanted to come and talk to you face to face. Calypso...She isn't in the picture anymore."

"Seriously? You up and leave her after everything? Or did she make a fool of you this time?"

"They would never abandon each other," Ayai whispered, placing her hand on Justin's knee, trying to calm him. "Raphael, what happened?"

"Hades has her." He could barely muster the strength to speak, as if speaking it out loud would concrete its reality.

"What do you mean he has her?" Justin gritted his teeth and curled his hands into fists.

"She was captured by him. He promised to keep her alive."

"Is this about the prophecy?" Ayai asked with tears in her eyes. Raphael's forlorn head shot up and he made eye contact with her. His eyes begged the question, how do you know?

"What prophecy? Someone, tell me what is happening!" Justin yelled.

"When Hades created the vampire race, it came at a price. The three Fates prophesied that through the lineage of vampires, a male would become the king and a female the queen. These two would have a purpose to Hades, but ultimately, the queen would betray and kill him, ruling over Hell." Raphael exhaled, wondering if he could have spared Calypso's life by truthfully telling her the prophecy.

"You knew this would happen? That she was going to be trapped in Hell forever?" Tears broke through Justin's eyes as he attempted to jump Raphael. Ayai was quick to her feet and braced herself against him, holding him back.

"So that's it? You're just going to leave her there to rot? Who knows what he'll do to her! You liar, you bastard! You knew this would happen, and you let it happen! You never loved her!" Justin screamed and his words reverbed off of the wooden walls.

"Justin, please," Ayai sobbed. Emotions poured out of her

body as she felt for Calypso, Raphael, and herself. She would have been trapped by Hades if she had become the queen.

"I cannot change fate's course. All I can do is check on her and keep on Hades' good side. I didn't come here to cause distress; I just thought you should know." Raphael exited the house and disappeared into the night. Justin crumpled into a ball on the floor and pounded his fists.

"It's not fair," he spoke after crying for a long while. Ayai rubbed his back and nodded in agreement. "I never got to say goodbye; I never forgave her."

"Nobody is ever ready to say goodbye."

*

Calypso should have died from the lack of blood. She was unable to count how many days had passed since she was taken prisoner. The hunchback servant would crack the door occasionally and throw her a rat, which she would gladly feast on. She guessed she was fed daily or every few days. Based on the slowly growing pile of rotting flesh and bones, she had been fed for twenty-seven days, or possibly more.

Every moment, the demons tortured her. She relived her entire life in mere seconds, with the demons adding terrible horror to her memories. Even the most innocent memory of her mother's face was tainted with melting flesh and blood. She tried to close her eyes, but the images were etched in her mind. When her consciousness was exhausted and near sleep, they would begin the physical torture.

Vampires came in for this as the demons were not strong enough to inflict anything more than mental and emotional pain. A few elderly bloodsuckers were more than happy to bind Calypso with red hot metal. Her screams echoed throughout the entire castle as they brutally beat her, waited for her body to regenerate, and then attacked again.

Persephone was fed up by the torture. No room was silent from the prisoner's screams, and she hated it. Not even her chamber, the furthest corner away from Calypso, was safe.

Usually, torture would occur in the layers of Hell outside of the castle. Hades wanted to keep her close to make sure she wouldn't escape. Though in unbreakable chains, he did not trust her.

After hearing the screams for weeks, Persephone had enough. She dropped her fork during dinner as a shrill scream pierced her ears. The fork clanged against the ivory plates, making an equally loud and annoying sound. Hades had his eyes closed, and a smug smile hinted at the corner of his lips as he relished in his prisoner's pain.

"Are you ever going to do something with her?" Persephone huffed, clearly annoyed.

"What is the rush?"

"The rush is that I've had enough of listening to her wails! I can't even sleep in peace. She has tarnished my own chambers." Persephone glared at him as he chuckled in amusement. He rested his feet upon the golden feasting table.

"Shall I take her tongue? That would quiet her, don't you think?"

"I think you shall decide what you are doing with her. People might think that keeping her prisoner is a sign of weakness." Persephone cut a fig while she glanced at Hades, watching his nostrils flare.

"Who has mentioned weakness, or is this of your own accord?" Hades repositioned himself to sitting and glowered over her.

"Oh no, you are wise for keeping her here rather than entrusting anyone in Hell. However, I have heard the chatter of others as I pass by, wondering if anything will ever become of her. Or if you are too afraid to kill her."

Hades slammed a knife into the table, and Persephone pretended to flinch. His emotional overreactions were too easy to play with.

"I have trapped her, and she has given me no reason to kill her, so why shall I take her life?"

"Of course, you have always been fair, even to your most

unloyal subjects. Perhaps I can help; we can find a purpose for her together."

"How would you help?" Hades laughed.

"I could talk to her. Explain the gravity of the situation. She could have a change of heart. Of course, I would never trust her, but maybe someday she could serve a purpose in Hell. Enchained and under supervision, she would at least contribute something besides echoes in the walls."

Hades sat back to ponder while Persephone continued to eat slowly. She had to act mildly disinterested, or he would become suspicious. He finished his glass of wine before he slowly rose from the table.

"I'll grant you this. But you must have a guard with you at all times."

Persephone nodded in gratitude as he left the dining hall. She exhaled loudly once he had left earshot, as she had not expected him to grant her request. She had been nothing but perfect since returning from her own prison, but she knew he would always distrust her.

After finishing her meal, she made her way to the sinister section of the castle, filled with screams and torture. Calypso's room was evident as the vampires terrorizing her left the door cracked. The smell of blood and other bodily fluids made the hallway reek, and the loud thumping of the beating made Persephone hesitate at the door. She had never experienced such a brutal punishment from Hades, nor had she witnessed many to this length and degree.

Three large vampires surrounded Calypso in a circle. She lay against a wall, barely conscious or alive from the looks of it. She wore a thin white robe, now completely stained in blood. Large gashes oozed across her forehead and whatever skin was visible. One of the vampires murmured something. Persephone did not hear as she was too horrified at Calypso's appearance, but she managed to smile and spit blood in his face in return.

The vampire tugged down his pants and approached her

roughly, Calypso's head bobbing to the side as he straddled her. He raised his arm to smack her, but Persephone cried out.

"Enough!" Her anger echoed through the chamber, and he stopped immediately. "Hades requested only mental and physical torture. He disapproves of your actions."

"Who are you to say what I can do to a prisoner?" He scowled at her in response.

She swiped her arm at him, and his head fell off. His decapitated body crumpled against the floor, and the remaining two vampires jumped back in alarm.

"I am the wife of Hades. You all seem to have forgotten my place and my powers. What I speak comes from the mouth of your master. You, bring his body to Hades and explain what happened." The older vampire quickly collected the body and rushed out of the room with the taller vampire trailing behind. She tapped his shoulder before he exited the room.

"Give her your blood."

"I'm not doing that."

"That is an order! Hades granted me a conversation with this prisoner. She is too beat up to move, let alone hold a coherent conversation. Feed her so she will heal quickly."

The vampire was not happy, as he was given explicit orders from Hades that no blood should be shared with Calypso. Persephone was in a murderous mood, so he knelt by Calypso and let her drink from his wrist.

"Anything else, m'lady?" he mocked her. She glared at him and nodded her head.

"Hades has requested for a guard to accompany me. Remove her chains from the wall. You will lead; we will follow behind."

This order he took with no hesitation and yanked the metal out of the wall. He dragged Calypso to her feet, who was already starting to heal. She was slow to walk and kept her head downcast.

"I figured you would be more grateful to be out of your

chambers," Persephone began.

"Oh, I am ebullient for your mercy. Thank you so much for sparing my life. I prayed their beating would finally put me out of my misery." Calypso's voice was hoarse, her trachea still healing from being choked.

"I'd hope so, too. I cannot hear your screams of terror any longer. Your presence has leaked into the entire castle."

"You can take that up with him. I did nothing wrong, yet I rarely receive a break from the mental and physical punishments."

The vampire leading pulled hard on the chains, and she flew forward, scraping her knees in the process. Persephone immediately grabbed the back of his hair and yanked him into submission.

"You are here to protect me, not listen to our conversation. Now shall I tell your master that you have disobeyed me like the other?"

The vampire shook his head and Persephone released her grip on him. Calypso stayed silent as they continued to walk through the hallway. The sounds of her chains dragging against the stone floor deafened her, a constant reminder that she was a prisoner.

Persephone led them to a bench seated in between a view of the hellfire and near the Elysian Fields. As Persephone sat on the bench, Calypso dropped to her knees and held her arms against the bench in a prayer position. She began to mutter in desperation, and Persephone leaned forward to make out her words.

"Why is light given to those in misery and life to the bitter of soul? To those who long for death that does not come, who search for it more than for hidden treasure?

"Sighing has become my daily food; my groans pour out like water. What I feared has come upon me; what I dreaded has happened to me. I have no peace, no quietness, I have no rest, but only turmoil."

"Repeating Job in Hell, quite ironic. I never took you for the religious type."

"I never was, but since I have been trapped here, every word of death has deafened my mind. Why must God let me suffer any longer? I have been punished for my misdoings long enough." Calypso sounded defeated, her voice weak, and her body trembled.

Persephone hesitated but leaned toward her to speak. "I know it won't bring you any comfort, but it's all a lie. Religion, Christianity, and the Bible were all made up by Zeus. He thought creating a grand book with rules and morality would help calm the human race of all their strife. To his dismay, he only created more problems. After that, we all took an oath never to infiltrate the humans again. Their issues would be theirs and not our own."

Calypso wanted to cry from the new knowledge but had no energy to weep. Instead, her body rolled into a long and painful laugh. Of course, everything she had ever known was a complete and utter lie.

"Well," she said finally. "My mother would have been very disappointed to find out Jesus Christ was none other than the God of lightning."

Persephone chuckled and motioned for her to sit on the bench next to her. The vampire stiffened but did not move.

"I will hold her chains. Stand over there. Keep watch on the hall, and make sure it remains empty."

He begrudgingly handed over the chains and stepped a few feet away, still close enough to jump into action if needed.

"Tell me about your mother."

"Why? It doesn't matter. Nothing matters anymore," Calypso whispered.

"Tell me about her; it will bring you some peace. She was religious?"

Calypso moved to sit on the bench but kept her distance from Persephone. "My mother's religion was based on a single act, so I wouldn't consider it undying faith. Growing up, I thought it would be enough to get her into heaven, but why would she need to roll off a mountain to go to heaven?"

She paused; the heaviness and sadness in her voice returned. "She and my father struggled with infertility for years. I was told they had given up and decided to take a vacation to get away from it all. They were on some exotic island; I never really listened to this story. My mother said that she was in the ocean, floating and crying to God about her childlessness. She had always wanted to be a mother and felt robbed of such a beautiful experience. She told me in that moment, she felt God come over her; she had never felt such euphoria or peace before. They came back from vacation, and she was pregnant. It was a miracle to them, and she dedicated every Sunday to God after that. Of course, I was dragged along as a child and was always told that I was a blessing from God. Now I know that couldn't be further from the truth."

Persephone looked away towards the hellfire as she processed Calypso's story. She touched her shoulder softly and briefly. "I know what it is like to lose a mother."

"Why, because you are trapped in Hell while she gets to frolic on Mount Olympus?"

"My mother is dead." Persephone's eyes darkened, hurt by Calypso's casual words. The hellfire seemed to crackle louder in her ears.

"Demeter? I'm sorry, I didn't know."

"You know, I have never seen her soul. When I was first informed of her untimely demise, I never left the Elysian Fields. I called out to her for months, begging her to reveal herself to me." Persephone's eyes clouded over as she relived every painful moment of crying out to Demeter with no avail.

"Why would your mother ignore you? I'm sure mine would, though. She wouldn't want to see me as a monster."

"Everyone else would say she is ashamed to look at me after killing herself. But I know the truth. Our mothers are the same, ashamed of the monster we have become."

Calypso hung her head in silence, trying not to let the overwhelming memories of her killings take over her mind.

"Regardless of that, you will never recover from the grief."

"That's what I thought for the longest. But now, I am happy she is dead. She will never know what I have become." Calypso picked at her skin as she spoke.

"Don't say that," Persephone said sternly. "You are a beautiful woman with amazing powers and gifts."

"Ah, yes, how could I forget? I can fly, run, and jump higher than any human. I can not only read minds but alter their thoughts. My incredible strength only comes at the price of murdering humans and feasting on their blood, never to touch the sunlight again, or I would burn to death, as I should be."

"All that may be true, but you were tricked into becoming a vampire."

"How was I tricked? I begged Raphael!" Calypso exclaimed. The guard threatened to move closer, but Persephone's glare kept him at bay.

"He manipulated you; he used your love for him to sacrifice your soul. If you truly knew this would be the end, would you have ever said yes? No, you would have kept your so-called boring life with Justin. You would have worked until you were old, had a few kids, and maintained your home." Persephone looked into her eyes deeply and it made Calypso almost want to believe her.

"Do you believe in destiny?"

"I believe in fate; I suppose destiny is just another term."

"Well, I know this was my fate. No matter what could have happened with Justin or even Raphael, I was always meant to end up here in Hell." Calypso shifted uneasily on the cold stone.

"Why do you say that?"

"After my parents died, I was lost. Physically, I moved from my hometown to live with a total stranger. I don't know how current you are with human relations, but moving to a new high school in the middle of the year is brutal. I remember it was my sixteenth birthday, just a few months after they had died. I was at a park in central Florida with a group of guys. I didn't like them, but they were generous with drugs, so I took advantage. I was so fucked up I stumbled over gnarly blackened tree roots. I tripped and cut my knees open, so I stopped along the river to wash them. As I was kneeling over and washing my wounds, the water turned red. Not like a red tint, the entire stream was the color of blood. I moved closer to look because I couldn't believe it. As I made out my reflection, I saw devil horns behind my head."

Calypso took a deep, shaky breath while Persephone pondered her story.

"You said you were on drugs?"

"I was drunk, but I know what I saw. I screamed and sobbed but the boys, they didn't see anything! They told me I was crazy and left me there by the river. I had to call Justin to come pick me up. His mom drove over an hour to get me and after that, I pushed the memory to the back of my mind. I've never told anyone else about it."

"If you believe your destiny is to be here, then you should claim it. Make something useful of your time."

"My destiny is being trapped in Hell. I do not claim it, though. Of course, you could say that with your jewels and robes. I've been robbed of everything I have, of everything I have ever loved!" Calypso's voice cracked, and she clenched her fists.

"Do you see this," Persephone motioned to the Elysian Fields. Calypso sat motionless in response. "There are millions of souls trapped inside this portal. It doesn't sound like heaven now, does it? Yet the souls are filled with eudaimonia; they are at peace. If you were to try to interact with one and explain the gravity of their entrapment, you would shatter their entire worldview. Of course, some know it, but they choose to believe that this is their home. A final resting place where their soul can finally be free, in their entrapment."

"What are you saying?" Calypso asked.

"Although you are trapped here, you are free. You no

longer have to serve as a vampire. No killing, mutilating, or drinking blood. Perhaps this time in solitude can ignite your powers and passion for what is beneficial to you."

"Even if I had something to offer to Hell, which I don't, Hades would never let me. All because of that damn prophecy, he will never cease my torture. I hate him! I made a few mistakes with him, but for him to be so cruel..."

"Enough. I will not listen to your slander." Persephone curtly ended the conversation and turned away from her. Loud laughter broke out at the end of the hallway, and she motioned for the guard to investigate. He scowled at her but turned away from them.

"Although he is my captor, he is still my husband. I loathe his anger and envy his powers, yet I still love him. I must love him; if not, I would rot away here." Persephone's voice was stern as she revealed her truth.

"Why are you still here? Can't you leave for a few months?"

Persephone laughed and shook her head. "Ah, the old wives tale. At one point, it was true. But I no longer have a reason to return to Earth. Every visit was so painful, as I knew I would return to darkness. The worst part was that my soul ached for him; I wish I could cut it out of my body."

"But why don't you hate him? He stole you from your family, trapped you here, and ripped out your tongue! You were trapped in a box for hundreds of years but still love him?" Calypso became frantic, her nails digging into her palms with rage.

"You don't understand, you foolish girl," Persephone spoke quietly, shaking her head at her innocence. "Of course, I was enraged at first; I hated the mere sight of him. But do you see where that anger got me? Trapped and alone. My love for him was blinded by my emotions. I must keep them at bay, as you must. Perhaps if you respect and admire him, he will treat you well."

"Why? He's ruined my life!" The chains loudly scraped against the ground as Persephone grabbed her chin, forcing their eyes to meet.

"You know nothing of ruin. Hades stole me from my one true love. He posed as Apollo, waiting to take me on a sunrise chariot ride. Only by the time I saw his face, it was too late. He dragged me to Hell, a pain you are most familiar with. He granted me my return but at a price. He begged me to eat something, for I was so weak running about the castle, trying to escape. Only when I returned to Earth, shackled by physical illness, did I realize that he had bound me to him. His blood was in the pomegranate; I bound myself to him for eternity." Persephone's grip grew tighter around her chin as she spoke more fervently.

"I could only visit for weeks at a time; seeing my mother sob uncontrollably and seeing Apollo, who I could never be with, shattered me. After years of trying to exist somewhere I couldn't, I gave up. I gave into him; I let him clothe me in jewels, bathe me in gems and perfumes. Eventually, Demeter killed herself out of sorrow, but I know it was him. I know he killed my mother, yet I still bed him every night. I please him, as is my wifely duty.

"Do you see now what you must do? You must forget about your anger and forget about your past. Otherwise, you will torment yourself as much as the demons who abuse you."

Calypso's mouth dropped open, and she shrugged herself out of the Goddess's grip. "He killed your mother, and you still choose to love him?"

"He did not kill her but was complicit in her murder. It doesn't matter now; all that matters is that you control your hatred and emotions and find your place in eternal suffering."

"Why did you bring me here? All you have done is tell me to accept the destiny of slavery and to love my master!" Calypso spoke frantically, her body tingling with anxiety. Every atom felt like it exploded inside of her.

"I'm telling you to escape your mental shackles. Calypso, you are here for eternity. You can spend it repeatedly being abused, or you can make something of yourself, even as a chained servant."

"Eternity." The word rolled off of Calypso's tongue slowly.

Her mind had never fully accepted the severity of the word. Even as a vampire, she had no concept of infinite time. To imagine being trapped in Hell forever, never to see Raphael again, was more than heartbreaking.

Adrenaline raced through her body as she became furious with Hades. Having no one to direct her anger to, she lunged at Persephone. She fell backward, and the tension on the chains snapped them, freeing Calypso's arms.

Persephone smacked against the floor. Her eyes widened as the crazed beast jumped onto her. Her head cracked against the stone wall, making her pass out immediately.

Calypso sank her fangs into her neck, slurping greedily. She pulled away momentarily to judge her incoming enemy. She took another deep drink before turning to slam the guard against the ground. He jumped back up immediately, but Calypso was too powerful.

Fueled by the blood of a God, she thrust her hand into his ribs and ripped out his heart while he rushed toward her. His body froze and crumpled immediately. By now, she knew she had little time left, so she would have to act quickly.

She grabbed Persephone by the wrist and dragged her limp body toward the Elysian Fields. She hoisted her body up and began to force her head toward the portal. Calypso felt the air shift as it began to open up, accepting the particles of the body. Persephone regained consciousness as the portal began to suck her in, and she gripped Calypso tightly.

Hades appeared behind the combat and yanked Calypso by her hair. She was dragged off of the ground and released Persephone as she screamed in pain. Persephone crumbled to the ground, holding a hand to her still bleeding neck.

Hades slammed Calypso into the wall, destroying her face. His whole body heaved with anger as he quickly raced down the hallway.

Calypso did everything in her power to release his grip, but she was no match. Persephone caught up and grabbed his arm, trying to stop him.

"Please," she cried, "This was my fault!"

"She tried to kill you!" His voice shook the castle walls. "If I had been a few seconds late, I would have lost you. No, this has gone on long enough."

Hades continued into a quiet, relatively unused section of the castle. He hadn't stepped foot into this area in thousands of years, which terrified Persephone.

"Hades, please, I'm begging you! You swore you would never do this again." She pulled against his arm desperately as he kicked open a creaking wooden door. The room was pitch black and musty. The smell of fear and decay lingered from the last victim; Pirithous's skeleton lay strewn across the ground.

"I will repeat what I told you last time." Hades thrust Calypso into a large black chair made out of stone. She struggled against him as he held her down.

"Anyone who threatens to take you away will be met with this fate." Tears poured out of Persephone's eyes as the rocks attached themselves to Calypso's body. Tiny golden serpents slithered through the cracks and wound around her ankles and wrists. The snakes continued to coil until they covered almost every inch of her body.

Calypso's screams ended abruptly as her head fell to her chest. Her brain and body fought as hard as they could until the spell overtook them. Every memory, thought, and image in her brain was erased. Her consciousness became nothing more than a barren desert.

Hades watched as her soul left her body, then turned toward his wife. She stepped away from him, betrayed by his unjustified actions. He pressed her into the wall, holding her hips and breathing in her scent.

"I can never lose you; just the thought of it frightens me to death," he whispered into her ear. She tried to squirm away, but his tight grip and the smell of seduction and cedarwood kept her glued to him.

He kissed her neck, where her wound slowly healed. He sucked at the remainder of the drying blood, a true delicacy for him, and she arched her back in response. He rubbed his thumbs over her tightly stretched dress, erecting her nipples. She finally gave in, opening her chest and legs to receive him.

"You always protect and love me, even when I don't understand," she whispered into his lips.

"Enough talk; I can't control myself around you any longer. Although we've done this in the open plenty of times, I want you to myself tonight." Hades cradled Persephone in his arms and led her away to his chambers.

She nuzzled herself into his shoulder, catching one last look at the stupefied vampire. She would rot away, never to be remembered more than a bad dream. Along with it were Persephone's dreams of the prophecy being fulfilled.

Chapter 19

Hades was abruptly awoken by one sharp knock on his chamber's door. He scowled in response but assumed it was urgent; otherwise, the messenger would face instant death. His servants understood the rules perfectly: Do not bother in private quarters unless it is a truly urgent matter. One knock suffices, and you will wait for a response.

He grabbed his slacks from the ground and stepped into them. Before exiting the room, he caressed Persephone's cheek and tucked the heavy duvet around her body. She was a beautiful, perfect angel in a deep sleep after his aggressive and passionate lovemaking.

Judas Iscariot awaited him in the hallway, his chronically shaggy hair falling over his eyes. He opened his mouth to explain himself but was cut off by a distant female cry. Hades' eyes blazed with fury in response.

"I stood watch at the door as you instructed me, Master. No soul dared to enter the hall. I must have stood there for a few hours before I began to hear a strange noise. It piqued my interest, yes quite so, yet I never opened the door for fear it was a trick! Soon enough, the gurgling sound turned into moaning and then into the screaming you now hear. I was fearful to leave guard, but I wouldn't trust anyone else with the duty you lay upon me. I knew you would be interested in this development."

Hades nodded in response to Judas's soliloquy and started down the hallway.

"Good work, Judas."

Judas hid his smile. Recognition from his master was rare, though he had been a loyal companion for thousands of years. Jesus Christ, played in part by Zeus, struck him down and sent him to Hell immediately after his betrayal. He demanded Hades give him a suitable eternal punishment for his actions. Hades determined he would be an excellent addition to his council.

Hades reached the opposite end of the castle in no time,

with Judas trailing behind him. His fury was evident in his throbbing temple and clenched fists. He threw open the door, which cracked against the wall.

A faint light from the hall illuminated the bleak room and shone on the quivering woman. She winced in response to the light and continued to tug her arms against the barriers. Her wrists were grotesquely destroyed as she had removed multiple layers of skin trying to escape. Her legs were in equally fair shape, with blood dripping down to her feet.

"Please, help me," her voice was so timid the words barely escaped her lips. Hades towered before her, inciting a deep fear inside her soul. He stood motionless, examining her tattered state.

"I, I don't know who I am," she continued. "I don't know where I am or why I am trapped here!"

"You have no recollection of your past?" Hades asked in a monotone voice.

"No, I try so hard, but my mind is blank. I have shooting pain if I try too hard."

"What is your name?"

"I don't know!" she cried out. "I don't know." She repeated the phrase louder and louder until she broke out into a deep sob. Hades squatted down to her level. He wiped one of her tears, and she made eye contact with him.

Her eyes glazed over as she became lost in his irises. He searched her soul and found total emptiness, no subconscious thoughts of vampires or even her human past.

"Remarkable," he whispered, his thumb lingering on her cheek. "You have no memory, yet you remember how to talk and breathe."

Calypso struggled against the chains again, and Hades moved to take them off.

"Sir," Judas warned from the doorway.

"Do you know who I am?" Hades asked as he began to break the golden snakes woven around her legs.

"No, sir," she responded. "You must be powerful, but I do not know you. Have we met before?"

"How do you know that?"

"You have an air about you, one that demands respect. Your stance is large and muscular; you must be some sort of king."

"My name is Hades. What does that mean to you?"

"I, I don't know," Calypso whined in frustration. "All I know is that you, Hades, have saved me, and I am eternally grateful."

Hades finished ripping the chains off of her hands, and once she was free, Calypso sank back into the chair. Hades stood back and waited for her to make a move. She squished her face in concentration, but her body made no movement.

"Get up and walk," he commanded.

Calypso sat motionless while her arms lay folded around her waist. "I don't know how to."

"Judas." He entered the room and scooped her into his arms, his face of disgust in plain view. Calypso began to cry again as he led her out into the hallway, following behind Hades.

It was a time of rest in the castle, with few demons, vampires, and servants wandering the halls. The few who were aroused quickly pressed themselves against the walls as the group passed. They all had looks of fear and dismay painted across their faces.

They entered the chamber where Calypso was previously held. The stench of blood and vomit filled the room and made her gag in response. Judas placed her on the ground, and she sank against the wall as if she had no bones.

"Hades, don't leave me, please!" she cried out as he turned away from the door.

"Your name is Calypso," He responded as he slammed and locked the door.

*

A few weeks passed, and Calypso's body began to

desiccate. She could not move and hardly had any thoughts. She could only stare into the darkness and remember her name and Hades. She repeated them constantly, trying to bring up a memory, but nothing came. Eventually, she heard footsteps outside of her chamber and sighed in relief. She sat up straighter as Hades and an old man entered the room.

"Hades, thank God you are here! You have to help me!"

He folded his hands in front of him while the smaller man peered around his tall frame. He wore broken glasses and had a crazed look in his eyes.

"We are here to help you, to give you a purpose." A smile toyed at the edges of his lips.

"Oh, thank you. I cannot be thankful enough! Thank you for giving me another chance. I know I did something to wrong you or someone else, but I can't remember. I will do anything you ask of me, I swear, please."

The man stepped closer to her shriveled body, and she winced in response. She was fearful of the new person, but Hades' presence reassured her. He drew a test tube from behind his back, filled with a black, sluggish liquid.

"Drink, my darling, and everything will go away," the man croaked.

Hades grabbed the vial and pushed him aside. He bent next to Calypso, and she stared eagerly at her hero.

"Don't be scared," he whispered to her. "You'll do anything for me, remember?"

"Yes, I'll do anything for you," she repeated. She opened her mouth, and Hades emptied the vial into her throat. He jumped back as he knew her body would twist and writhe in pain.

Liquid fire shot through her body, similar to when she became a vampire, not that she could remember. Her arms and legs convulsed, and her pupils rolled back into her head, leaving only her sclera visible. After a few minutes of thrashing, her body came to an abrupt halt. She gasped as her back arched, and she rose to a sitting position.

Calypso blinked rapidly as her vision returned to normal. Her thin and bloody body was already filling into a more voluptuous figure. Hades and the strange man grinned down at her, and she smiled in response.

"I feel so much better; how can I ever repay you?"

She slunk onto the ground and wrapped her body around Hades' legs, hugging herself closely to his groin.

"Follow me," Hades ignored her and turned away. "We will get you settled into your new environment."

Hades led down the hallway, with Calypso skipping and giggling behind him. The man followed closely behind, observing his specimen carefully. She ripped off her stained and tattered clothes, exposing her naked body. She tossed her hair over her shoulder and winked at the man who stared at her.

"I would say the potion has worked, but there is only one way to confirm." He licked his lips as Hades paused to unlock two heavy golden doors. They creaked open and revealed a large furnished room.

Dozens of women and a few men hid in the shadows as Hades entered the room. They had existed long enough to know the rules: stay away unless you are called forward. A few had previously rushed toward their master and were met with immediate death.

Calypso examined the room in front of her. Elegant cloth couches lined the room, and white marble covered the ground. Chains, ropes, multiple types of sticks, and flogging equipment hung along the walls. She turned back toward Hades, unimpressed with the room, and her eyes begged for attention.

"Melvin, thank you for your work. You are no longer needed." The man paused before exiting the room, mumbling crazed rantings down the hallway.

"Finally, just the two of us," Calypso grabbed his hands. "What about them?" She glared at the eyes that stared back at her.

"Play nice; these are your succubus brothers and sisters. They will make you feel welcome here."

"I want you, not them!"

"You will have me, but you will also receive anyone else who comes in here to request you. Do you understand?"

"Yes, anything you say."

"Very good, now; show me how grateful you are." He barely finished his sentence before Calypso dropped to her knees.

*

"A fucking sex demon?" Her deafening shriek made Hades wince. His slight movement made him avoid a glass that Persephone threw, crashing into the wall behind him. She continued to scream and throw expensive perfume bottles and other trinkets he had acquired for her over the years. He allowed her to express her anger for a short period, then he stepped toward her and held her wrists tightly. She struggled against him as she tried desperately to free herself and scratch him.

"They have a name, you know."

Persephone spit at him, and he slapped her in response. She fell into her vanity, holding her swollen cheek as Hades rubbed his hand.

"Calm yourself; this is our panacea; we no longer have to worry about her."

"Calm myself?" she whimpered and picked herself out of the mess.

"You know this has been the discussion of the council for weeks, deciding what to do with her. We all agreed it was in my best interest to keep her alive and to give her a purpose rather than have her rot away in a chamber. It was communally decided that a succubus would be the most mindless servitude, with no risk to her rediscovering her vampirism."

"She's still a vampire?" Persephone turned away, hurt, but still clung to his every word.

"Yes, but she will no longer need blood to sustain herself. As I said, she will never remember what she is."

"Can you just admit this is about you and how you want to fuck her?" She turned back toward him, her nose scrunched and eyes watering. "You claim this to be a whole council issue, but I know you've always wanted to."

Hades shook his head in disbelief and stifled a laugh, knowing it would not help their situation. His wife had rarely shown so much jealousy.

"I want to hear you say it out loud! She's beautiful, and you did this so you could fuck her."

"Her beauty is none compared to your own. You are the entire ocean with a depth and intensity impassable to the human eye; she is none other than a stream, pouring into you and giving you her life force."

"So you admit it then, that she is beautiful."

"Of course, all vampires are beautiful. You know this: evil takes only the most beautiful to couple in the shadows. I will keep my promise to you as I have before." Persephone scoffed, annoyed he had brought up their centuries-old argument. He had promised he would not commit intercourse with the succubus other than fellatio. According to him, it kept his loyalty to her while still giving him the freedom to enjoy his Godly powers.

"For once, I wish you would choose me like I have chosen you. I have given you *everything* you have ever asked of me, but you can't give me this." Her voice cracked, and she lowered her gaze, quickly leaving her chambers and rushing into the hallway.

She pushed past others with tears in her eyes as she made her way into the grand entrance room. She sat on her throne alone and sighed as she planned her next moves. Hoping her outburst was believable, she retrieved her knife, tucked underneath her chair. It was slender and elegant, one of her first gifts from Hades to be used for protection.

She replayed their fight in her mind, analyzing his facial expressions and tone while mindlessly twirling the blade in her fingers. Her dissociation caused her to miss the entrance of a visitor completely. He gave a cough, which startled her, causing her knife to clang loudly against the floor. Persephone quickly bent over to grab it, pricking her fingertips as she recognized his face.

"Raphael, what are you doing here? You haven't come around in a while."

"When your other half is stolen from you, there isn't much motivation to visit."

Persephone faked a smile at him as she returned her knife to its sheath. She motioned for a guard to come forward and whispered into its ear. It exited the room quickly, and she stepped down the stairs slowly to meet Raphael.

You know I have only done as I was asked.

"Your actions are not excused," he growled with a clenched jaw. He refused to acknowledge their blood connection after she betrayed him. She turned away in anger and was met by Hades. He gave her a questioning look, reading the hurt on her face, and she glared back at him.

"You know what he's here for."

"Raphael, I would inquire about your reasoning for showing up unannounced, but we both know why that is."

He forced a smile on his face and nodded. "I have given both you and her space long enough and feel it is time for me to return."

"You have been gone such a long time, almost two months?" Hades motioned for him to follow, and Raphael kept up with his long strides.

"I've had to keep myself busy. I've ended a few vampire clans, as you know. I didn't think to ask for your permission; rather, I dealt with them myself." Raphael kept his gaze forward, looking only at the stone floors ahead of him.

"I was interested, as I did not know that the Las Vegas clan were disobedient."

"They were not, but I did not approve of how they handled themselves."

"So you burned them all alive?" Hades asked with no malice in his tone, only the harshness of the truth.

"I needed to send a message. I am still the King of

Vampires, even if she has left me."

"You were the king for how many hundreds of years before you came into her life? My son, you must realize that you and I are different from the rest. We are powerful, and the women in our lives add to that, but we do not need them. I am still the God of the underworld without Persephone, am I not?"

"Of course, sir, but—" Raphael stumbled over his words, thrown off by being referred to as kin.

"You do not need to show such a force of power or dominance for your kind to know you are in charge. They know your position has not changed, and you will still obey me and enforce the rules with or without a queen. If anything, they should honor you more, as you have kept your position and morale strong even amidst a challenging time.

"I respect you myself, as does the entire council of Hell. You may have had some differences with them before, but they all admire your dedication. I don't know anyone in my ranks who could handle the pain you deal with such grace."

Raphael remained silent and nodded, although Hades wasn't looking at him. He knew they were walking toward a different part of the castle, which made him anxious.

"You have been gone so long time that I was forced to take action into my own hands. We tried for so long to break her. I wanted her to admit her wrongdoings so we could move forward. She refused. No matter how hard the demons pushed her physically and mentally, she rejected all chances of forgiveness. Her howls drove the entire castle mad, especially Persephone. She convinced me to let them converse. That she would be able to help her find a place in Hell besides that of a prisoner."

"What did you do to her?" Raphael growled.

"I found Calypso broken out of her chains, draining the life out of her. She attempted to kill her by forcing her body into the Elysian Fields! I had no choice. I had to take her where I have taken others—to the chair. She should have died, Raphael, but again, to my surprise, she was alive. Able to talk, but no memory whatsoever. She couldn't even walk when I commanded her. The council was in sessions for days on end until we figured out what we could possibly do with her."

Hades stopped outside of the gold-plated doors Raphael knew too well about. He had only visited the chambers a handful of times but was aware of the activities that occurred inside.

"No," was all he could muster the strength to say.

He collapsed to his knees, his shoulders weighing him down. Hades picked him up by his shirt collar and forced his head back to look into his eyes.

"I know this isn't what you wanted to hear, but it is better this way. Calypso is alive and has a purpose. She has no memory of the pain she endured or put others through.
She is happy, and you can still enjoy her."

Hades swung the door open and forced Raphael inside. Eyes flickered at both of them from the shadows, but nobody approached except Calypso. She lay elegantly across a red velvet couch before she strolled toward Hades. She was allowed the unique privilege of coming to him without being called.

"Have you...did you..." Raphael struggled to get out the words. Hades' subtle nod made him turn away and bite his palm, careful not to draw any blood. His world was crashing down onto him, threatening to strangle him at any given moment.

"What can I do for you, master?" Calypso asked in a sultry voice. She paid no attention to his counterpart, who tried not to gawk at her naked body.

"I would like you to meet a friend and take good care of him. She is still yours," he whispered into Raphael's ear before leaving the room.

"You must be special; Hades never brings anyone in here for me. What's your name?"

"Raphael." His voice was ice cold. He stared into her eyes, begging her soul to remember him. Her coy smile and glassy eyes gave nothing in return.

"Raphael, what a beautiful name. What do you want me to

do?"

"Nothing, nothing, I just, I need you, Callie."

"Callie?" She took a step back and scrunched her forehead in confusion. "No, my name is Calypso."

"I know, come here." Raphael stepped forward and wrapped his arms around her, muffling his cries into her hair. She held him for a short while, allowing him to express his emotions before she began to kiss his neck.

He balked, not wanting to receive affection from her in an altered state, but quickly gave in. It had been so long, and she was here, freely offering herself to him. He couldn't resist; he threw her against the couch and passionately kissed her as she moaned and met him with equal action.

As he undressed, he imagined they were back in his penthouse, rolling around the stone floor next to the coffin. He imagined her as a human as he thrust into her. She arched and moaned in response, pleasing him as she had been created to do.

*

"Ayai?" Justin called out to her from the living room. She tended to a bonfire outside on the back porch.

Summer was around the corner, so they were taking advantage of the last few cold nights. It was ironic, hating Hell but enjoying fire, but this was different to her as she was in control.

Justin stood in front of the television, remote clenched in his white knuckle. His eyes were wide, and it looked as if he had seen a ghost. Ayai smiled and cocked her head at him, surprised that anything had caught his attention as he usually ignored any shows they watched together. She glanced at the screen and saw the news was reporting about a serial killer on the loose in Santa Monica.

The reporter showed blurred pictures of bodies. They were covered with a white sheet, but it was painstakingly obvious that the corpse's heads were missing. The images switched to photos of the deceased, young Caucasian women with long red or brunette hair, all with similar features and smiles.

"They all look just like her," Justin muttered, his eyes still glued to the television. The television switched back to the reporter standing outside at a park in front of yellow police tape. He advised that all women stay indoors, heed the newly enforced curfew, and call with any information.

"Raphael," Ayai rubbed her temples as she paced throughout the room. It had to be him, based on the women's appearance and brutality of the murders. But he would never do something so bold and messy without reason.

The shifting of rocks by the bonfire let them know he had arrived. Justin was the first to reach him, slugging his fist into his face, although he was already on his hands and knees. Raphael took the punch and fell against the ground dangerously close to the fire, tears stinging his eyes.

"What did you do?" Justin screamed as he continued to hurl punches at the lifeless vampire. Ayai managed to pull his arms behind his back and drag him away.

"Raphael? Raphael!" she yelled at him to get up. He lay blankly, staring at the fire, refusing to move. Dried blood stained his shirt, and his clothes were a disheveled mess. This was highly unusual for him, as he took great pride in his appearance.

"It was only a matter of time before the news got out." He remained lying on the ground, back toward them, as he gazed into the flames.

"Why did you hurt those girls?" Ayai asked, her voice full of distress, afraid to know the answer.

"All I see is her; she is everywhere. She haunts my dreams. I see her in the streets while I wander at night. I see her and pull her close; then I see the truth. It isn't her and will never be her. My anger consumes me, and I lose my temper," Raphael began to shake as the images of him feasting and decapitating the women played in his mind.

"I know this is hard for you, but can't you visit her?" Ayai released Justin, sensing his anger had slightly diminished.

"Calypso isn't there anymore."

"What do you mean, where is she?" Justin asked. The winds shifted and blew smoke into his face. His nose scrunched and eyes began to water.

"She is there, her body is. But her mind and soul are gone forever. He...he wiped her memory and turned her into a succubus." Raphael struggled to speak the words into existence. Ayai turned away as tears flooded her eyes, and Justin struggled to comprehend.

"If I visit her, all I see is him taking advantage of her," Raphael shook with fury. "He smiled when I asked if he touched her, if he tainted my queen!"

"What are you doing here? We have to go to Hell now and kill him!" Justin's mind began to turn, thinking of every possible way he would dismember Hades.

"I've already thought of that a thousand times, but I can't figure out the execution."

"Stop, both of you!" Ayai exclaimed. "You are both idiots; nothing can be done now."

"Are you crazy? We have to do something! She can't be Hades' sex slave; I won't allow it!" Justin yelled back at her.

"You won't allow it? She wasn't yours in the first place! Since when do you care about her? The last thing you told her was that you hated her and would never forgive her for what she did to you."

Justin's face turned red, and he balled his fists, stomping back into the house. Ayai waited until he had disappeared to sit next to Raphael.

"You know you cannot do anything. That is why you are acting out. He would kill you, and you know he is on guard, waiting for you to mess up so he can do the same to you."

"I am the King of Vampires. If I take a whole legion with me..."

"If you take every vampire in existence with you, not only would they all die, but he would keep you alive to purposely torture you for all of eternity. You are powerful, but you are not a

God! I can imagine how painful this is for you, but maybe it is better this way." Ayai uneasily turned over a few rocks in her hand.

"How could you say that?" Raphael asked.

"She has no memory of you or of the terrible acts she committed while a vampire. She cannot long for you or even human existence as she does not know either exists. I know you love her, but maybe this is what you need to move on with your life."

"How can I move on, knowing what is happening to her? She is the love of my life."

"You moved on fine when I left." Ayai was curt, and Raphael felt an instant shame.

"I still loved you, though," he whispered.

"Maybe that is true, maybe not. Regardless, you never tried to find me or even speak to me in my mind. It can be the same with Calypso. Just imagine she left and you don't want to find her. Raphael, I truly am sorry. She doesn't deserve this fate." Ayai gently rubbed his shoulder and stood up to go back inside.

Justin needed her comfort now, though she wasn't sure how to give it to him. She watched Raphael momentarily before she turned away, still shocked and hurt over what had happened to Calypso. It could be her in the bellows of Hell, but she was spared.

Chapter 20

The endless nights in Hell grew longer as Hades became absent more frequently and for longer periods. Persephone questioned him, and he gave vague excuses: traversing the landscapes of Hell or getting caught up in a frivolous discussion among the rankings. She knew the truth, however, that he visited his prized possession as frequently as he could stow away.

He let her sleep in her own room instead of demanding that she sleep with him. He only did this when they had fought or when he was already given pleasure by someone else. She tried not to become jealous, but she couldn't help it. She was his wife, yet he enjoyed entering other women; lest she try the same, he would behead any man who looked at her too long.

Persephone was driven mad by this; she began to hear him moaning even though she was far away from the room of succubi. She would sit in solitude in the grand library, trying to think of a way out of the hellhole. Although the books of Atlantis and Great Alexandria filled the endless shelves, she could find nothing on vampires turned to succubi or anything close to her situation. She knew it could be reversed; it had to be, as with any spell or potion. She had been around long enough to know there was always a loophole out of witchcraft.

She slammed a book down as his moan entered her mind again. Dust swirled around her face, but she paid it no mind. She stormed out of the library and made her way to the dark area of the castle. He had left the door cracked open. He was so careless and in a rush to see his servant. She stood a few feet away, enough to stay hidden but close enough to view what happened inside.

Hades lay naked, his bushy and muscular legs straddled against the couch. Calypso rocked against his beard as she pleasured him. His moans were not in her head this time; instead, they were audibly shouted. Persephone watched in horror as his toes curled and his eyes shot open. He slammed her head further down his sheath as his thighs pumped beneath him. He immediately grabbed her waist and repositioned her to face him.

"That has never happened before." His whisper felt like a scream in her ears. Calypso giggled as she caressed his chest hair. "You are mine, and mine only. No one else will ever have the pleasure of your company again."

Persephone couldn't help but gasp out loud and disappear by the time the two lovers peered out of the cracked doorway. She stormed down the hallway, pushing past souls who clogged the entryway. Her husband had been so busy fucking recently that he had lacked judging the new souls, leaving them to roam and howl around the castle. Usually, Persephone cared about their final resting place and prayed they were not tortured, but now they could burn for all she cared.

As she sat weeping on her throne, she remembered who she was. She was a God, and she was upset over her forced lover taking pleasure in mind-controlled sex. She began to laugh; her rocking movements ceased the tears.

She straightened herself and looked forward; the time to regain her strength was now.

She closed her eyes and whispered his name. She knew he would not be immediately responsive but did not expect him to take days to show her attention. She sat calling to him, day after day. She barely left the throne, awaiting his arrival. After multiple days of being ignored, she called a dream demon to her side. She whispered her desires, and they vanished to wreak havoc. Shortly after, a frenzied Raphael appeared.

"Finally, what took you so long?" she cooed.

"You," he growled at her. "You terrorize my night, demanding that I visit you after you destroyed my life! I let your shrill voice fill my head, but I ignored it. Until you sent that damn demon, penetrating the only time I can rest and forget about the hell I live in. You sent *her;* she was with me, loving me, only when I opened my eyes it was your face!" His body shook with rage, and she grinned back at him, knowing her plan had worked.

I needed to get your attention. I know how to get Calypso

back.

"Why should I listen to anything you have to say?" He shouted back at her. She stepped down from her throne to stand eye-to-eye with him.

"It's not just you who suffer. Do you not think I feel guilt daily for finding favor with him but for erasing her mind? I captured her soul; yes, I know that, and I have been trying to figure a way out of it ever since. You do not need to trust me, but at least try for her. Her soul is still there, you know; it is just trapped. She will come back to you."

Raphael was stunned at her empathy and decided he would follow her. He was desperate and had no other choice. As much as he wanted to destroy all of Hell and Hades, he knew in his heart it was an impossible task.

Persephone held his hand as they walked through the halls.

You must listen carefully. Do not act out against Hades, or he will suspect a betrayal of your loyalty. She must drink your blood, but it cannot be noticeable. If he figures it out, he will kill you both.

As Raphael digested the information, Persephone opened the doors to the chamber where Hades and Calypso lay. They had barely spoken since she caught him ejaculating into her mouth, though they both knew the sever it caused between them.

"He is here to see her," she said loudly, making Hades' head lift and acknowledge them. Raphael stood rigid, watching as Calypso moved her lips up and down his cock.

"Please, take over. I was finishing up."

He stood frozen, unable to walk forward. Persephone grabbed his hand again and walked him into the room, pushing him down onto the ground a few feet away from Hades.

"I want to have fun, too." Persephone made eye contact with Hades as she unbuckled Raphael's pants. He immediately blushed and turned toward Hades, knowing that any relationship with his wife was forbidden.

Hades pondered the sight before him, assumed it was her frivolous way of getting back at him, and decided to allow it.

"Please, don't deny yourself pleasure."

Persephone began to kiss his inner thighs as Raphael shifted uncomfortably underneath her. He made sure his hands were far away from her and refused to make eye contact, so he stared at the ceiling above them.

You are going to get us both killed!

Remember, she needs a little bit of blood.

"Get off," Persephone stood up and faced her husband. "He is mine." She shoved Calypso away from his groin and sat on his lap. Hades smiled at her, loving her jealousy for him, and kissed her passionately.

With her master attended to, Calypso slunk toward Raphael. He shook with anticipation as she slowly ran her fingers along his legs up toward his chest.

"Please," he whispered as he grabbed a fistful of her hair and motioned her down to his cock. He tried to stifle his groans but was unable to. He was met by a glance from Hades, and his face turned red in shame. Persephone sensed the discomfort and straddled his lap to kiss his neck, blocking the view of the vampires.

Raphael saw that Hades was out of view, so he quickly pulled down on Calypso's hair, making her teeth grate against him. He bit his hand to stifle his cries of pain, but he yanked her down again until he felt his flesh tear.

Calypso continued to suck against him, moving faster once she tasted the blood. The taste exploded against her tongue, and she tried to pull more out of him.

Everything hit her at once; her head exploded in pain, and she dropped to the ground next to him. She stayed silent as she writhed in pain, holding her head as if that would prevent the excruciating agony. As her memories returned, Raphael noticed a flicker of recognition in her eyes.

"Calypso," he mouthed as he lay over her, still trying to

mask Hades' view.

"Raphael," her voice cracked, and a single tear rolled out of her eyes. She cupped his face in her hands, his glorious face she thought she would never see again. He was here, with her, naked on a cold dungeon ground. The same grounds where she was beaten, tortured, and made into a mindless sex demon to be raped repeatedly. The horror of it all made her want to curl into a corner and die; she just wanted the pain to end. She quickly realized that it would never end and would haunt her psyche forever.

Raphael sensed her anguish and kissed her gently, trying to keep her in the present with him.

"Mon chérie, I never doubted that you would come back to me," he whispered.

Her voice cracked and he placed a finger over her lips. She cried as he caressed her dirty, sullen face.

Hades let out a long moan as Persephone performed some act, which made Calypso jerk her head to the side.

"He did this to me." Her words grew in power, and Raphael hurried to push her against the ground.

"Shhh, it's okay; let's go home."

How can you tell me its okay? After everything he has done to me! Everything he has done to us.

"Please, just stay with me," he whispered and tucked a strand of hair behind her ear.

"He did this to me!" she yelled, grabbing the attention of the nearby demons who lurked in the shadows. She threw Raphael into the corner, releasing a strength neither of them knew she embodied.

Hades continued to bounce Persephone on his lap as he watched Calypso stand and shake with fury. They made eye contact and he grinned.

She catapulted in the air toward Hades, who threw Persephone off his lap—the moment he yearned for had finally come. Drawing a long knife from underneath the couch, he plunged the blade into her chest as she landed on him.

Raphael was frozen, screaming in horror as he watched the blade exit through her back. Her body went limp as soon as the knife pierced her heart, ending her short-lived, everlasting life. Hades held her in the air, grinning through the blood that speckled his face. He threw her body onto the ground and stood up to redress himself.

Raphael's continued screams echoed throughout the chamber and bled into the hallway as servants began to gather to view the commotion. His vision blurred and he nearly passed out as he watched a thick, white liquid fly onto Calypso's naked corpse. Hades grunted with release and zipped his pants before bending down to remove his knife, then stuck his hand into her gaping wound to pull out her motionless heart.

"Calypso, the Vampire Queen, is dead. The prophecy has been fulfilled." Hades' words echoed into every vampire's mind, causing an uneasy stillness in the night. Raphael's tears stopped as Hades strolled past him, looking down his nose at the quivering shell of a man.

Persephone crawled over to him, rubbed his shoulder, and spoke to him, but he heard nothing. He could focus on nothing other than her naked, soulless body. She had come back to him, only to disappear forever moments later. It was too much to handle.

A white sheet was draped over her body, and Raphael lay next to her corpse, stifling his cries as the sheet became soaked with blood. It seemed so cruel of the body to continue to ooze after life had left it.

"Get up. You need to get her body out of here." Raphael picked up her body, so weightless now, and kept his face shielded through the hallway. He caught sight of Judas Iscariot and other council members but chose better judgment to walk behind Persephone, who threatened the onlookers with her stoic countenance.

You cannot bury her. You need to take her body to the ocean.

Bury her? The thought hadn't crossed his mind, having to throw his beautiful dead queen into a pile of dirt in the ground. No, he only thought about taking her to their coffin, where he would lay next to her until he would desiccate into nothing. He would die nobly next to her side, holding her hand and breathing in her scent, basking in the memories of the past.

Raphael! The ocean!

He stopped once they were in an empty part of the hallway and glared at her.

"Why should I trust you? You told me all she needed was a little blood, and she died!"

"Have you seen the looks on their faces? They want to crucify her and mutilate her body. Imagine the vampires on Earth! Surely, they will come searching for her body, to humiliate or use in some sort of ritual. I did not know her well, but she doesn't deserve that. They will tear you apart to get to her, even if she is dead. They will not rest until they have seen her dead body themselves, then they will tear it apart like wild animals. If you take her to the ocean, she will be safe. Fly out to deep waters, far away from any land, and let her go. She will sink to the bottom, and the fish will eat her decaying skin. No, it's not beautiful, but her body will be safe there. She will nourish others, and her body will not go in vain. Please, Raphael, if nothing else, please listen to this." Persephone teared up as she spoke, which Raphael couldn't comprehend. He nodded blankly before turning away to teleport out of Hell.

Persephone made her way to the grand entry room, where countless servants poured in, desperate to glimpse the heart Hades paraded in the air. He sat triumphantly on his throne, wearing his crown, which he only wore on rare occasions.

She made eye contact with him and nodded her gratitude that the battle was finally over.

*

Cold air pierced Raphael's skin as he flew at light speed toward nowhere. He had immediately teleported to his penthouse, and when he saw the rising sun, he fled into the ocean. The blood-soaked sheet had flown off miles ago, so he stared at her corpse.

Her eyes were closed, thankfully, and her face finally looked peaceful, no longer troubled by the weight of the world or eternity. He still longed to lay by her side until he passed, but he figured this would be the best way to let her go. Persephone had been right; legions of Hades worshiping vampires would love to mutilate her body. On the other hand, the vampires who secretly despised him would use her body to try to raise her from the dead or worship her carcass for being brave enough to try to kill him.

Raphael slowed down once he began to feel weak. Judging from the lack of land and cool air, he figured he was somewhere in the northern Pacific Ocean. He floated down until the white-capped waves splashed against his feet. He wanted to make sure her last descent was peaceful. He sobbed as he took one last look at her perfect body, blemished only by the gaping hole in her chest. He took her cheek in his hand one last time and wept onto her face. His tears rolled down her neck, and he could taste the lingering blood on her lips.

"I'm so sorry," he breathed into her lips. "I will never forget you, my love, my queen. My life will never be the same without your presence."

His few words felt empty and meaningless in the grand scheme of what he wished he could say to her. There was no point; he spoke to a shell. Her soul was gone, and he would never be able to find her in an afterlife.

He lowered her body gently into the water, watching as she sank below the visible waves. He waited momentarily, half hoping she would swim back up to the surface, gasping for air. Of course, his imagination was useless, as he would never see her again. He wished he could return to the moment he first saw her, reading on a bench on a humid night.

Chapter 21

It was remarkable; she had seen her face before. Daphne pondered at the pale skin and red hair that floated around her head, creating a halo. Could it be her? She had to find out quickly before anyone else saw. She grabbed an arm and drug the body into a thick patch of grass underneath a rock. Bubbles caressed her body as she sank into the sand, slowly rocking with the current. She had to find him fast, but he was infinite and elusive.

How could she grasp his attention without calling the attention of the others? He was always flanked by numerous nymphs and the like, thinking that if they could swim in his presence, they, too, would be graced with his powers and immortality. She suddenly remembered the sacred conch; of course, she could use it to direct his attention. She glanced at the partially hidden body one last time before swimming off in search of the shell.

It took her a while to find one, as she was in a vacant area of the ocean, but she eventually found the large pink shell and dug it out of the sand. Sticking her fingers inside of the hole, she scooped out the slimy mollusk and gently placed it on the sand, apologizing for disturbing its rest. Flapping her tail quickly, she propelled herself to the top of the water and ascended with the shell in hand.

After a few attempts of blowing into the spiral and hearing nothing, she was finally able to produce a sound. Daphne was unprepared for the lung capacity the shell required to create the deep tone, as she had never needed to use it. She blew into the shell until she was breathless and convinced her message was received, then she floated on her back to try and catch her breath.

"What is the meaning of this?" A merman popped his head out of the water, half scaring her to death.

"I needed to signal Poseidon; it was the only way I knew how."

"You know the sacred conch is only for emergencies."

"Of course, I know that; I am in his rankings as well, or have you forgotten? I have been around since before the tides have changed, no need to lecture me on the matter." Daphne glared at him while he pondered her words.

"Well then, what is this emergency?"

"Why did Poseidon not come himself? The emergency is for his ears only," Daphne insisted. "There is no crisis in the ocean or on land, but something he must view for himself."

"I need more information than what you give me."

Daphne paused, not wanting to reveal more than she should to him.

"I found a body. He may have sentimental value to it. Please, tell him I found it and that I know he needs to see it. I will meet him at the large boulder near Kanton."

"Kanton? That's hours from here!"

"Correct, I know he dwells in the southern section of the waters; I'll make the journey easier for him. Hurry now, let's not keep him waiting."

Daphne dove back under the water, lurking under the waves until she watched the merman swim away. She quickly swam back to her rock and threw the limp body over her shoulder. She swam in the current, moving south quickly along the jetstream. The extra weight of the body made the task strenuous, but she was prepared to make it to her destination quickly. Once she felt the temperature warm slightly, she rose to the top of the water and paddled her way to a large boulder that stuck out of the water. She slung the body onto the rock, then helped herself on so she could pull the woman further onto the rock.

The body had become shiny, and though she had only been submerged for a few hours, the decay process had already started. Daphne looked upon her with pity and then decided to make a trip back to the bottom of the ocean to grab grass and plants to cover her.

She returned with fistfuls of sopping grass to cover her chest and lap area. As she was finishing the arrangement, a loud splash made her turn her head.

"Daphne." Poseidon greeted her with a single deep word.

"My Lord, it's been too long," she bowed her head in respect. He smiled at her, holding his strict expression, but she felt his warmth.

"I was told you requested my presence for a body." He swam closer to the rock, and she moved slightly to block his view.

"Yes, you are alone?"

"Correct."

"Sir, I have no good way of telling you this, but it is your daughter."

Recognition flooded his eyes, and Daphne moved to the side so Poseidon could climb the rock. He towered over her and stood above the corpse, tilting his head as he examined her.

Daphne was formerly tasked at Poseidon's castle, where she grew in the rankings based on her loyalty and hard work. One day, Poseidon had confided in her about his adulterous relationship with a human, creating a child. Nobody could find out; the community he had created worshiped him, and if they knew of his scandal, it would destroy them. She had agreed to closely monitor the child and its mother anytime they were in or near water.

Daphne left the castle and set off to the east coast of America, where she waited year after year for them to enter the water. She knew their faces but could also sense when their skin would come in contact with the ocean. As he had requested, she never reported to Poseidon but only monitored them from afar. She had not seen or felt Calypso in years until she had reentered the water as a corpse.

"Here, take this," Poseidon pulled a thick blade out of his belt and turned to face her. Daphne grabbed the handle, her arms shaking with the weight of the knife.

"Cut a single line over my heart."

"What?" she exclaimed.

"Daphne, the time for balking is not now." Poseidon

kneeled so she could reach him and pointed directly at his heart. She grimaced as she punctured his skin.

"Deeper," he commanded. She shoved with all of her might and felt the blade connect with his ribs. She gasped as he overlapped her hand and pulled the knife down, creating a large wound in his chest.

Watery silver blood oozed as she removed the blade, and it clamored against the rock. Poseidon inserted both of his hands into the wound and pulled his skin and bones apart. Daphne turned her head away in fear and disgust, ready to hurl herself into the water.

"Pick it back up. I need you to cut a section of my heart. A small section of my heart, now!" Each word pained him to speak, but he showed no affliction.

Daphne whimpered as she lifted the knife into his chest again, pushing the blade deep until she connected with his pulsating muscle. She pulled the blade downward and removed it slowly from his chest, the small piece of organ attached to the end. Her hands shook as she held it far away from her body.

Poseidon removed his hands from his chest and grabbed the piece of his heart, which seemed minuscule in the size of his palm. His wound became smaller due to his instantaneous healing, and he sat down next to the corpse of his daughter. He placed the section of heart inside the gaping hole of her chest, pushing it in with his two fingers.

Daphne watched in awe as her cells began to form slowly, suturing up the jagged cut that ran through her center. It was a slow process, taking a few minutes to close the wound fully. The body was still, with no movement or breath that could be seen. Daphne began to think it was a fluke, perhaps something to do with Poseidon's powers, until she saw the stomach of the corpse rise.

It rose once, twice, then the body jerked up into a sitting position and projectile vomited water. The seawater came out of her mouth multiple times, streaming out of her nose and mixing with a putrid stomach bile.

Calypso felt nothing but pain. She could not see, hear, or breathe; her mind thought of nothing but the excruciating pain in her chest and head. She blindly thrashed around as her body automatically moved, removing all of its contents from her stomach. Her nose and throat stung with lingering salt, and after gasping multiple times, she was able to breathe.

She continued to gasp with her mouth, slowly hearing her own panicked breathing along with waves. The feeling came back to her hands, and she felt a slimy and cold surface, a rock based on its jaggedness. She forced herself to blink but could not see anything besides darkness.

Daphne removed herself from the rock and floated nearby, waiting for a confirmation nod from Poseidon indicating that she was free to go. She would continue to guard the secret of his child with her life.

"Where am I?" Calypso coughed out. She could now see shadows, nothing more than a prominent dark figure in front of her.

"You are safe now," a deep voice spoke in front of her. She winced and pulled her legs close.

"Where am I? Hades told me there was no afterlife for my kind."

"Hades did this to you," Poseidon spoke as a fact, not a question.

Calypso blinked again and finally perceived the man in front of her. He was tall and muscular, similar to Hades, but his long curled hair was white, and his beard matched. He was shirtless but wore tight black pants with a waistband and a large knife on his hip.

"You are a God," she whispered. She was sure of the fact. He carried too much resemblance to her mortal enemy.

"Calypso, what is the last thing you remember?"

A wave of pain washed over her body again and she vomited as she remembered Hades' smug smile as she died.

"I was captured and held prisoner for a long time. I don't know how long, but it felt like years. I had a chance to escape and took it, but *he* did something to me. I lost my memory; I lost everything. I couldn't walk, but I could talk.

"I didn't remember my name until he told me. Then, he turned me into a sex demon. Making me serve him and others until Raphael came back. I didn't remember him, the love of my life, until I tasted his blood. All of my memories came back, so I tried to kill Hades. The last thing I remember is seeing his face, and now I am here."

"Who are you?"

"Who am I? Who are you, sitting here, superior, and asking me all these questions?"

"Who are you?" Poseidon asked again. "Where did you come from, your family?"

"My name is Calypso. I am an orphan. My mother and father died when I was a teenager. I am, or I was, the Queen of Vampires. Now, you answer my question."

"You are wrong about one thing, Calypso. You are not an orphan."

"I've had enough of this," she muttered. She scanned her surroundings, planning to escape from this conversation, but realized she was stuck. She could fly, perhaps, but felt weak and didn't know if she could fly after dying. "You're telling me that my mother and father didn't get blown off of a cliff? That's news to me and could have changed the trajectory of my entire life."

"No, they are dead, but he was not your father. He raised and loved you, but he did not provide the sperm to create you."

Calypso stared blankly back at him. He nodded, and she closed her eyes tightly, already knowing the words that would come out of his mouth. A warm breeze blew in the night around them but she still shivered.

"Calypso, my name is Poseidon. I'm sure you have heard about me, the God of the oceans. I take pride in my title. I am a God, so I listen to prayers occasionally. One day, I heard your mother's prayer, crying out for a child. I came to her as the sea foam, gently embracing and impregnating her. Of course, she assumed it was her husband, and that was how I wanted it. I wanted nothing to do with her and her child; I wanted only to do my duty as a God.

"I made sure you were both taken care of. I watched you grow, every summer coming back to the water. I rescued you when you almost drowned as a toddler. I got too close, which is my fault. I should have never returned to see you or her. That's how he found out.

"My brother, Zeus, is a very jealous type. He, of course, has plenty of earthly women with whom he has joined over the millennia. However, his wife Hera, is even more jealous. She took it upon herself to murder every woman he had ever been with. Zeus found anger in this and decided to take it out on me. He found out about your mother but never about you. He thought I had laid with her while she was married and with child, so he killed her. He spared you, as he did not know that you were mine. I never fought back, though I wished I could, to save you from the same fate."

Calypso sat silently, slowly shaking her head as she digested his words. "You are my father—the God of the oceans. Your brother, my uncle, killed my parents. And you, I'm assuming, saved my life somehow?"

"I did. Your partner dropped you into the ocean; what a smart boy he was, and I found you. I gave you part of my heart so that you would survive."

"You said you spared me from the same fate, but you didn't." Calypso smiled and stifled a laugh, wanting to explode over the irony of the situation. "Here I am, dead or alive now, but I was dragged to Hell. I was a traumatized human, and I died to become a vampire. I murdered ruthlessly until Hades got ahold of me. Then I became bound to his will; how is that any better than dying and having my soul stay with my parents?"

"I didn't realize that saving you would entail you becoming

a monster. I never intended for that to happen." His eyes sparkled with sincerity.

"Maybe not, but it was inevitable, with the prophecy and all."

"Prophecy?"

"Surely you have heard of it; Hades created the vampires against the Gods' will, and a prophecy was born that one day, the Queen of Vampires would betray and kill him." Calypso scraped her fingernails aimlessly against the rock.

"Of course, I know of it; I argued against him for creating such an abomination. But it shouldn't have been you."

"What do you mean? I am the Queen of Vampires, and I have tried to kill Hades. Raphael knew I was to be queen when he discovered me. He sensed it in my soul."

"What he sensed was me. You are a demigod, and he felt your power."

Calypso's chest tightened and she looked away. Her mind swirled and she felt nauseated.

"A demigod, is that how this works? If that were true, why did I never have any powers until I became a vampire? Wouldn't Hades or Zeus have sensed that?"

"I was very particular in my creation of you. I ensured that your heart and soul would be protected for this very reason. That the demigod powers would never appear unless they were activated."

"Activated how?"

"Did you ever have any unusual experiences with water while you were human?" Poseidon questioned.

"I saw my reflection in the river once, but it wasn't me. It was the devil."

"You were prophesying your fate."

"Huh, and I thought I was just drunk this whole time."

They sat in silence, unsure of what to say to each other. She liked him, her newfound father. His resemblance to Hades made her quiver, but his face was kind. The moonlight gave him an angel-like halo. She appreciated his honesty with her.

"Now that you have my heart, your powers will manifest to their full extent." Poseidon broke the silence.

"What does that mean? Am I still a vampire?"

"Technically, yes, you are. You still have the blood of Hades flowing through your veins, and now my heart."

"A demigod vampire, I'm sure the Fates never prepared for this."

"No, I'm sure they didn't." He chuckled. "You know what you must do now?"

"I can't," her voice cracked. "I can't face him again."

"You can and you must." His voice and face became stern, his knuckles gripping the handle of his knife.

"He must pay for his crimes against humanity, for what he did to you, my beautiful daughter." His face darkened, and she saw the same blackness in his eyes that she had seen in Hades'. He seemed genuinely upset, although they had just met.

"You don't know me; you don't know what I've been through! I'm grateful for your heart, I suppose, but you can't expect me to follow your wishes just because you granted me life."

"You are right; I don't know you or what you have endured. But I will tell you this: the fates are never wrong.

If they prophesied you killing Hades, then you will do so."

"Trust me, I would love to put an end to him, but how?"

"I will not pit you against my own brother. You have been in his company; you should know his weaknesses. Don't rush. Learn how to act as a demigod.

"You'll find you have a whole new world of opportunities. Master blocking your soul and switching bodies. Perhaps there you will find your plan." Poseidon dove into the water, returning above the waves to marvel at his daughter one last time.

"Wait!" she called out to him. "Hades, he's your brother. You are my father. That means he is my uncle." Vomit trickled up her esophagus and threatened to spill out over the incestuous thought.

"Hardly." Poseidon laughed. "You humans have such preposterous terms. Incest does not exist amongst us Gods, we prefer to keep our bloodline pure. Calypso, I'll see you again in Mount Olympus. I'll be waiting for you." He gave her a half smile and disappeared under the water.

Calypso sat on the rock until the stars began to fade away. She picked herself up and flew away with nothing but anger burning in her heart.

Chapter 22

Calypso landed in the lower region of Giza with a few hours of nightfall left. Her first mission was clothing, as she was still naked. She quickly stole a tan tunic that hung on a laundry line. She had chosen a small and rural Egyptian town, away from the bustle of the main cities. There were still a significant number of houses in the village, most of which were made of yellow adobe.

Dust smacked against her bare feet and covered her body as she slowly strolled down the main dirt road. The village was alive, though dark, with lights and music streaming from most houses. She heard the laughter of men in the distance, snarling her lip at their insolence. The town was near the Nile River, and she was acutely aware of the sound of the flow.

The relentless thoughts of humans continued to enter her mind, and she closed her eyes to visualize their owners. One thought made her stop in her tracks: the thought of murder. It came from a woman a few houses over; Calypso instantly appeared a few feet from the porch. She made herself invisible so she could observe without being seen.

A beautiful dark-skinned woman sat on the porch and scrubbed clothes in a washing basin. Thick, curly hair bounced off her shoulders as she scrubbed the dress meticulously. It was already cleaned, yet she had to work out her anger somehow. As Calypso walked closer, she noticed a stark purple bruise under the woman's eye. Though her skin tone mostly covered the bruise, the swelling was noticeable.

A quick glance into the woman's mind and she discovered the bruise was from her abusive husband. She scrubbed the dress to make sure the blood stains had disappeared. She wanted nothing more than to slit his throat, but she was weak compared to him and would never step out of her place as a wife.

Calypso appeared behind her, inhaling deeply as the sweet and strong smell of pumping blood intoxicated her. With her fangs bared, she was ready to tear into her neck but stopped herself. Instead of feasting on the beautiful woman, she would become her.

Stepping in front of the woman, she made herself visible again. The woman was not as startled as Calypso expected, with only a slight gasp and shutter up her spine. Calypso stood motionless, examining every detail of the woman's face. Her golden, almond-shaped eyes, slightly curved nose, small pink lips, and the curves of her collarbones. She was a beautiful queen, and Calypso would use her wisely.

*

By the time morning arrived, the woman was dead at the bottom of the Nile. Calypso had drained her blood, soaking in her youth and beauty, then dug herself a hole near the house.

When night fell again, she emerged from the sand as the woman. Her husband shouted at her as she pushed open the creaking door. She grabbed his scythe that hung from the wall and instantly sliced his throat. She straddled him as she carefully cut his heart out and placed it into a small satchel. Finally, she grabbed a white scarf and covered her face before walking into the night.

The covering was not unusual for the culture, but she wanted to conceal her face as she was a human who had just committed murder. Calypso did not want to use her powers more than she needed in case landwalkers or demons were nearby.

She was on a mission, traveling South to the Temple of Seti I. She walked overnights, keeping a slow human pace, and stopped at dawn at hostels to sleep. She had stolen the little money left at the house and managed to buy herself a bed and a measly meal each morning.

She received plenty of curious looks, wondering who the covered nomad was. Women rarely traveled alone through the cities, but she was no ordinary woman. After almost two weeks of traveling, she reached the town of Abydos.

The sky was dark, with an empty moon and thin clouds covering most of the stars. A smile cracked through the dust caked onto her face. A large temple lay in front of her, but she had no intentions of going inside. She walked around until she reached the outside of Osiris's chapel.

Thousands of years ago, humans made the pilgrimage to the temple to worship Osiris, the God of death.

She dropped to her knees, laying prostrate facing the walls, and began to speak in Latin, granting praise to the God of death. She took the hardened heart out of her satchel and began to dig a hole to bury it. Once she placed it inside, she removed the scythe from the belt under her dress and drew it across her palm, squeezing blood into the hole. She felt the wind shift behind her and knew it was time. She continued to shout in Latin, raising her arms in praise as she was dragged to Hell below.

The demons who captured her immediately bound her in chains and put her in a trance. They forced her to the ground; one stayed with her while the other went to fetch Hades. They explained the situation to him, discovering a woman who practiced dark arts and worshiped Osiris in Egypt. They knew he would enjoy such a unique specimen. Her beating heart made her even more worthy.

Hades slowly examined the beautiful woman placed in front of him. He tore off her facial covering, revealing her symmetrical face. He grabbed her chin and forced her gaze upward into his eyes. Calypso glossed over her eyes, pretending to be lost in a trance. He read her soul, finding nothing but the thoughts of the woman before Calypso murdered her.

Hades released her and demanded that she be cleaned and kept away from others until she was called for.

A few days passed before he called out to Raphael. A month had passed since he slayed his enemy, which he figured was more than enough time for his servant to grieve.

He called for the woman to be presented in the grand room. She stumbled in, wearing the same dirty dress she wore when brought to his castle, though her skin was remarkably cleaner. Her golden eyes were glossed over, and her lips partly pursed, awaiting her next command. She knelt in the corner as she was directed.

Persephone walked into the room and noticed his latest captive. She examined her quickly and glared at her husband.

"Another woman to feed your incessant need of flesh?"

"My landwalkers brought her as a gift to me. Very rarely do you find such a beautiful woman worshiping death anymore. She brought her husband's heart as an offering to me, romantic, isn't it?"

"Hardly." She scoffed.

"I'm feeling generous; she is a gift to Raphael."

His name caught Persephone's attention, and she turned back to him. "Do you still trust him?"

"Of course, he is my most loyal servant. His time for anger has passed, and this gift will bring in a new era for him. The time for sulking is over."

"As you wish." Persephone nodded at him and walked out of the room, taking one last glance at the woman frozen in the corner.

Raphael appeared moments later, bowing his head in respect to Hades. He flashed a wide grin and stepped down from his throne to greet him.

"How are you holding up?"

"As well as I can be." Raphael stood stiff, not imitating his master's charisma.

"I've been surprised not to see you inflicting pain on any innocent souls. Quite unlike you."

"I learned from the best, didn't I?" Raphael faked a smile and struggled to keep his anger suppressed. "Besides, I no longer have a purpose. I'm surprised you haven't done away with me."

"You think that poorly of me?" Hades' face darkened, and Raphael dropped his head in response. "You have done more than your purpose, which is never-ending loyalty to me. You could have stopped her, but I have forgiven you. I understand your loyalty to her was unwavering, but now you are able to switch your focus back to me.

"Come, follow me. I have an offering for you—a tribute to a new era, one where we men of power rule over everything. Now that *she* is out of my way, I have big plans for us."

Persephone lingered in the hallway, and Hades' speech intrigued her. She walked back toward the room's opening and peered around the corner.

"Step forward." Hades called out to the woman. She struggled to her feet, still bound by the chains, and walked forward toward him.

"I don't want anything to do with her, or any other woman for that matter." Raphael turned his face away, ignoring her beauty and pulsing blood.

"She is my gift to you, and you will sacrifice her for me. She is one of the few humans left who still honors me, even if she calls me by another name. Take her, drink her blood, you know you want to. Save some for me; I've been craving fresh blood for weeks."

Hades undid her chains and the woman absentmindedly stepped into Raphael's arms. He brushed her curls out of her face, taking pity upon her dazed face. She smelled sweet, like the fresh air of Earth, and he breathed deeply into his fistful of curls.

He leaned her back and bit into her neck slowly, savoring the hot blood that splashed his tongue. He hadn't fed since Calypso died, so he became ravenous after his first taste. He pulled back instantly, not wanting to drain her.

"Don't stop," she spoke slowly, and Hades belted out a deep laugh. His boisterous howl blocked out her next words, but Raphael saw them on her lips. "Mon chérie."

He gazed into her eyes but received nothing in return. He must have imagined those words; Calypso was too ingrained in his brain. After his subtle pause, he bit back into her neck and sucked deeply, moaning as she arched into his chest. It had been too long since he felt a connection with his victim. He wanted to lay her on the floor and take her as his own but stepped back and wiped her blood off of his lips.

Hades stepped in and pulled the woman into his arms. She was weak, stumbling, and barely able to hold her body weight. Raphael drank much of her blood and made sure to leave a gaping wound for Hades to drink from.

Her head rolled backward, and the whites of her eyes showed as Hades nuzzled into her neck. Without biting, he wrapped his lips around her bleeding jugular and lapped his tongue into her wound.

She enjoyed it, him feeding on her; he could tell by the way she drew her body closer to him. She couldn't resist the pain and ecstasy she felt, and she tore at his shirt, ripping it and feeling his bare chest.

He hardly noticed as she felt for his heart, puncturing her nails into his skin. He was so engrossed in drinking her blood and feeling up her luscious body that he didn't sense the change in her body. Her body tensed as she shed the face of the woman she had gazed upon in Egypt.

Hades pulled back slowly and stared into the brown, fiery eyes of Calypso. Recognition filled his face but it was too late. Her hand plunged into his chest, wrapping her fingers around his heart. A look of fear appeared on his face, something he had never shown before. She let out a roar as she jerked her hand out of his chest, removing his heart.

His body slowly crumpled onto the ground as she stepped backward. Raphael stood a few feet away, watching in disbelief. His love had returned from the dead. Persephone, who had silently watched the whole event, ran from the hallway and dropped next to Hades.

"He's dead," she called out.

"Calypso." Raphael ran over and embraced her. She kissed him back, still holding Hades' heart in her hand. "How?"

"We don't have time; we need to dispose of his body. Now!" Persephone yelled. She dragged him by one arm, and Calypso and Raphael each picked up a leg to help her carry him into the hallway.

The hordes of Hell were petrified as they walked past with Hades' limp body. Calypso held his heart above her head, parading her victory. Persephone brought them to the Elysian Fields. She huffed as they lifted his body and threw it into the portal. He disappeared quickly, and Calypso threw his heart in for good measure.

"I don't understand," Calypso said to Persephone.

"You cannot kill a God that easily. He would become alive again in only a matter of minutes. We had to trap him in the Elysian Fields, or this would have all been for nothing." Persephone stared into the empty fields.

"So that's it? He is trapped, he can't escape?"

"Precisely. Unless another God plans on dying anytime soon, he could escape while they enter. But he is now dead, gone from Hell and of this Earth."

"Hades is dead," Raphael quietly murmured. His mind swirled and he wiped sweat from his forehead.

"Come, we must crown you." Persephone grabbed Calypso's hand and rushed back to the grand entry room. The news spread quickly throughout the castle, and hundreds of entities crowded the room.

"I can't do this," Calypso hissed as Persephone dragged her up the stairs of the thrones. "I don't want to rule over Hell!"

"You must; you killed him. Now, announce yourself."

Calypso gave her one last glare before she stepped forward. She glanced at Raphael for comfort, who still reeled from the events.

"I, Calypso, the Queen of Vampires, have killed and overthrown Hades, the God of the underworld." Her voice echoed into Raphael's mind, and he took a step back, bewildered that she knew how to do so without any instruction.

"I have completed the prophecy set by the Fates. Now, I am to be crowned ruler of the underworld. I do not accept this fate for myself. I direct ruling leadership to Persephone."

Persephone looked at her knowingly and stepped forward. She grabbed her hand and raised it up, Hades' blood staining both of their palms.

A wave of nausea overtook Raphael, and he had to push his way through the crowd to escape. He was deafened by the equally rejoicing and angering shouts of Hell. He made it into the hallway before he collapsed onto his knees and vomited.

Calypso found him there hours later after she had thoroughly discussed matters with Persephone. She was to be in charge while consulting and keeping Calypso in decisions. She sat next to him and placed her head on his shoulder.

"He's gone; we can finally live freely." She whispered into his ear.

"What does this mean for us?" Raphael shifted uncomfortably under her weight.

"This changes nothing. I love you, and now we can travel the world freely, never having to fear Hades again." She looked deep into his eyes and his heart skipped a beat. He wanted to believe that everything would be okay though his world was rapidly shifting.

"All I've ever wanted is to spend my eternal breath surrounded in your glory." Raphael intertwined his fingers with hers, returning her gaze. "You seem different."

"She is, can't you tell?" Persephone appeared and laughed, a bright glow shining off of her face. "Your vampire is also a demigod."

Raphael looked at Calypso in disbelief, and she nodded. "How did you know?"

"I knew you were of water when you told me of your childhood. Of how you prophesied. That's why I told Raphael to drop your body into the ocean. I knew he would find you."

"What is she talking about?" Raphael asked.

"Poseidon is my father. Persephone knew I had to die to step into my powers fully."

"Powers?"

"I can turn into others just from looking at their faces. I shielded my own soul from Hades. I'm more powerful now; I rarely need any blood to survive. I can connect and move freely in the water. I finally feel like myself."

"I'm so happy for you." Raphael tightly squeezed her hand, fearful for the future.

"Go, you lovebirds. You've done more than enough for me; enjoy yourselves." Persephone winked at Calypso, and she smiled back at her. Raphael envied their newfound God connection.

"Where shall we start?" Raphael kissed her neck, and she arched into him.

"Take me away, take me to paradise where we can love endlessly and forget everything."

About the Author

Makenzi Rivera has been writing stories since she was a young child. She lives in Florida with her husband and clan of animals. When not daydreaming, she enjoys traveling and spending time in nature.

Co-Author Toasty